COLLATERAL LOVE

MELISSA KUNZE

Contents

1

PROLOGUE

If you looked up the term 'brother' in the dictionary, you would get something like:

"A male who has the same parents as another or one parent in common with another."

This definition was the only one that seemed to make sense to me when it came to talking about my brother, Clay. He was born before me, thirteen months to be exact. We shared the same mother and father and had the same blood coursing through our veins. This was how we were rightly related to one another.

If you kept scrolling down the list of definitions, you would also come up with:

"One related to another by common ties or interests."

Clay and I always had the same love for things like Chinese takeout on Sunday nights and trashy reality television shows. We were both book worms with common interests of pursuing English degrees at NYU and dreaming up futures with book signings and frazzled hair as we tried to reach a deadline. Clay was a morning person who was all smiles and wide eyes at seven in the morning. I was the same, only liking to sleep in a few extra hours.

And we both shared the same love and utter adoration for each other.

But the final definition of the term 'brother' that scared me the most was this:

"One of a type similar to another."

Sure, Clay and I had so many physical features that were similar, what with the auburn locks and bright, baby blue eyes. We shared freckles dusting along the tops of our noses and through our cheekbones, almost dotted in the same exact spots. We dreamed the same futures for ourselves and liked some of the same foods.

He was my older brother, the one who inhabited this Earth before me and the one who was supposed to show me the ropes when I was too young to understand everything. Older brothers were supposed to stick up for you in the school yard against bullies and annoy you to no end when you were home with one another.

But somehow, the roles of our stand points in this family were reversed as we got older and high school became the turning point in both of our lives. My brother was no longer the protector, but the coward. I was no longer the little sister who could hide behind her big brother, but the one who was standing in front of him and protecting him. I wasn't allowed to run to Clay when I had a problem or an ex boyfriend that needed a stern talking to. He wasn't the strong one with a sturdy figure or the one who annoyed me to the fullest when we were home alone.

As high school became harder and the bullies became more full of themselves, the times at home were always eerily quiet and almost soul-shuddering, like you knew something was bound to happen that would crack the foundation we all took so long to build. He would sit in his bedroom in the blinding silence and surround himself with his thoughts and nothing more than a simple cough or two came from behind that wooden door for more than a year.

That's why the final term in the dictionary scared me the most.

Because the moments I had with Clay weren't always this scary and quiet. I could remember him pulling me on a bright red wagon during one summer when were six and seven. He took me to my first ballet and got me backstage passes for my favorite band the day I turned fifteen. We collapsed onto the living room couch with Chinese takeout on Sunday nights and stuffed our faces until we couldn't fit anything more into our bodies. He'd tell me about how his latest play was coming along and I would tell him how my current English essay was going.

At one point, we were so close that we decided to take our dreams one step further, attending NYU the year after each one of us graduated. I remembered him talking about how he would test it out for me, making sure he was my tour guide when I finally managed to graduate a year after him. He was in the process of buying dorm room furniture and applying for scholarships to help my parents when it came to the heavy weight of their financial status. But he didn't even need it, because I knew he was smart enough to get a full ride.

And all of that changed at the shuttering thunder in school that day.

If the term 'brother' meant that the person in question was similar to you, then I was fearful of the day I would end up just like Clay had; unnerving, broken and completely insane.

We shared so many common loves and wanted to be the same things when we grew up. Our physical features made it easy for those around us to tell that were related, the freckles and bright eyes always true telling features. Because of these similar traits and uncanny features, did that mean that I was going to end up like him one day? Would I turn against everyone around me and crack underneath the deep pressure that I couldn't bear to tell anyone?

It's all I can think about as I'm sitting here on the docks, my feet skimming just above the waterline and shivering lightly from the icy, small waves. I can't help but think, will I have the same fate as Clay? Will I become a massive form of self-destruction and a raging monster to those I loved the most?

As my eyes drift across the expanse of water, fifty five and a half miles away from the civilization I was currently drowning in, I see the county prison. Bordered by high brick walls and dark, caramel rusted barbed wire, it was scary enough to make me quiver against the wet wood of the dock. The sun was setting behind it, still not making the dark clouds that were permanently set above it part ways for a moment. No matter how beautiful the surrounding area was, how much they cleaned up the outside or how the florescent lights from inside the jail shined through the windows and bounced off the waves...it would always be a place of utter fear.

I'd always hate to look at that place across the water because of who now inhabited it. He had gotten what he wanted, an escape from his old life and a way out of the misery the people he cherished the most surrounded him in. He was no longer being pushed into lockers and beaten up outside of school for the life choices he decided to make. He had no contact with the world outside of that rusted, worn down building that housed the worst of the population in Riverton.

Before they booked him and gave him the satisfaction that he wanted, I remembered him saying, "Now I get to escape this mental prison, Callie."

The irony of his words was now hitting home. He had escaped the mental prison he had been buried under. He was no longer subjected to the things that cepressed him, angered him and made him hate himself for who he was.

But now Clay was in a physical prison, one he had thrown himself into.

And the only thing I had left to ask him was, 'Was the escape from the mental prison worth this?'

2

— ◦ —

CHAPTER 1

Two months before...

The first time I noticed something changing in Clay was the first day of varsity football tryouts.

"Keep up, Tollson!" Coach Ramsey shouted from the sidelines, his signature clipboard that was piled to the brim with play sheets tucked underneath his arm. He was pointing a finger in the direction of jersey number 54, Clay's from the previous year.

I was sitting on the bleachers, mango iced tea in between the heels of my Doc Martens, with my elbows on my knees and hands cradling my face. As I watched, I ran my finger over the sweat from the glass, absentmindedly wandering off as I pretended to watch my older brother run across the Riverton High football field. Sweating bullets underneath the beating sun, I was just wishing I could be back in my car like earlier with the air conditioner on blast and the radio turned way up.

Clay wanted me here for moral support, feeding me some words about my being there acting as his good luck charm. I whined about it for a good hour and a half, asking if I could just sit in my car instead of on the bleachers in the hot sun, but he wasn't having any of it. He just whined right back, practically down on his knees to watch him while he tried out for the team.

So here I was, basically sweating off the double cheeseburger I'd just devoured before I came here. I looked down to jersey number 54, my eyes casting back and forth as he ran from one end of the field to the other, just skimming past the touchdown line each time. The coach was making them do sprints each way, having them touch the goal line every time they got to one end. Here I was complaining when Clay was probably dying beneath his helmet and pounds of shoulder pads.

"Pick it up, men!" the coach hollered one more time. I sipped from my drink, noticing Clay look to the coach with a bitter expression that I could just make out underneath all of the metal bars in front of his face.

My heart broke a bit for Clay. He spent most of the summer and the months before it practicing from dawn until dusk to make his plays perfect. He pushed himself to the point where he almost broke his leg just a few weeks prior to this event, twisting it while sprinting down the front lawn during an exercise technique. He wore my dad's old jersey like it was the only thing keeping him alive and tried to bench press just like the guys who were already on the team for years.

It was hard watching him push himself the way that he was because, as much as I hated to admit it, he wasn't like the other boys on the team. Clay was a drama nerd, keeping most of his focus on memorizing lines from scripts and putting on shows in front of the whole school every few months. He liked to read books and immerse himself in plot lines just like he was living inside of the pages. When he graduated this year, he wanted to go off to NYU and pursue a degree in English studies.

Meanwhile, the football team consisted of macho teenage boys who couldn't pay attention in class for more than twenty seconds. While Clay was reciting lines from the top of the stage on Friday nights, the football players were off at house parties and hooking up with every cheerleader and shameless slut they could get their hands on.

Clay didn't compare to the guys on this team. But somehow he had gotten this idea in his head that if he joined the team that he would be popular and no longer the victim of high school bullies and jackasses who liked to judge from first glances. I tried to convince him that trying out for a team full of unintelligent knuckleheads wasn't the answer to fitting in, but he wouldn't budge. He just pushed himself harder and harder as summer neared the end of its twilight nights, swearing he would become something other than the lead actor in the school's fall production.

It hurt watching him run up and down that field with all of the other guys around his age, simply because he was doing this for all the wrong reasons. This wasn't supposed to be the reason why you joined teams or pushed yourself to get something done. He should have been doing this for himself because he loved football or felt like he needed a change of scenery from the drama department.

But he was only doing this for the other people at school who felt the need to make my brother the poster child behind their target practice.

"Tollson!" Coach Ramsey shouted to my older brother, waving him over from the field as the other guys ran past him once again.

While they were on lap thirty-four, my poor brother was trailing behind with a mere average of about twenty in the past half hour.

My brother snapped his head up, a grim look taking over his features as he glumly jogged over to the coach. Ramsey pulled the clipboard from underneath his arm and used an arm to wipe off the sweat beneath his red cap.

I couldn't hear my brother from where I was seating on the bleachers, but I could see the way his face contorted as Coach mumbled some things to him underneath his breath so the others wouldn't hear. He listened intently, hands on his hips and shoulder pads pushed up near his neck, tapping his cleat against the artificial grass. I watched as the sour look on his lips became more twisted the more the conversation went on. Coach was very physical with his words, gesturing a lot with his hands and wiping his face every once in a while against the end of summer heat.

I bit my thumbnail impatiently, praying he wasn't about to give Clay some bad news. Without thinking about it, I was clinking my iced tea bottle against the edge of the bleacher seat, making an annoying metal clanking sound the heavier my taps became. If Coach told Clay he wasn't about to make the team, it would mean another eerily silent day back at home without another word from him for the rest of the night. And it was Sunday, our day. I didn't want that to happen.

With a final pat on the back of the shoulder, Clay made his way towards the fence that was separating the player's benches from the multiple bleachers. He ripped off his helmet with angry force, throwing it down on the grass as he packed up his water bottle and iPod into his duffle bag. The fear burned in my stomach as I continued to watch him move his stuff around.

Hopping over the rest of the bleachers and making my way down the seats, I almost fell against the fence in front of him and clutched the chain links in between my fingers. Cautiously eyeing him down, waiting for a response from him first, the fear was boiling higher and higher.

"Clay," I said slowly. "What happened? What did he say?"

He spat his mouth piece to the floor and zipped up his bag quickly, not making eye contact. "Nothing. Absolutely nothing," he spat, throwing the bright blue bag over his still padded shoulder.

Clay started walking down the field against the fence, already being sucked into his own little world as he went. I followed him slowly, my fingers trailing against the warm metal. Gulping loudly, I asked, "What did Coach say, Clay?"

We made it to the exit of the field, an open parking lot coming into view. There were only a few stray cars lined up where the concrete started, most just from the boys on the field. It was the end of summer, one week before school officially started, and everyone else was soaking up the rest of the sun and jumping into their pools for one last swim.

"I didn't make the team!" he shouted, casting his arms into the air with frustration. "Is that what you wanted to hear, Callie? You said I wouldn't make it and I didn't. I hope you're happy," he seethed, hanging his head as he made his way to my car.

I let him walk ahead of me, afraid of what he might do under his current mood. Hanging back as I walked, I whispered, "I never said you wouldn't make it. I just warned you that those guys were a lot different from you..."

"That much was pretty damn clear, wasn't it?" he yelled as he threw open the passenger side door of my cherry red Toyota Camry and chucked his belongings inside.

"Clay, you still have drama. You even told me the other day that you were excited to get started on the fall premiere," I encouraged him, hoping he would drop the topic of this stupid football dream and go back to being the brother I grew up with.

"That's not the..." he went to scream, but was cut off by an awfully familiar voice from behind me.

My skin raised in miniature goosebumps as Carter Wayland, the lead quarterback, walked right past me when he spoke. "Well, you tried little buddy," he chuckled, his broad and muscular chest bouncing up and down lightly.

"Now's seriously not the time, Carter," Clay said somewhat sternly. He had lost the vicious tone he was using with me and his face dropped somewhat as Carter came closer and closer to him.

My heart pounded harder and harder against my chest the closer Carter got to him. He walked liked a predator haunting his prey, almost swooping in silently for the kill. Clay backed up slowly against the now closed passenger side door, his body almost molding to the paint.

All I kept thinking was: Please don't, please don't.

"What made you think you could come around my territory and try out for my team, Tollson?" he asked, venom practically slipping from his tongue as he got in my brother's face.

Clay's auburn short locks were pushed up in all directions from his football helmet, the sweat drenching the area right above his thick, dark brows. I watched as the fear in his hazel eyes seemed to overtake him. My brother looked so small against Carter's six foot five figure towering over him.

"I wasn't trying to come to your..." he gulped.

I winced as Carter gathered a handful of Clay's jersey in between his fingers, bringing them almost nose to nose, chest to chest. "What makes you think your gay, stage prancing ass could even make it on my team?" he seethed.

"Carter!" I piped up, trying to gain his attention and direct him away from my now cowering brother. Clay already knew that he didn't stand a chance if this went down the path he was so painfully used to.

But Carter didn't even flinch at my plea, only clutching the jersey tighter. I could see Clay quivering beneath him, showing no strength like an older brother should. That should have been me there, being in the claws of an older girl in my junior year as she spat some derogatory words in my face. He should be the one coming to save me from the pain, not the other way around.

"Listen man, I didn't mean to do anything to piss you off," Clay breathed furiously. His hands were plastered against the door of my car, not once moving to push Carter off of him. This was only because he knew if he even tried to disengage Carter's hands...it wouldn't end well.

With one swift movement, Carter had flung Clay onto the black-top of the parking lot, Clay's head just missing the pavement. I felt like the air had been knocked out of me. It was going too far now, this being just the first step in a series of throws and punches to come. I knew better than to let Carter go any further, this having happened multiple times before. But I just couldn't seem to unglue my frozen feet from the ground as I watched this unfold.

Carter fell to his knees so he was hovering over my brothers quaking body, arm already thrown back and hand clenched into a tight fist.

"Carter, stop! Please don't do this!" I shouted, finally finding my footing and running over to him.

"You know better than this, Tollson!" he shouted, letting the fist collide with my brother's slightly tanned cheek.

My heart stopped as I heard the faint crack of Carter's fist against my brother's face. Hot tears made their way down my cheeks as I watched Carter hold my brother's face with one hand and let out another punch.

"Stop it! Someone help! Please!" I screamed, my voice coming in high pitch tones and desperation.

Clay tried to fight back, pushing on Carter's rough chest. But it was of no use to him. Carter was built like an athlete, muscular and strong, while my brother was scrawny and lacked enough muscle to stand up against the school's quarterback. Carter just pushed Clay back down to the ground and punched him in the jaw once again. Bright red blood started to trickle from slightly opened wounds on Clay's face, dripping down his cheek and into his hairline.

"Carter!" I shrieked, my iced tea bottle slipping from my slick fingers and crashing onto the concrete beneath me into a million painful pieces.

"I thought I showed you," he threw another punch, making me wince. "Your place," he huffed out.

Before throwing a final punch, Coach Ramsey came running out after I screamed once again. I wasn't even sure how he heard me over his booming voice and rowdy players, but he was breathing heavily as he made his way towards the scene. Immediately, Carter jumped up from Clay's sagging and bloody body.

"What the hell is going on here?" Coach Ramsey shouted, ripping his hat off and revealing a graying, receding hairline.

"Nothing, Coach!" Carter shook his head quickly, denying the obvious evidence laid out right in front of everyone.

He almost gaped at Carter. "This doesn't look like nothing, Wayland!"

I got down to the ground to Clay's level, my heart breaking over and over as my eyes fell upon each heavy and ripped wound. While the coach and Carter continued to yell back and forth at one another, I slowly ran my fingers over his face, trying to get him to respond to me.

"Clay? Can you hear me?" I asked, feeling like the outside world hadn't existed while I surveyed my brother's broken body. His favorite red and white jersey was covered in blood, wrinkled from Carter's handprints and fight.

"Mm," he moaned beneath me, bringing a shaky arm around his middle where Carter's knee had been dug into his ribcage.

"This is no behavior of a star athlete, Wayland!" Coach Ramsey shouted over my words to Clay, waving his hands boisterously in Carter's face as he spoke. "There is absolutely no explanation for this type of action!"

"Coach, I didn't...I wasn't..." he muttered on, looking sullen all of the sudden like a child being scolded by a parent for stealing from the cookie jar. He showed no remorse for what he had just done to my brother.

"What are you going to say? You weren't thinking? You didn't know what you were doing?" Coach rambled on, his wrinkled face becoming redder as he yelled on. I could see his blood pressure rising from beneath his skin just by watching him. "I've heard every single excuse in the book before from you, Wayland. You want to keep your spot on this team? You better shape up and learn how to act like a man, because boys do not belong on my team!"

"Coach, I'm sorry!" Carter said hurriedly.

He just shook his head at him. "I'm not the one you should be apologizing to." After his final words, Coach threw his cap back on and pulled out his clipboard, making his way back to the field to baby-sit the newcomers to his fall lineup.

I pushed Clay's hair away from his eyes, mussing it back with the help of the sweat from his forehead. I cringed as I saw more scars coming into view, blood now trickling from his cheek, jaw and above his eyebrow. I suddenly wished I carried tissues or something in my clutch, this way I could at least help him in some way. Casting my eyes towards Carter's towering figure, I saw him look down at me. He was blocking the sun, painting a shadow of his body behind me.

"He needs help!" I yelled, gesturing towards his sluggish body still lying against the scolding hot pavement.

Carter just shrugged. "And?"

"But Coach just told you…" I went to say, but he shook his head at me, rightfully cutting me off.

"Coach isn't here anymore. He'd never kick me off of that team. I'm the most useful player there. He just threatened me because he didn't want to seem ignorant in front of you."

"You are such an…" I snapped.

"Asshole?" he finished for me. "Save it, Callie. Nothing I haven't heard from girls like you before. Your brother deserved it. He knew better than to come around here. He doesn't belong here," he shrugged once again, not even looking down at my hurt brother before stalking off in the direction Coach had went.

More tears pooled at the rim of my eyes as I tried to pick up Clay's head with my hand at the back of his hair. He groaned as I pulled him to a sitting position, rubbing his jaw with a scuffed hand filled with scratches. The blood switched directions, leaving the sides of his cheeks and sliding down to his chin. He used the sleeve of his already bloody jersey and wiped it against his face, not too sure where all of the cuts were.

"Come on, let's get you home, Clay," I breathed, trying to pull him up with my own weight.

Before I could though, he shrugged me off roughly, pushing my hands away from his arms. "I've got it!" he boomed, rubbing his face again with his sleeve and placing his hands against the edge of the sidewalk to steady himself as he began to stand up on his own.

"Clay," I murmured, not trusting his bruised body and trying to hold onto him again just in case. But he just shook me off once again, shaking his head in a look of disgust as I did so.

I knew he had every right to be angry right now, seeing as how he was just beaten up in the school parking lot without an ounce of fight left in him. In his mind, he was supposed to be the strong one, all conquering and able to step into any fight that he was put up against. He wasn't supposed to be quivering underneath the hands of another guy just the same age as him. He was supposed to know how to fight back and how to stick up for himself.

Growing up as a book worm and automatically shy kid, Clay never got along with other kids his own age very well. He was always reserved, too stuck in his dreamland of novels and socially awkward around others. While most guys his age went out to parties on the weekends and spent their senior year grouping up with friends and making memories, Clay was stuck in his bedroom or at rehearsal for the next play coming up. He was judgment bait, the more masculine guys at Riverton reeling him in like a rightful catch.

They called my brother gay, a pansy, a fairy for being the star in plays and dressing in tights for roles he stared in. Clay never had a girlfriend or many friends even, so other guys at school always pinned him as the socially absent kind and a closet homosexual for his actions. None of this ever made sense to me, seeing as how my brother still dressed like a guy, in jeans and t-shirts, just like the same people who made fun of him. Sure, he wasn't interested in sports and didn't go out much, but he was still a person with a heart of gold who would do anything for the people he loved.

He didn't deserve the crap people around him handed to him on a daily basis.

I sometimes just wished he didn't take out his anger for the actions he couldn't control on everyone else, especially me. I was the one who stuck up for him when times got hard, pushed the bullies out of the way and dragged him away from situations that raised obvious red flags. Yet, I was always the one he ignored when he was too angry to deal with everyone.

"Let me just at least help you to the car, Clay," I whispered cautiously, slowly moving my hands to his shoulders.

But he snapped his head around to me as he finally planted his feet on the blacktop, shooting me the deadliest of glances. "I got it, Cal!"

I shook beneath his taller figure, wrapping my arms around myself as I nodded my head in agreement. He walked past me and to the car door, every so often moving his hand beneath his bruised jaw. I bit onto my thumbnail once again, using minimal strength to drag myself to my car.

The ride home was covered in a shattering silence, the only sound being groans coming once in a while from Clay's side of the car. Out of the corner of my eye, I'd see him wipe more blood from his face while looking in the shielding mirror and trying to un-wrinkle his favorite jersey that was now completely ruined.

Even if he did manage to get the stains out, iron the wrinkles to smooth creases and wash away the pain from that jersey, he would never be able to forget this day. Every time he would slip it over his head, he would see a dried blood stain or have a moment's flashback to this very instance, just like all the others, where he was something less of a man in his own eyes.

I just wished I could reach over the center console and wrap my fingers around his hand, squeeze it and show him how much he truly meant to me. Moments like before didn't matter to me. The only thing I cared about was his well-being and whether or not he was hurting. I didn't care that he was getting beaten up when he was supposed to be fighting back. I could care less that I was the one sticking up for him and not the other way around. He was still my older brother and I still admired him for who he was to the bone.

When we finally reached home, my shoulders able to drop as he escaped the car as quickly as possible, I felt a strange sense of fear run through my veins.

Today was Sunday. On Sundays, we always camped out in the living room while my father was at his weekly AA meetings and my mother was working the night shift at the hospital just down the road. We had the whole house to ourselves and we would order Chinese takeout, eyes glued to the television as episodes of the Real

World repeated on re-runs throughout the night. It was our only time to vent to one another, truly ask how the other was doing. I knew he was pissed off. I knew he was upset about everything that had happened. But I was still wishing he wouldn't run into that house and slam his bedroom door, signaling that the night wasn't about to go as planned.

Hurriedly, I turned the key in the ignition and shut off my car. I packed all of my things up into my clutch and threw the mirror back up against the roof. Throwing the door shut as soon as I was out, I jogged up the driveway and burst through the front door. Clay's duffle bag was thrown next to the doorway, his schoolbag following the path of his self-destruction as it was deposited on the couch that wasn't too far from the opening of the living room walkway.

"Clay?" I called into the dreary silence. All of the lights were off in the house, the only source coming from sun casting in through the living room windows. He never answered back.

I walked past the living room archway and into the kitchen, already maneuvering throughout the room to find the Chinese place's menu that housed our usual orders. Pulling my cellphone out of the pocket of my white laced denim shorts, I started walking to the first step that led upstairs.

"Clay, I'm about to order from…"

But I couldn't finish my sentence because I was met with the gut-wrenching slam of his bedroom door. I squeezed my eyes shut at the sound, clenching the paper menu in between my nimble fingers. It was hard to tell if the feeling coursing through me was sadness or pure anger for what was going on with him.

I wasn't angry that he was ignoring me, just a little sad that this Sunday night was the first in years that we wouldn't be abiding by tradition. The main reason behind my anger was the lack of respect everyone at Riverton High seemed to have for my admirable older brother. He offered the world so much. He lived the way he wanted, enjoyed things differently than most like him did.

Just because he wasn't the 'normal' he was treated like the outcast he never set out to be.

And I feared the day that he would finally crack.

Chapter 2

One Month and Three Weeks Before...

Today marked the first day of school, my junior year and the hardest year of high school yet.

To say I was far from thrilled was an understatement. All junior year meant was being piled to the brim with SAT study textbooks and level-headed college decisions. Teachers constantly reminded you of the deadlines to sign up for the multitude of dates lined up in the year, tying in useful vocabulary tactics and calculator-free math problems. All anyone would care about in the next few months leading up to our first taste of prom were the numbers in bold print on your computer screen that somehow determined your scored intelligence.

Clay told me all about it last year when he was thrusting his face into the pages of the official study guide and practicing example problems every night after his other homework was already finished. He would complain about the utterly impossible wordings of English problems and stupidity behind a test marking how smart you were to the college admissions offices.

The first few days of the official start week hadn't been so terrible. Most of the classes consisted of supply lists being handed out and outlines for when certain chapters needed to be read by. I'd barely opened a textbook since I walked through the metal double doors on Monday morning, which was a good sign. I'd much rather focus on prom in April than the haunting SAT at the first week of November.

"I have news!" a familiar high-pitched voice erupted behind me while I fiddled with the lock in the North hallway.

Only deterring my gaze from the mission in front of me to show her I was listening, I grumbled beneath my breath as the wretched lock still wouldn't budge. Her pixie cut blonde locks barely bounced as she jumped on the balls of her feet in excitement. The dark make-up clouded her lids and her perfected cat-eye was lined perfectly above her top lashes. A smile danced across her lips as the words begged to burst from inside of her.

When she didn't respond right away, I said, "What news?"

"Carter Wayland just asked me out!" she squealed, her books almost falling from the crevices of her fingers as she continued to move like a jumping bean next to me.

I immediately dropped the lock from my hands, freezing at the mention of the school's quarterback who just so happened to beat the crap out of my brother just a week ago. Turning on my heels slowly, I looked at her carefully.

"Carter Wayland...he..." I went to say, but she was already nodding her head fervently.

"I was just coming out from Physics and he was waiting by the door. Carter Wayland was waiting for me of all people!" Marnie squealed, her eyes alight with a sort of excitement I hadn't seen from her in a while.

I closed my eyes, taking in a breath to give myself time to process this information. Marnie was my best friend, one who had been there for me during the hardest of times. She was there when my father first decided to attend his AA meetings, stayed on the phone with me for hours when I needed to vent about Clay's ever-changing personality over the past few months and was the all-knowing social butterfly who had introduced me to all of my former friends.

I found it gut-wrenching, the thought of crushing her hopes by telling her that Carter was the man behind the fists that were constantly wailed against my brother. She knew all about Clay's lack of acceptance in school and all of the times I had to protect him from everyone else around us. While she loved my older brother like her own, I didn't have the heart to spoil her excitement.

Nodding in a silent agreement with my inner conscience, I murmured, "That's great, Marn."

Much to my dismay, she smiled even broader at my acceptance to her news. "I mean, I know it's a long shot that we'd even be in a relationship or anything but...I'm just so excited! Who would've thought that someone like Carter Wayland could like me?"

She said his name like he was the epitome of a god, succumbed by his killer good looks and athletic physique. I was almost waiting to hear that breathy sigh like one a fan girl would emit when she came into contact with a gorgeous lead singer to a band. But all she did was push her textbooks up higher in her arms and let another smile slip through her features.

I turned around from the conversation and fiddled more with my lock, finally managing to click it open and grant myself access to my textbooks. Letting my fingers dance over the tops of the hard covers,

I located my Anatomy book and slammed the door shut when I settled it in my arms.

Without looking in Marnie's direction, scared I might blurt last week's events to her on accident, I continued down the hallway to my next class. She followed behind quietly, her spiked Jeffrey Campbell's clicking against the linoleum floor.

"You're awfully quiet today," she mused, catching up to my quickly retreating figure. "Normally you would be jumping up and down with me over something like this."

I just shrugged, shifting my books uncomfortably. I wanted to come up with a conversation topic that would change the direction of this conversation and save me the horrific details of retelling Clay's story with a certain boy's name in the cliff notes. She wasn't budging though, just continuing to walk next to me with a pushy look in her eyes.

"Go on. Out with it, Tollson," she urged, gesturing with a hand. "You know you're no good at lying."

Sighing heavily, I stopped in my tracks, almost making Marnie fall into me. She collected herself quickly though, demonstrating impeccable balance on her high heels. "Clay got into another...incident last week after football tryouts."

She gaped me, her glossed lips a perfect 'O'. "What happened? Is he okay?"

I shook my head solemnly. "He was pissed about not making the team when we were on our way out to leave. C..." I stopped myself before the name could be put into full form. "Some guy came out from the field and beat him up pretty bad. Clay couldn't even fight back."

As I finished the re-telling, I was almost choked up thinking back to last week. I felt so helpless as I watched it all unfold before me. Compared to the massive football player and my older brother, I was a twig. If I was stronger, more prominently built than that asshole who laid his hands on Clay, than I could have saved him from the humiliation and hoard of hurt he was experiencing.

"My God," she murmured lifelessly, her eyes like a deer caught in the headlights. "Poor Clay can never catch a break, can he?" she frowned as she tried to play out the situation in her own mind. "Who was it?"

Now it was my turn to look like a deer at the hood of a car passing down the street. Shaking my head furiously I said, "I'm not sure!" I was sure it came out too rushed, my words jumbled and not well thought out. "Some guy on the team, I guess."

"Do you remember what he looked like?" she asked hurriedly, not giving up until I painted her a picture of the guy who did it so she could kick him where it hurt too. "I'm friends with Kyle Stafford, the one who plays like linebacker or something. If you remember what he looks like I could totally give him a piece of my mind."

I shook her off. "Coach already let him have it when he caught him. I'm sure it's all dealt with by now."

"No," she gasped. "He was caught? What did Coach do? Is he benched for the season now or something?"

You could tell that everyone at Riverton was far too emotionally invested in the football team's lives. Whenever someone else was benched or injured for the season, it not only affected the player at the receiving end, but the hundreds of students who made up the population of the school. Millions of questions would ensue like how long the team would be in a bind and what exactly he did to make this happen. We protected our guys like brothers and sisters.

Riverton was a small town, quaint with minimal people and loose boundaries. It was bordered from the rest of civilization by a mass expansion of lake, circling us like sharks. The only time you could get across the lake and over to Moreland County was by a boat at the all too familiar docks on the edge's point or by an almost abandoned bridge to cross the threshold that everyone rarely used.

This meant that you couldn't hide a thing in this town. Your secrets were always on display for the rest of the population to see and being comfortable with your peers seemed to be the only option. Housewives would mill about with their girlfriends, gossiping about the latest teenage drama that I hadn't even heard of yet. Most of the fathers around here were friends, golfing on Saturday mornings and cracking open beers in their backyards. This only left their children to join the circle of collaboration. The kids here practically grew up with one another, grade school companions and forever long best friends. This was also how Marnie and I had become so close, having grown up with one another since preschool.

So whether you liked it or not, everybody was your friend.

Our quaint, little town left little to the imagination and not many places to go for entertainment so the school's weekly football games during the fall seasons were what we all looked forward to the most. Even if you couldn't stand to watch the sport unfold, it was enough to split some cheese fries with friends in the freezing cold with your asses frozen to the bleachers, surrounding one another with mindless chatter.

I gave her a look that read something like, 'I have no idea', before continuing down my path to class. She hurried behind me, her heels still tapping aimlessly, and was breathless by the time she could form her next question.

"How's Clay doing?" she asked, trying to keep up with my pace.

"Not too good," I responded truthfully for the first time in this conversation. "I tried to step in to stop it, but neither of them was budging. He hasn't spoke to me much since it happened. He skipped our Sunday nights twice already. He just hides away in his room, ignoring everyone like it's our fault or something..." I muttered off, angrily shaking my head as I walked on.

When it first happened, I allowed Clay his space for the time being. I knew he was upset about being the receiver to idiotic bullying once again. The gay jokes hurt him more than anything, he once told me. So I figured I'd give him some time to cool off before trying to invade his personal space once again. But after three or so days, he still wasn't speaking to me or my parents. He just grabbed his designated foods from the kitchen for meals and used the bathroom every once in a while. Whenever he came into contact with any of us, he'd brush right past and pretend like he hadn't even seen us in the hallway or in the kitchen.

Now I was just angry that he was giving me the brunt of his issues. I was the one who tried my best to protect him and deter him from things like that happening. Whenever he needed to talk, I was always there to listen until he couldn't let anything out anymore. We cried together, laughed together and trusted each other with the deepest of secrets.

So why was I being shunned for trying to love my brother like I knew he needed?

Marnie's hand on my shoulder had me freezing in my tracks. Still quite out of breath, she turned me around to face her with a concern blazing in her eyes.

"Did you ever think..." she breathed, finally catching up to her lungs. "That he's probably embarrassed?"

"Of course he's embarrassed. He's being bullied by guys who are practically the same age as him. Who wouldn't be embarrassed by that?"

She shook her head, slinging the strap to her bag further up her shoulder before continuing. "I didn't mean that. What I'm trying to say is...he's probably embarrassed because his little sister is always saving him."

I took a step back like she'd slapped me or something. "I don't do it to..."

She put up her hand to stop me. "I wasn't saying that! All I'm try-ing to say is that he's an eighteen year old male. They're supposed to be able to stick up for themselves. It already sucks that he's the butt of every joke and is always getting the crap beat out of him like that. You saving him...his little sister...probably just hurts his ego more than it already has been."

"So basically it's my fault that he's not talking to me?" I boasted, my tongue sharper than a tack. I hadn't meant to snap at Marnie. It just slipped out with the anger I was hoarding around for a week.

"Callie, calm down. I wasn't trying to imply..."

Before she could finish her sentence, the familiar dark-haired, cocky boy sidled up next to her. Placing his arm around her shoulder and squeezing her to his side, he raised his eyebrows at the obvious tension he just walked into.

"Catfight, ladies?" he asked, a sketchy grin slipping onto his lips as his finger traced small circles on Marnie's arm.

"Piss off, Carter," I snapped, a snake ready to bite on its prey. It took all of the self control within me not to drop my textbooks and make a run for his precious face. I'd reconfigure it just like he'd done to my poor brother.

His eyes widened just a bit, not really surprised by my reaction. "Whoa, someone's a little on edge aren't they?"

"Well when a certain asshole football player felt the need to..." I trailed off as I watched Marnie's face configure against my words. She went from ecstatic to having Carter wrap his arm around her in front of the others in the hallway to somewhat displeased at what was unfolding in front of her.

It was the top code in the rulebook of best friends that you had to try your hardest to get along with the boy the other was dating or crushing on. What kind of person would I be if I ruined the first exciting thing for her? It was obvious she was already hooked onto Carter, even before their first official date, and what I could have said would have abolished any hope for happiness for her.

I just couldn't do that to her.

Waving him off like an annoying fly in my peripheral, I muttered, "Never mind."

He raised his thick eyebrows at me once again, almost mocking me for not being able to finish what I was about to say. He knew if Marnie wasn't in the middle of us that he'd be getting the brunt of everything I had been going through with Clay since his first day of high school. Carter was monster that was creating a whole new side of Clay that I had never seen before.

Clay grew up being picked on by the kids near the sandbox, all the way up to his last day of middle school and being pushed into the skinny lockers that lined the chipped walls. He went into high school after that summer thinking he was finally able to be himself and create another version of Clay Tollson that other people would actually appreciate and adore. There was a bubble of positivity radiating around him that I knew was about to pop as soon as he walked through the doors of his new school.

He must have forgotten that most of the town went to the same schools together all throughout their middle and high school years. We only saw transfers once every few years, save for a few loner types that snuck in without notice. Carter Wayland strode through the halls of Riverton the moment Clay did, a slick smirk already planted on his lips and a force to be reckoned with. One look at my brother and it was almost like they were destined to be mortal enemies until the last day of school during their senior year.

And ever since then, Carter hadn't let Clay slip from his fingers. Sometimes he had others help him when it came to scaring Clay out of his wits. Other football players would join in, most Carter's closest friends. But most of the time it was just Carter and Clay, head to head, with a winner clear from the beginning of the first punch.

My disgust as I watched him glance at Marnie with an all-knowing smile bubbled in my stomach like bile. So badly I wanted to jump in between them and give him back what he'd given Clay. But all I could do was stand back and watch with a twisted smile to show my best friend that I was happy for her...no matter how much I hated the guy she so clearly adored.

"So where would you like to go tonight, beautiful?" he murmured in her ear, just loud enough for me to hear him. It was like he knew this was getting underneath my skin. When he pulled back from her face and looked towards me, I wanted to kick that smirk right from his face.

A look of shock overtook her features. "I...I'm not sure. Wherever you want to go is fine with me!" she squeaked.

"I've got just the place in mind. Be ready by eight Friday night," he said, rubbing more concentric circles on her arm and probably making her want to melt in a puddle right in front of him.

Biting back my disdain for this situation, I pulled my textbooks closer to my chest and looked to Marnie. "I'm going to be late. I'll talk to you later."

She nodded silently, her eyes softening as she watched me turn to go. I knew she wanted to continue our talk about Clay's well-being and probably apologize for the way she worded her concern. We never left a conversation open-ended like that.

But I kept walking away anyway, careful to watch my steps as I went because I could feel Carter's eyes burning a hole into the back of my head. I know I didn't scare him the least bit, me being the scrawny, five foot five girl that I was. He was the head player on his sports team with muscles large enough to lift almost two hundred pounds. He probably laughed at me more than he feared me.

Deep down though, I think Carter knew. He knew that I was nowhere near finished with him. If he so much as even looked in my brother's direction again, I wouldn't stop until I released the payback on him that he rightfully deserved. The conversation may have been finished because Marnie was in the vicinity.

But the riff between us was nowhere near close to ending.

4

CHAPTER 3

Two Weeks Before...

"I just can't believe it you know," Marnie rambled on, gesturing wildly as we made our way to lunch. "We've been dating for a month now and I feel like I know him."

Trying to restrain myself from rolling my eyes in front of her, I sipped from the bottle of tea in my hand and kept quiet while she continued to go on. For the past three hours since I picked her up for school this morning, she hadn't shut up about her and Carter's one month anniversary coming up. Of course, they weren't officially a couple or anything, but she thought he would be asking her any day now...or so she kept repeating to me every few minutes.

"He's just so down to earth and kind," she sighed, looking up towards the ceiling like she was thanking God himself for bringing such a special guy into her life. "He pays for the bill every time we go out. He introduces me to his friends. He listens to me drone on for hours about stupid things," she shook her head like she was in utter disbelief. "It's crazy. Isn't it?"

I almost spit out my drink when she looked over to me for a response. In the past few hours she had been droning on about Carter, she never once looked to me for a reaction or a word in edgewise.

I was just expected to nod along to her elongated story-telling and just pretend like I was listening when I really wasn't.

To tell you the truth, I could barely manage to bite down on my tongue and not let her in on the secret that had been haunting me since their first date last month. Although Carter made it his mission to be in the presence of Marnie every single time I was in a room with her, he seemed to be losing the signature smirk and paid more attention to Marnie than to me. I felt like he had an ulterior motive, suddenly treating me like I hadn't existed when he was the one constantly beating on my older brother. At first, I kept thinking he was using my best friend as a way to get back at me for calling him names and reminding me who held the upper hand here. But as the weeks went on and he was becoming immersed in everything Marnie Matlin, I couldn't help but think he was truly falling for her and not just using her against me.

I still didn't like the fact that a guy like Carter was courting my best friend around and acting so oddly different with her. No one knew how long this 'nice' streak of his would last in their relationship. And before you knew it, as much as I hated to think about it, he could be wailing on her as well.

"Um," I stuttered, taking my time to screw the cap back on my bottle to form a logical response that didn't involve spilling the beans. "Yeah…it's crazy how close you two are getting."

She sighed dreamily once again, clasping her fingers together and clinking together the many gold and silver rings she was wearing. "I can't wait to get to lunch to see him!"

This time I couldn't hold back the eye rolling. "You just saw him an hour ago, before English. Remember?"

She waved me off nonchalantly. "That's so long though!" As we walked by the girl's bathroom on the way to the cafeteria, she halted in her tracks. "Give me a second! I have to pee and I want to freshen up before we see Carter."

Before I could respond, she was already pacing towards the door and leaving me alone in the silence of the hallways. We were already ten minutes late for lunch and the other students who didn't have lunch at this hour were seated in class. Basking in the first bout of peace I had since this morning, I fell against the row of lockers with a lengthy sigh.

I didn't know how much more of this secret keeping I could take. I was so used to telling Marnie everything, known for not keeping quiet about my secrets for too long. It felt like an eternity, only keeping this to myself for about a month. Carter had been wailing on my brother for four years now, being the main reason behind Clay's anger and sudden instances of sadness whenever I was around him. He treated Clay like his own personal punching bag. How could a guy who was so insanely kind to my best friend be so vicious to my brother?

The only plus to this new boy toy of Marnie's was that Carter hadn't laid a hand on Clay since the time at football tryouts last month. He still stared him down in the halls if my brother ever passed us while we were together. Maybe it was a territory thing again, making Carter feel the need to remind Clay who was the boss here. But I had an awfully horrible feeling that had been boiling in the pit of my stomach that Carter was only withholding his punches for a time that was going to be ten times as worse later on, when Clay was least expecting it.

Clay seemed to be returning back to his former self, all smiles and positive attitude when he came from drama rehearsal or when he was bringing me home food when Mom and Dad were out for the night. Our Sunday rituals came back to life with Clay full of stories about the new secrets surrounding his next play and how much he knew that he was going to snag the lead from underneath his arch nemsis, Jerry Torren's, nose. He was asking me about my classes, helping me with homework and nudging me about new cute boys in my grade.

He was back to being the brother I loved and admired. But I just wasn't sure for how much longer. Good things like this only lasted so long, right?

"What the fuck did you say to her, Callie?" a masculine voice broke me out of my reveries as he came stomping towards me in the empty hall. He was sporting his traditional leather jacket that was taut against his muscles and dark jeans, colliding together to make him the most mysterious and fearing boy on campus.

I immediately shrunk back to the lockers. "What are you talking about?"

Carter was in my face now, both hands on either side of my face against the cool metal. He was breathing heavily and his nostrils were flaring as he prepared himself to speak once again.

"She's been asking about the guy who kicked your brother's ass. She won't stop bringing it up! It's been a month and she won't knock it off. Now what the hell did you tell her?" his voice boomed as he slammed a hand against the locker, next to my head. I jumped in my place, my skin lining in the bad type of goosebumps, almost like a warning.

I shook my head viciously. "I didn't…" I stuttered. "I didn't…say anything…to her. I swear!"

His nose was almost touching mine, his heavy panting hitting me in the face and blowing my bangs out of the way. "You obviously…" he trailed off, catching his breath. "Said something to her. She just keeps bugging me about a kid who could have possibly hurt your brother. And I'll tell you what. I don't have a problem doing it again if this keeps going on."

My heart had leaped into my throat, my lungs feeling like they were on fire as I breathed. I couldn't get my muscles to stop shaking as his face seemed to drift closer and closer towards me. I knew he was known to beat on other guys, but I still wasn't sure if he would make me his next victim. My nervous limbs were making it apparent to him that he had me by the collar, almost like he could smell my fear.

I swallowed down the tears that were threatening to slip over the edge and tried my hardest to square my shoulders in my bravest pose. "I swear to you, Carter, I didn't tell Marnie anything about you. She knows what happened with Clay but she doesn't know who did it. I just told her it was a player on the team."

"That doesn't make it any better!" he barked, slamming his hand again and causing me to jump in place once more. "She won't quit unless I tell her it was me! I swear to God, Tollson, if you ruin this for me…" he shook his head, his eyes reading nothing but a vicious threat. He backed away just a bit to give me a small bit of room to breathe. Pointing a finger in my direction, he said, "You'll regret it, Callie."

A large hand fell over Carter's shoulder and threw him off of me, slamming him against the lockers I was already quaking on.

The metals clattered against one another and seemed to resound around the once silent hallways. When I finally regained my breath, I looked over to see Clay holding Carter against the lockers with a hand on Carter's broad chest. I gasped at the surprise, the reversal of this situation.

"Don't you dare lay a hand on my sister, Wayland!" Clay shouted, all trace of fear gone from his eyes.

This was the first time that this had ever happened. In my lifetime, no matter the playground bullies and piggish boys who laid their hands on me, Clay never took it upon himself to save me from those types of situations. He just stood back on the sidelines because he knew I didn't need his help. I could handle the scary scenarios far better than he could. This was the first time I was seeing him stand up for something other than himself.

"What are you going to do about it, Tollson?" Carter urged, his face smug and lacking any trace of fear as my brother pushed him back into the lockers once again with hidden force. Clay raised a hand to him, his fingers clenching into a fist I'd never seen on him before. "Do it!" he teased. "Hit me, Tollson! See how far you actually get!"

I was hoping some type of sibling telepathy would kick in as I chanted a mantra in my head: Don't do it, Clay. Don't do it. Clay was already throwing a hand back, poised for the fight that was about to ensue. I was flinching as I watched him hesitate for just a moment. I was almost sure he had somehow heard the chant I was feeding to him. That is, until he was a moment too late in halting his actions and Carter had turned the tables on us all.

"Carter, don't!" I screamed, cursing the teachers in the adjacent rooms who somehow hadn't heard a word of this going on yet. They could spot a student whispering underneath their breaths all the way in the back of the room, but were overlooking danger near their classroom.

Carter was now in Clay's place, pushing him against the row of lockers and sticking his arm on Clay's neck. I could practically feel the pain Clay was enduring as Carter's elbow seemed to dig into the side of his neck. The longer he stood there, the paler my brother's face got. He was sucking the life right out of him.

"Look who's not so tough now," he taunted, his elbow still pinching at the skin on Clay's neck.

As I watched Clay's eyes become heavy and his face lack less and less color, I raced over to Carter and pulled at the arm that was choking my brother. Carter wasted no time in throwing me away from him, almost making me lose my balance.

"Carter, stop!" I continued to beg him, wishing I was physically strong enough to win this battle for Clay. "He can't breathe!"

"Looks like both of the Tollson kids need to learn their place then, huh?" he said to Clay, his face inching closer to Clay's as the tint of rose that was normally on his cheeks drained second by second. He pushed his arm further against Clay's neck and squared off his jaw as he spoke. "You know who always wins," he said through clenched teeth.

Clay started grabbing at the sleeve of Carter's leather jacket, desperately pulling and not succeeding. He was moaning through the loss of breath, trying to gasp on every inch of air that he could.

"You're going to kill him!" I shouted again, praying someone would finally notice the commotion in the halls and come out to rescue my slowly falling older brother. The more color drained from Clay's face, the shorter my breaths became. "Carter!"

I was getting sick of using his name, sick of seeing him and sick of him hurting my brother. If he was having such a hard time getting along with him, why couldn't he just walk away and pretend Clay didn't exist? Beating him senseless was achieving nothing other than harming an innocent life. Carter had to make everything a freaking battle, one that he always knew he would win.

Maybe that was it...that he got the satisfaction of winning. Football wasn't enough for the star player and next level ladies man. He already had the world at his feet, but he wanted it all on a damn silver platter.

"I don't know how many times I have to tell..." he seethed again, but a feminine voice cut through the shouting and his words, making the world freeze around him.

"Carter..." she gasped. My head flung in her direction, seeing my best friend almost crumbling to the ground before us with a hand on her gaping mouth. She looked close to tears as she watched this unfold.

Carter immediately dropped his arm from Clay's neck, shaking off in his jacket and crumbling in front of her eyes. Clay gasped for the first full amount of air that he had access to, throwing his hands to his neck in desperation. I immediately ran over to him as he started to fall to his knees onto the floor. Wrapping my arms around his middle, I clutched onto him like he was my only anchor to the world.

"Baby, I..." I watched as Carter shook his head, the frown so eminent on his lips. He almost looked close to tears as well as he walked over to Marnie who pushed him off quickly.

She closed her eyes, the silent tears that were pooling now cascading over the rim and drenching her cheeks. "The football player who hurt him before...that was you?" she cried, hitting his arm when he tried to reach out for her again.

He just looked at her, doe-eyed and defenseless now. "I wasn't...Baby you know that I..."

"He's like a brother to me, Carter! And you hurt him!" she screeched, getting in his face now as she tried to wipe away the traitor tears that were messing up her perfect made-up eyes.

A classroom door opened then, making me curse the teacher under my breath for being so immensely late. "What's going on out here?" Mrs. Wayans piped up from across the hall, hands planted firmly on the hips of her lengthy skirt. When no one answered, each one of us too invested in our opposite prospects at the moment, she tapped her shoe against the floor to get our attention. "If you're not out of this hall in two minutes, I'm sending you all down to discipline."

After shooting us one last warning glare, she clicked back into her classroom and shut the door quietly behind her. Looking down to Clay once again, I saw that he was still clutching at his throat, but regaining much more air than before. The tinted pink was coming back to his cheeks and he looked like he had life in him once again.

"We're done, Carter," Marnie murmured in the heavy silence. At her last word, the look of utter disappointment and heartbreak crossed over Carter's face for the first time since I've known him. No longer was there the cocky smirk or the lusty eyes. He was just a broken boy with nothing but a broken heart to show for it.

"Marn, don't do this," he begged, reaching for her again. But she just shook her head and walked over to my brother's hunched figure. Slowly unwrapping my arms from around his midsection, I let Marnie pick him up gingerly and guide him down the hall. She rubbed gentle circles on his back and held his arm the entire way. He never once pushed her off or screamed at her for saving him.

Although I was somewhat jealous that she got to help him without complaint, I flashed back to the words she told me not too long before this. He was tired of being saved by his little sister. It was embarrassing enough that these types of things were happening to him, scarring him little by little as the days and the fights went on. As much as I wanted to be the one to pick his pieces back up for him, I had to let someone else take the reigns right now.

As I got up from the floor and dusted off the back of my leggings, I took the time to look over at Carter's disengaged face. It was like I watching all of his emotions paint pictures across his face, letting me in for just a moment to view the guy who normally had the toughest of exteriors. His face shifted from heartbreak, to sadness, to a look of lost concentration. Then...all of the sudden...his eyes became hard as they moved from Marnie's retreating figure to look at my own. His body became stiff and his jaw clenched as he conjured up what he wanted to say to the girl who he always felt the need to blame for his own mishaps.

"I warned you, Callie," he seethed, his teeth clenched once again beneath his plump lips. "You and the other Tollson are going to regret this."

I backed away slowly as his figure seemed to become larger and scarier the more I was in its prescence. I wasn't sure what this revenge would be, whether it be on myself or Clay, but I knew it was the furthest from whatever I could imagine.

"Callie, are you coming?" Marnie called to me. I quickly turned around to see her watching me with a look mixed with sadness and utter anger.

"Yeah, coming!" I called to her, backing away from him quicker now and watching my wiggling footsteps. He was still eyeing me down, his fists tight in large hands.

"You and that faggot brother of yours better watch out," he warned, giving me one last threatening look in those dark blue eyes of his and turning to walk down the opposite end of the hall. He threw the door open with aggressive force, allowing it slam against the wall as he continued to walk down the staircase.

As I jogged down the hall to meet Marnie and Clay, I couldn't help but keep replaying his threats over and over in my head. Carter wasn't one to forget his grudges, always keeping you in the back of his mind if there was score that wasn't settled yet. I knew he would never lose track of Clay and I, always keeping an eye on us even in the shadows. He would make us pay for being in the middle of him and Marnie, no matter how little involvement we truly had in the situation.

But I wasn't prepared for the commotion he would actually allow to unfold.

5

CHAPTER 4

One Week Before...

The eerie sense of being watched was catching on quick in the last few days.

Wherever I went in school, it almost seemed like a camera was sensing my every move, behind walls and around corners of the halls. Even if I was sitting in c ass, there was this strange feeling that a pair of eyes was on the back of my head, burning identical orbs into the back of my head. I would eat a bite from my sandwich in the café and it seemed like the pair of eyes bit along with me. I'd flick a piece of hair out of my face and the eyes would flick along with it.

I couldn't do a single thing without the creepy sense of a second person noting my every jostle.

Ever since the day in the hallway where Carter had almost choked the life out of Clay, it had been a quiet week. Clay was recovering slowly, a few purple and blue bruises dotting along his collarbone and near his Adam's apple. He was sending smiles to others and treating me like he always had before the fights happened. But the way his smiles didn't seem to crinkle at the ends of eyes made me believe that there was something much deeper going on in Clay's mind that I would never understand.

Those times in his bedroom where he locked himself away from the rest of the world, not speaking to anyone and choosing to blanket himself with strangely silent air, always made me wonder what it was he was thinking about. Every moment he remained quiet was a moment longer that he wasn't opening up. Instead of talking to someone about what was going on in his head, he was making the decision to let his thoughts swallow him whole.

How long could someone bow down to their inner voices before they cracked underneath the pressure?

Along with the scary stalker feeling, Clay's ever odd behavior and Carter's disappearance came Marnie's overwhelming sadness over her break up with Carter. For the past week she had been hanging her head as she walked to class with me, less verbal and more depressed than I had ever seen her before. It wasn't like Marnie had time to think a rational thought last week before dumping the boy she was falling for. She just ended ties as soon as she saw the monster he truly was behind those mysterious dark blue eyes.

For years, Carter Wayland had a way with words and a physical attribute that made it so easy for others to get along with him and believe everything he said. He could bat an eyelash and make a girl swoon. He could make up the biggest lie from the top of his head without much hesitation and used his physical beauty to make the girl leave their doubts about him behind the heels of their shoes. I didn't know why God graced him with the traits of a liar and fearful shadow, but there had to be a spec of karma waiting for him behind a corner somewhere.

Marnie was just another one of those girls who was spellbound by his charm, falling head over heels before he even took her hand in his.

She wasn't speaking much as we spent time together. If I tried to engage her in any type of conversation I could to stem her away from thoughts of a certain football player with a mean streak, she'd just mumble a one-worded response and continue her frowning. I wasn't used to seeing her like this, so lost and feeble. I was used to the bubbly Marnie with the eccentric cloud that always seemed to follow behind her. She was always the one making me feel better, so I wasn't sure how to help her come out of this funk.

Sitting with my head in my hand while I stared mindlessly at the fair blue lines across my notebook paper, I kept replaying Carter's words in my mind. The pair of eyes glued to my every move and belonging to an unknown patron only had me fearing his threat more than before. I was wondering if he was the one watching me or if he hired someone for the position of making me creeped out. Were they waiting for me to be alone? When I turned that corner, was the person whose eyes had been burning holes in my head waiting for me?

A small, folded piece of paper was slipped onto my desk, interrupting my fearful daydream. I immediately flicked my head up to find the person who'd given it to me and met eyes with Grayson Foster. His striking grey eyes met mine before they looked down at the note that was now in between my fingers.

"Carter told me to give this to you," he said quietly, looking around the room like Carter was suddenly added to the class's roster.

My heart raced at his words, almost unable to open up the folds and read the note. With my fingers already noticeably shaking, I said, "Why did he make you give it to me?"

I didn't mean for it to come out like I was angry that he chose a guy like Grayson to hand me the note. It was more of a feeling of surprise than anything else.

I knew who Grayson Foster was, having been in the same school with him since we were little Kindergarten kids playing on the monkey bars. He was the shyer one in the population of Riverton, always immersed in his sketchbooks and baseball games. Being the star pitcher on Riverton's well-known varsity baseball team, practically everyone knew who Grayson was. I just hadn't gotten the chance to talk to him very often, let alone be able to call him a good friend of mine.

A small blush crept up at the base of his neck, making him pull at his collar. "I don't know. I was just walking into class and he told me to hand it to you and not ask any questions. I can't exactly say no to my captain," he grinned sheepishly.

There Carter was again, involving more individuals in his issues and finding more people to blame for his misfortune. Along with being the star quarterback for the football team, he was also co-captain of the school's hockey team and captain of the baseball team. I seriously couldn't escape that guy no matter what I did.

I nodded unevenly, swallowing audibly as I cast my eyes down to the paper still shaking in my hand. Nervously unfolding the flaps of lined paper, I pushed my hand down on it against the desk to even it out. Slowly, I read over the carefully written scribble.

Don't think I forgot, Tollson. Fear threaded through my veins like a liquid, causing me to freeze in my seat. Looking around the room just like Grayson had done before me, I half expected Carter to be seating in the seat just on the other side of me, taunting me even further. Before anyone was able to read over my shoulder, I quickly balled the paper up in my hands and thrust it into my bag.

"What did it say?" Grayson asked, trying to peer over at me while I zipped up my bag.

I shook my head vehemently. "Nothing. Some stupid joke," I said hastily.

And I was wishing it was. If it was some stupid joke I wouldn't be scared every time I walked down the halls and fearful of the day he would truly make me and my brother pay. Carter was so skilled at making people feel beneath him, always making sure it was known that he had the upper hand in any event. What was he getting out of this? Was this just a thrill for him? Or was he actually seeking out a revenge for Marnie breaking up with him?

"You don't look so good. Are you alright, Callie?" he asked, his eyes soft as they ran over my flushed face.

That was the thing about Grayson. He carried his heart on his sleeve and was always there for someone, even if he didn't have the slightest clue to who they were. Grayson and I knew about each other, but never got the chance to really get to know one another underneath the exterior. Yet here he was, acting like my best friend in my time of my need.

I found myself regretting I had never gotten the chance to know him before all of this.

I nodded my head quickly. "Just great."

"Because you know...if you need..." he went to say, but I lost attention to him when Marnie came pacing into the room with her eyes cast down towards the floor and tears evident in her normally bright eyes.

She plopped down in the seat right next to mine and avoided eye contact with me at all costs. Surrounding herself with books, she kept taking out papers and pens from her book bag and pretending like she was focused on getting herself prepared for class. I couldn't ignore the sniffles coming from her end or how she kept wiping underneath her eyeliner every so often to dry away the tears.

"Marn…" I said softly, my eyes flickering to the front of the room at our Advanced Algebra teacher, Mr. Coolson, to make sure I wasn't about to get caught. Much to my luck, his back was turned to me as he wrote free hand problems on the board before him.

Marnie continued to pretend like she hadn't even seen me, her eyes casually going from the board to her paper as she wrote down the problems. Her hand was flying at warped speed, so unlike her normal half-attentive personality when she was in this class before.

"Marnie, what's wrong?" I whispered, tapping her arm and maneuvering my head so I could get a better look at her hunched over figure.

She coughed lightly and shook her head. "Nothing," she murmured, her voice scratchy and thick with tears.

I watched her with impatience, wanting her to just open up to me already. She knew by now that there were no secrets between us, something we had practiced over the years. Her other hand, the one furthest from me, was tucked underneath the desk and she kept trying to hide it from view. With my eyes now trained on the hidden arm, it slipped from underneath the desk just long enough for me to see that it was blotchy red with a purple bruise branding itself against her peachy skin.

"What happened?" I gasped, my eyes never leaving the marks on her arm.

Her eyes bulged as she glanced to where my eyes were trained on and she pushed it further from view, her leg bouncing considerably now. "What are you talking about?"

"Marn, stop! What the hell happened?" I urged, my voice becoming sharper. I hadn't noticed how loud I was until a few pairs of eyes looked over in my direction with curiosity.

"Ms. Tollson, is there a problem?" Mr. Coolson asked, pushing his thick framed glasses further up his nose as he turned to watch our encounter. His electronic pen was poised in his large hand, impatiently bouncing as he waited for me to respond.

I shook my head quickly. "No problem, Mr. Coolson. Sorry," I blushed briefly before sinking back into my seat to avoid the multiple pairs of eyes that seemed to be growing the more time he spent looking at me.

"Very well then. Please refrain from more outbursts in the future and focus on the assignment," he stated, gesturing towards the row of problems behind him and turning back around to finish his work.

Uncapping my pen with my teeth, I sunk further into the seat and started writing out the problems so everyone watching would realize that the show was now over. I couldn't help letting my eyes drift over to Marnie's injured arm every so often, wondering who had done that to her in the twenty minutes we had been apart before this class.

"Carter tried to get back together," Marnie murmured once again, hiding her face with her hand as she peeked over at me. Her eyes were sullen, filled with unshed tears as she relived the memory. I sat up in my seat and watched her intently. "When I kept telling him no, I tried to walk away and he grabbed me."

I took a sharp intake of breath. First my brother, then me and now Marnie? And Marnie was supposed to be the girl he was so into at the moment. He made it clear that he wasn't happy about the break up, mostly because he was just starting to form a relationship with her that he didn't have any plans of ending any time soon. How could he hurt the one girl who lifted him so high on a pedestal?

"What an ass," I hissed, shaking my head in bitterness. "What makes him think he can hurt everyone like this? Where does he even get off acting like that?"

"I don't really want to talk about it, Callie. It's already hard enough with everything else that happened," she sighed heavily, slinking back into her seat as she focused back on the board once again.

I gaped at her. "But it needs to be talked about, Marn!" I whispered loudly under my breath, glancing back at Mr. Coolson's turned body. "He's hurting all of these other people and no one's doing a damn thing about it. All because he's on the freaking football team! That doesn't give him a pass to do this!"

"You don't think I know that! I mean, Jesus Callie, one minute he was this perfect guy who was gentle and kind to me, listened to me and waited on me hand and foot. The next thing I know, he's got Clay up against a locker threatening to end his life. It's all coming at me from different directions and I can't keep up! Let alone get him in trouble right now," she hissed back underneath her breath, shooting me a glare that read, 'I'm done with his conversation.'

"What, you're worried he'll be benched for the season or something and cost the boys the game?" I snapped, I gave her a sideways glance while copying down the math problems with little concentration. "I'm pretty sure my brother's life means more than a stupid game, Marnie!"

"I never said...!" she shouted, obviously fed up with my relentless words.

"Ms. Matlin! I thought there wasn't an issue?" Mr. Coolson asked, glaring at her over the top of his glasses. "If something needs to be resolved, I'm sure the dean down in disciplinary can help you out with that. But my room is not the place for this!"

She was about to say something as an apology but stopped herself. Instead, she said, "You know what? I think I will go down to disciplinary." She gathered up her books and shoved the contents into her bag, slinging it over her shoulder and standing up from her desk chair. "Anywhere's better than here right now," she muttered before stalking out of the room and slamming the door behind her.

Some of the people around us were chattering and laughing at her outburst, probably already fueling rumors to be spread around later on. I just watched the door that she exited, instantly regretting the way I came at her like that.

I felt like I wasn't myself lately, snapping at people left and right and always being nervous when I walked through the front doors of school. The stress of my brother's downward spiral and fearing the day that Carter would officially get his revenge was wearing me to the bone. I kept imagining all of these horrid scenarios that only led to negative outcomes. Nothing seemed to be going right and I kept wondering when it would all end.

Instead of Clay cracking underneath the pressure, I was worried I just might before him.

Lunch had reared its ugly head and I was in search of Marnie, considering I hadn't seen her since she left class earlier in the day. I searched the North and South wings where most of the junior's lockers were and found no sign of her. After failing to find her in the girl's bathroom and at the café tables, I was worried I'd really pissed her off and she was either still dithering in the disciplinary wing or she had enough and went home.

In my trek to find my best friend, Clay ran towards me as I was making my way to the staircase to eat lunch by myself. There was a solid smile gracing his lips as he neared me, his auburn hair flying in different directions against the wind he was creating. Pushing his backpack strap further on his shoulder, he skidded to a halt in front of me and looked like he was about to burst with news.

"Hey, Cal," he said, almost in a sing-song tone. My eccentric brother was back and at full force.

"Hi, Clay..." I trailed off, raising a curious eyebrow at him as he bounced on his feet. What the hell had gotten into him?

"How's your day going?"

Crossing my arms over my chest, I said, "It's alright. I'm actually trying to find Marnie. Have you seen her?"

He nodded his head. "Just saw her in the West Wing, by the front office. She looked like she was about to go to lunch."

Feeling somewhat better about knowing where she ended up, I nodded at his statement but gave him a quizzical look. "What's going on with you?"

He gave me a confused look, one I knew he was faking. "Me? Oh, nothing..." he waved me off.

"Really? Because it looks like you're about to explode if you don't let out whatever you're hiding?"

"Okay!" he breathed out excitedly. "I can't take the suspense anymore. I have a date!"

My eyes almost fell out of their sockets due to utter shock. I tried to keep my jaw from dropping and seeming inappropriate, but I couldn't help it as it fell just a little. "With who?!" I screeched.

"Lily Powell," he boasted, his teeth shining through as he broke out in the broadest grin. "We're going to that house party together this weekend."

My heart dropped in my chest. That definitely wasn't the answer I was expecting.

Lily Powell was co-captain of the cheerleading team, bloody beautiful and about as sharp as a piece of rubber. She sported the routine long, blonde locks that seemed never ending. Her makeup and style was always ridiculously perfect and from rumors on the mill, she got it on with most of the football team…one time including Carter Wayland at a party back in her sophomore year.

Clay must have not known this information because he was bursting at the seams with excitement for the first time in four years. Either that, or he was too thrilled to go on his first date that he overlooked this fact. I could tell that this wasn't a good idea, considering Lily's past with Carter and the reputation she had as being friendly with most of the other guys on the team.

"Clay…do you think this is such a good…"

He cut me off as he let his smile drop into a frown. "Why do you always have to do that?"

Jaw dropping once again, I said, "Do what?"

"Shoot down any good thing I have to tell you about. First football tryouts and now Lily. I'm trying to have a normal life, Callie," he huffed, his eyes becoming hard with hurt and anger.

"That's what I've been trying to show you, Clay! You do have a normal life. Just because some jerks don't agree…"

He shook his head at me. "Why can't you just be happy for me? Just once?"

"I am happy for you! I'm just trying to look out for you!" I yelled, throwing my hands in frustration.

"Well I can look out for myself, Callie! Jesus Christ, I'm sick of you treating me like you're the older sibling here."

"Clay..." I went to say, my words hanging off the edge.

"I'm going out with Lily whether you like it or not. I'm done letting you dictate my every move."

And then he walked off, in the same direction he came, most likely to avoid having to walk down to lunch with me. He ran a hand through his hair as he went, frustrated with what he thought was over protection. On my end, it was just me looking out for my older brother who had a tendency to stumble into situations he wasn't fit enough to handle. He kept misunderstanding what I was trying to do for him as something other than love. He was becoming more annoyed the more I pushed and I could practically feel him drifting further and further away from me.

Whether he liked it or not, I would be at that party this weekend to keep an eye out for him. Something was churning in my stomach that was telling me this wasn't a good idea. All warning signs were pointed in the worst of results and I couldn't ignore it when it came to Clay.

I had to be there to protect him.

6

Chapter 5

The Night Before...

Although tonight's mission was clearly in pursuit of my brother on his 'date' with Lily Powell, Marnie and I had made it just a bit more fun for ourselves.

It had been about a week since our outburst in the middle of math class and she was still on edge with me. She wasn't back to the normal, bubbly girl I was so used to. She kept saying she had to 'focus on her homework' whenever I invited her over to hang out after school and didn't talk much when we were together throughout the day. I knew it was something much bigger that was bothering her, and not just the fact that I basically barked at her for not reporting Carter's behavior. We had fights before, most that lasted nothing longer than a day or two.

So something was eating her away inside, I just couldn't place my finger on what.

I was hoping it had nothing to do with the fact that she and Carter were finished. He wasn't anywhere near good for her, let alone enough of a man to keep around. He was a cocky, selfish bastard who got thrills out of scaring other people senseless. The way he was acting towards Marnie in their relationship was nothing short of a façade he must have put on for every girl that came in his path. You couldn't believe anything he did had any positive justification behind it.

Carter Wayland would forever be the nastiest form of a monster.

While Marnie was still upset about things she wouldn't clue me in on, she still accepted my invitation to crash the house party at one of the team player's massive houses. We made it enjoyable for us, me picking out somewhat slutty outfits to wear and her doing daring things with my eye shadow and lip stick. Even though her smiles were faltered and her eyes weren't as bright as before, she was still trying her hardest to make this night better for the both of us. The smiles, however small, were still there.

"Do you want to tell me what's going on with you lately?" I asked gently as she applied more dark eye shadow to the base of my lid.

She paused for a moment, her brush hanging in mid air as I glanced at her with one eye. She focused on all other parts of my face that didn't include my wandering eye.

"Um...I'm not sure what you mean."

Sighing heavily, I said, "Marn, you know exactly what I'm talking about. Ever since Carter grabbed you up like that this week, you've been...somewhere else."

She switched colors on the palette, giving the creases of my eyes accentuations while she determined what would be the best way to key me in on what was bothering her. After she blew on the brush a bit before placing it on my eye, she murmured, "Carter's just been acting weird lately."

"What do you mean 'weird'?"

I wished I could fully look at her instead of keeping my eyes shut for this makeover of hers. I wanted her to know that she had my full, undivided attention if this was too hard for her to talk about.

"After he gripped me up in the hallway the other day...he's been following me around campus a lot. If it's not him, it's one of his football buddies. I keep feeling like if I make one wrong move...he'll come after me or something," she breathed, setting the palette down and finally letting me open my eyes.

When I did, her eyes were back to the sullen, almost sunken look like she hadn't gotten sleep in weeks. She expertly covered the dark circles with concealer and made her eyes look beautiful beneath all of the make up, but I knew her long enough to know that this wasn't just some small thing to be overlooked.

"Why didn't you tell me?" I asked, placing my hand over hers that was lying limply on my plush carpet.

Her mouth quivered. "He told me not to tell anyone what happened with..." she trailed off, picking up her now somewhat healing arm and putting it back down again. "And then he had all these people following me and I thought if they heard me talk about him..."

Quickly bringing her in my arms, I tried to reassure her in the best ways I could, despite my own discomfort that I had yet to tell her about. "What do you think he's going to hurt you again or something?"

I felt her shake her head on my shoulder. "I don't know!" she cried. "I don't think he meant to hurt me the first time. I mean, Callie...I've seen him when we're alone together. He's always so gentle with me and he treated me like I was glass that could break or something. I think he's just scared of damaging his reputation and being kicked off of the team."

As she pulled back, I shook my head at her. "That doesn't give him the right to scare people like this."

"People?"

I let out a breath I didn't know I had been holding and let my shoulders sag. "I think he's been following me, too."

"How do you know?" she gasped.

"I just feel like someone's always...watching me. I can't escape it. And when you were taking care of Clay that day he had him against the lockers...he said me and Clay would regret ruining his relationship with you," I mumbled off, casting my eyes to the floor.

I should have told her sooner, clued her in on Carter's harsh truth finally coming to light. Maybe then we could have fixed this situation sooner, nipped it in the bud before things got too drastic.

"And then he gave Grayson Foster this note to give to me saying he 'didn't forget' or whatever..." I shook my head again. "He's insane, Marn."

She breathed what seemed to be a sigh of relief. "I'm glad someone finally agrees with me."

Gapping at her like a fish, I said, "I thought you liked him!"

She giggled a bit, the sound a relief to hear after being resigned to watching her mope for the past two weeks. "I did! But he's seriously insane. Did you know that he told me he was, 'The best I would ever get'? How cocky can you get?"

I laughed along with her, not questioning Carter ever uttering those words. He treated everyone like they had to bow down to him before he snapped. Much to his dismay, he actually wasn't God's gift to the world. I was just glad my best friend was finally seeing what he was capable of and wasn't letting her former feelings get in the way anymore.

Corey Palmer's house reeked of weed and beer.

Stepping into the team kicker's house on this Sunday night, I had to twist myself in a maze of sorts to get around the multitude of beer cans thrown around and bodies mangled with one another on the arm rests of couches in the family room. The party was being thrown on a school night because the team had won their latest match against Moreland County and knew just the way to celebrate...by getting drunk and forgetting all about it by the morning.

The smoke in the air was heavy, covering the party-goers like a thick blanket and making my lungs tighten at the smell. Sweaty bodies were grinding against one another in provocative motions, signaling that most would be declaring they were getting a room sooner than expected.

"Where's Clay?" Marnie shouted from behind me over the thumping bass and rowdy people lining the room.

"I'm trying to find him!" I shouted back, making a human chain with Marnie in hand to get through the mass of kids shrieking and babbling on drunken thoughts.

After avoiding a far from sober girl who was ready to start a fight with someone, that someone clearly being me, and maneuvering back outside to the porch out front, I had to squint beneath the darkness outside. As my eyes adjusted, I noticed Lily's blonde hair gleaming beneath the street lights with a familiar boy in hand.

I hadn't seen Clay before he left for his date, due to the fact that he was ignoring me after our fight at school earlier on in the week. I wanted to be able to spend more time with him, especially because he was in such high spirits about the date and was no longer spending long hours locked away in his bedroom. But I couldn't help but grin when I saw how much effort he put into his outfit choice for the night and his neatly done hair.

He was dressed in a mint green polo and dark jeans, almost making his slight tanned skin glow even further. His hair was pushed up just a bit at the front of his face to keep the little locks from fraying in his eyes. His large hand was firmly clasped into Lily's, both of them sporting flirty smiles in one another's direction. Neither of them had noticed Marnie and I practically stalking them on the front porch, so we continued to watch Clay's first date unfold.

"They're so cute together!" Marnie squealed quietly next to me, hiding herself behind a wooden beam that supported the small roof above us. She was bouncing on the back of her sharp heels, balancing herself on the metal railing in front of her.

As much as I wanted to agree, that sinking feeling of my heart plummeting to the depths of my stomach was overshadowing any hope of this going well. I couldn't help but question why they were out here when they could have been inside enjoying the party. Or else, why spend your first date at a house party? And I knew Lily enough to know that she never passed up a good party. She liked to get smashed to the point where she barely knew the name of the next guy she slept with and seemed to enjoy the fact that people had to tell her what she did last night instead of her figuring it out on her own.

From a distance, she didn't look drunk at all, walking in a straight line and never stumbling over cracks in the concrete. They looked to be keeping up quite the conversation, both of them laughing at something the other said. Watching them seeming to enjoy each other almost had me believing that I was just worrying too much and being a negative Nancy.

That is, until Carter and his army of men came striding up to Lily and Clay with devilish smirks on their faces. Carter had his hands stuffed into his pockets and the guys behind him seemed to be waiting for the signal word to pounce.

My heart was on overdrive, pounding mercilessly against my chest and allowing a cold fear to drain in my veins. Gripping onto the same wooden pole Marnie was hiding behind, I tried to stay put and not seem like the over-protective little sister Clay so rightfully hated to be around. My teeth were making a permanent dent in my bottom lip as I heard Carter laugh heartily.

"Well, Clay..." he laughed as he looked over at Lily. "I see you've finally decided to switch roles."

"I never said I was gay, Carter. You were always the one making up that rumor..." Clay trailed off, his voice trembling as he tried to keep his cool and not bow down to him just yet.

"Because I just couldn't understand why a guy would want to wear tights and prance around on stage like a fag," he rambled on, his cocky smirk never leaving his lips as he spoke. He was eyeing my brother like a lion settling in for the kill of its prey.

This made Clay drop Lily's hand roughly. "I'm not a fag!" he shouted, his back becoming taut as he straightened up and pre-pared himself to receive payback for the rebuttal.

"You better calm down, Tollson. I told you that you would be getting revenge for what you did to my relationship!" he pointed a hard finger in Clay's chest, pushing him back just a bit. Carter followed his slightly falling body, the boys behind him moving like machines in unison.

"I didn't do anything! You were the one..."

But Clay never got the chance to finish his sentence. A deafening crack resonated throughout the street as Carter's fist collided with Clay's jaw. The air left my body as I watched Clay fall backwards towards the concrete from the force of the hit. His arms flailing and his face already bleeding, he tried to save himself by skimming the ground with his elbows.

Without thinking about it twice, Marnie and I ran towards the scene and I immediately got in Carter's way as he stalked towards Clay's body once again. Pushing him on his chest, his lip curled in frustration.

"Get the hell out of my way, Callie!" he growled, not daring to push me again with Marnie in view.

"Carter don't do this to him!" Marnie cried from somewhere behind me.

"Corey, get her out of the way!" he shouted to the guy in the pack behind him, the one who owned the house that was serving the party for everyone else. Against my retaliation with swift kicks and missing smacks, two hundred and forty pound Corey picked me up from the ground and took me out of the way.

"Let me go, Corey!" I screamed, arms still flailing about. He finally placed me down on the grass, my ass plummeting hard against the ground. Before I could protest anymore, he was making a run for Clay, getting on his knees to punch my brother in the stomach.

It was almost ten against one, and my poor brother was on the receiving end. No one else was out here except Lily, Marnie and I, who were basically useless against the entire offensive football team.

"Stop it!" I shrieked. "Let him go! He didn't do anything!"

"Shouldn't have overstepped your boundaries again, Tollson. I warned you time and time again," Carter growled, wailing on Clay's innocent face once again.

"Marnie, get help!" I screamed once again, Marnie flying off just as soon as I let the words out.

"Carter, you said you just wanted to talk to him. You didn't tell me you would do this!" Lily cried, tears streaking down her cheeks as she watched him ruin my brother. "Carter, stop!"

Each boy got their shot at Clay, swift kicks to the ribs and hits to the eyes and cheeks all coming in a jumble of noise and grunts. I was sobbing at this point, tears streaming down my face like an ongoing waterfall. I was on the verge of throwing up as the blood became more prominent on the bland concrete floor. I could define each crack of bone and break in skin. It was repulsive and appalling, making my heart break into smaller and smaller pieces the more I watched this unfold and couldn't do a thing about it.

Clay's moans and pleas for them to stop became more sparse and less loud as the fight continued, Carter seeming to get enjoyment out of sucking the life out of my brother's body. I was wishing I was stronger, taller, more defensive...anything to help save my brother. He was so helpless, so unfairly paired against a bunch of guys who could probably bench press five of him alone.

With my eyes still focused on the scene before me and my ears so tuned into the damage of my older brother's body, I almost didn't notice as multiple guys ran out from the party and towards the resenting football players. I didn't recognize half of them, most probably from other schools and random passerbys who were friends of friends.

Most of the fighters were pulled off; Carter being the last one to be drug away from my brother's half limp body. When I looked up at Carter's pissed off eyes, Grayson Foster's face came into view behind him, wrapping his arms around Carter's middle and begging him to stop fighting. Carter tripped over his footing, almost falling backwards as Grayson drug him off.

"What the fuck are you doing, Foster?" Carter barked once he got back on balance turned around to face Grayson's panting body.

"You're about to kill him, Carter!" Grayson bellowed through heavy breaths. The exertion of pulling away his much larger teammate taking most out of him.

"This isn't your fight to get into!" he shouted back, pushing Grayson back with less force than he had used on Clay.

I sprinted towards Clay's still body, sobbing further as I stepped into pools of blood lining the cracks in the concrete. He had sharp cuts against his cheek and jaw line, his one eye already becoming puffy and bruised. He had an arm over his middle, probably hurting in his ribs as well. His body was covered in shoe marks and dirt, his once stylish mint green polo now rumpled and destroyed with blood and dirt.

"Clay! Clay, I'm so sorry," I cried, picking his head up gently from the ground floor and cradling it. "I'm so sorry."

"How could you do that?" I heard Marnie shriek, looking up at her through clouded eyes. She was in Carter's face now, not the least bit scared of him now that more people were watching around us. "He hasn't done anything to you! Why do you always pick him to torture?"

"Oh he deserved it and you know it!"

"You know, I didn't break up with you because of them! I broke up with you because you're a prick!" she shouted, stabbing him in his muscular chest with a finger.

Carter's bewildered expression overtook his features, his eyes wandering around the growing crowd of people coming out from the party and wondering what was going on. Some people were shaking their heads at him, others overly drunk and chanting for another fight to happen. Only a moment's span of regret was in his eyes before he shook it off and gave a look of nonchalance.

"Fuck it. I don't have to sit around and listen to this. Come on, guys. I know a better party outside of the city," he gestured to the boys to follow as he pushed himself through the crowd of onlookers and walked down the street from the scene.

Marnie ran over to Clay and me, kneeling down over his body to run a gentle finger over his profusely bleeding cuts. "Is he okay?

"Clay...are you?" I went to ask, but he pushed himself up from the ground with shaky arms.

With little strength, he tried to push my hands off of him, knocking himself back into Marnie for a moment. "What did I say about always pushing yourself into situations?" he yelled over a coated throat, spitting out a mouth full of blood after he spoke.

"I wasn't pushing myself into anything!"

"What do you call what you just did? God, I can handle myself, Callie!" he went on, starting to get up from the ground on his own. The blood switched directions and started to trickle down his cheeks and on to his shirt. His elbows were scrapped and bloody from the fall, causing more blood to fall down his arms.

"You were about to be beaten to death, Clay! I couldn't just sit back and let it happen!"

"I could've fucking handled it on my own!" he bellowed once more, trying to regain his proper balance as he began to walk down the street. The crowd dispersed for him, unlike with Carter, and watched with curious expressions as I followed him.

I went to go after him but Marnie pulled me back with her hand on my shoulder. "Let him go, Cal," she murmured, her eyes soft as I turned around to face her.

"No! He's hurt. I can't..." I shook my head, ignoring her further pleas as I tried to go catch up to him.

"You're hurt, Clay! We need to make sure..." I called after him.

He turned around in his spot, a look set to kill in his former bright eyes. "Leave me alone, Callie! I can fucking fix this myself!"

It was the first time Clay verbalized his ignorance for me. He truly didn't want me around to protect him anymore. He was hurt, beaten, bruised and bleeding. Any other sister would be able to rush to the aid of their sibling, but not me. I felt my heart re-breaking all over again at the thought of him hating me forever for this.

"I was only trying to..."

"You were only trying to help! I know, Callie! That's the excuse you've used every other time before. Well guess what? I'm a big boy now and I can help myself. I know how to fix this on my own!"

And then he stomped off, wiping his face now and again with the bottom of his already ruined shirt and spitting blood onto the street. Crossing my arms against the chilly night air, I watched him walk further and further away from me, physically and emotionally. I wasn't sure where his head was at, how he would actually react to this later on. I wanted to follow him home and make sure he was okay. I couldn't take the thought of him being alone through this.

But the thought I really couldn't take was how he actually planned to fix this.

7

— • —

CHAPTER 6

D ue to the lack of care Clay had of talking to me for the rest of the night while he cleaned himself up and encased himself in his thoughts, I spent the night at Marnie's, where she offered me a change of clothes for the next morning and shoulder to cry on if I needed it.

I ended up not saying much else after my encounter with Clay, only murmuring a soft 'Goodnight' to Marnie before she fell asleep. While she snored on throughout the night, my mind was on a replayed roll of the night's events. I couldn't get the scene of the other guys beating on Clay out of my head. I kept rewinding Clay's words in my head on how he would fix this issue, over and over again until I could recite them word for word without a reference. How would he fix this? How did you manage to fix a broken boy like that?

On the way to Anatomy the following afternoon, I ran into Clay just as he was passing by to the South wing for English class. His face was hard, a dark bruise forming underneath the half circle of his eye and cuts still fresh against his tanned skin. He was carrying his backpack in front of him, his hand reaching in and out every so often like he was in search of something.

"Clay!" I called to him, noticing how his posture froze at the recognition of my voice. He paused in his steps and took a deep breath before turning half way to face me.

"What's up, Cal?" he asked, his tone on edge and his fingers still playing inside of his bag. My eyes kept falling to his actions, which didn't take him too long to realize and bring his hand out of the bag finally.

"How are you...?" I swallowed down my fear to his jagged response. "How are you doing?"

He sighed heavily, his nostrils flaring. Looking around at any place but me, he mumbled, "I'm fine." Now that his hand wasn't firmly planted inside of the bag, his fingers were drumming impatiently against the pant leg of his jeans.

"Are you sure?" I prompted, my voice soft and understanding as I looked up at him. He seemed to be looking for something in particular, his impatience carrying on through his jittery limbs.

"I said I'm fine, Callie!" he snapped, his teeth clenched and hands becoming quicker in motions.

That shut me up. I deliberated in my head on what to say next that could possibly make him forgive me for everything I'd embarrassed him over. I just wanted to make him see that I loved him so much and just wanted him to be able to be happy. If hitting bullies for him and stepping in between a fight was what got him to be safe, than I would do it. Nothing would stop me from keeping him safe.

The silence wrapped around us both, making this encounter become far too awkward for siblings to have to bear. Squaring off my shoulders and taking in a deep breath, I went to say, "Clay, I'm so..."

"Listen, Callie," Clay cut me off suddenly, his eyes intent on whatever he was looking at behind me. His fingers became quicker than lightening and his hand traveled back into his bag once again. "I've got to go. I'm fine. I promise."

Before I could even come up with a response, he was shoving past me and working his way down the hall. The determined look in his eyes triggered a warning sign within me that I couldn't ignore. He never looked this driven before.

I looked behind me for a moment, watching his retreating back move down the hall and mindlessly bumping into others without apologizing. Some of the people were forgiving, not caring much about an innocent bump, while others scowled at him and called after him with derogatory names. His hand was still in his bag, this I noticed by the crooked arch in his elbow as he walked off.

Shaking my head at myself for working him up so much and not being able to reconcile this difference, I finally turned around and pulled my books further towards my chest. I was almost going to be late for Anatomy, save for an extra two minutes or so to sprint up the stairs and towards the Science department, so I picked up my pace down the hall.

Right before I reached the doors towards the stairwell, Clay's voice caused me to stop in my tracks. My hand planted on the door with no motivation to continue just yet, I listened further.

"Thanks for last night, Carter!" he shouted above all of the mindless chatter in the halls. "I really appreciate what you did for me!"

"What the hell are you on about now, Tollson?" Carter barked back, his tone making it evident that he wasn't in the mood for another public display of in-affection.

"You know, last night..." he trailed off, waiting for Carter to say something close to an 'Oh yeah, that time I beat you up, right?' When Carter didn't respond, I was curious enough to see what was happening so I turned around. I was hoping he hadn't touched my brother again. Clay continued on without another moment's pause. "When you and the rest of the team thought it was funny to wail on me like that in front of the whole school?"

"I don't have time for your shit," Carter shook his head. I had a hard time seeing everything clearly, seeing as how they were all the way at the other end of the hall and Clay's back was to me. People pushed me out of the way as they ran up the stairs to their next class, but I couldn't move. Something was keeping me frozen in this instance.

Just as Carter was about to turn around and walk in the opposite direction, away from Clay and his rambling, Clay's arm moved and was now out in front of him. Some people on the opposite end of the hall shrieked and others ran in different directions to escape the chaos. I could have sworn I heard the word 'gun' but that would be impossible, right? How on earth would Clay get his hands on a gun? I tried peering around Clay's broad frame, but it wasn't doing me any good.

"I think you better stick around for this one, Carter..." Clay bellowed, one hand still out in front of him.

As more people came out of classrooms and closed their locker doors behind them, noticing what was happening, more screams reverberated throughout the halls. People came running my way, as far away from the encounter as possible.

"What's going on?" I yelled over the shouts and pleas for help. "What's happening?"

No one stuck around long enough to answer me, intent on getting the hell out of here. No matter how much I wanted to figure out what was going on, I couldn't move from my spot in front of the door.

Eventually, some people had managed to push me somewhat out of the way of the entrance to the staircases, but I still couldn't see what Clay was holding.

"Whoa...Tollson, there's no need for..." Carter backed away, holding his hands up in a form of surrender.

It was such a shock seeing Carter in this position, surrendering and waving a silent white flag to bow down to my brother. Normally it was the other way around, Clay on his back on the ground, admitting that Carter actually did hold the upper hand in the fight. From the distance, I could see his face drop significantly, fear rattling his bones.

"What, are you finally the scared one now?" Clay taunted, not moving from his place. I could practically hear the smile in his tone, the way he was enjoying scaring the crap out of someone like Carter Wayland who tortured him for years.

"Man, we can handle this a different way..." Carter urged, pushing his hands forward in a lame attempt to somehow make Clay go away. "It doesn't..."

And the whole world halted in that one, fleeting moment in Riverton High's South wing.

A single gun shot went off in the air, panging a hole of utter fear into the confinement of my heart. Screams erupted louder than before, people running for their lives in so many different directions it was almost hard to keep up. I saw so many familiar and unfamiliar faces drift past. I jumped a mile in my shoes, sweat already forming at the spaces above my brows and every crevice of skin. I felt my heart collide into my throat, making it almost hard for me to scream. That couldn't have been Clay. There was no way...

When my eyes managed to glance over to Clay after the initial shock, I saw him holding a silver pistol in the air, one lone finger still clutching the trigger. He'd shot it in the air, I noticed, and not at anyone just yet. A rather large hole was implanted into the short ceiling from his shot.

I watched as Carter tried his hardest to back away. He was shrinking into a little nothing as he quivered in his combat boots. No trace of a cocky smirk graced his lips, no swagger emanated from his body, no revengeful laugh came from his mouth. He was just shivering in Clay's view; just like I'm sure Clay wanted in the first place.

"Come on, dude. This isn't the answer…" Carter wavered off, his hands still up in a frozen plea of his life.

Clay lowered the gun now, aiming it square in the middle of Carter's broad chest. They were standing feet away from each other, but somehow the distance didn't hold an ounce of importance in this matter. I couldn't see Clay's face, couldn't make out what he was feeling through the shine of his eyes. Although a part of me wished I could see him face to face, I was almost grateful that I was so far away from the chaos and unable to make out what he was thinking. It was so scary, so bone chilling to realize that my brother was holding a gun in his once precious hands.

"And what else would the answer be?" he asked, cocking his head to the side in mock question. "Trust me. I've thought about this…plenty of times. It's the only answer."

I heard Clay cock back the gun with a simple motion of his hands. I was shaking so hard I could see my Doc Martens knocking together beneath me against the floor. So many people had run off, some I could still see quivering in the hidden corners of the hall and praying to whatever God they believed in. So much fear was on display, so much hope for life as they all watched on or hid themselves.

"Clay, don't..." Carter spoke my older brother's name for the first time years.

From day one of the bullying years, Carter Wayland never once uttered my brother's first name. He would call him Tollson most of the time, settling for fairy or fag whenever he felt the time to be appropriate. Maybe it was some crazy psychological thing, like if he said my brother's name he would be weirdly connected to him and no longer able to take out his frustrations on him. Or maybe he just hated my brother that much that he couldn't bear to say his name out loud.

Whatever the reason, this was the first time I was hearing him utter his name...and it was the scariest thing I'd ever heard in my life. The trembles in his letters, the sheer fear alight in his eyes...it was all too much to look at. Especially with my brother and a deadly weapon active in his hands.

And then another shot went off. My eyes immediately squeezed shut on instinct and more screams came to life. People who were hiding behind corners were crying into one another's arms, panting and sobbing uncontrollably all the while trying to remain silent enough so Clay wouldn't see them.

I couldn't stop shaking, couldn't keep my fingers still long enough as they rattled against my legs. My back was instinctively pressed against the wall I was pushed in front of, my nails now curling into the peeling paint. When I managed to open my eyes, my heart still lurched into my throat and my stomach heavy, the only person left standing was Clay.

The gun was still facing the same direction he had it pointed, right in the center of Carter's far chest, but no one was on the receiving end. My heart went from being caught in my throat to plummeting down into my stomach when my mind put two and two together. I couldn't bear to look down at the floor where I knew he would be. But I had to; I had to see if Carter managed to run when the gun went off. No matter how much I said I hated him, I found myself wishing that he made it out alive and untouched.

I gulped aloud, careening my head around the row of lockers to look down at the floor in front of Clay's still figure. Tears immediately pooled at my lids at the scene before me, but I couldn't flee from my spot. Blood was pooling quicker and quicker around Carter's fallen body. A small hole, right near his heart and expertly shot by my somehow related older brother, sat against his football jersey, right below his Captain's emblem that was sewn in.

His hands were awkwardly sprawled out around him, his mouth ajar just barely and his chest was far from moving. The blood seemed to seep everywhere around the hall, people still screaming and crying as the events continued to unfold. No one dared to move from their spots, no matter how much they wanted to escape the hell that had just formed inside what was supposed to be the next safest place to home.

I was full on sobbing at this point, not believing what Clay had just done. Carter wasn't a perfect person, always choosing to bring down his anger on my brother and acting like the world owed him favors all of the time. But I wouldn't have wished this on the worst of people, not even someone like Carter. He didn't deserve to be lying in a pool of his own blood like this, with my brother holding the gun.

I fell to my knees, my hands shaking against my legs as my body let out the loudest of sobs. It was so heart-wrenching and sickening, watching as the blood seeped further and further away from Carter's body, his body still not moving an inch. I couldn't even tell if he was breathing anymore. All I could make out was the blood and Clay's still standing figure over the scene.

"You see what happens when you fuck with the weird kid?" Clay suddenly shouted, flailing the gun around like he just hadn't altered a life and was instead using a plastic toy. "Anyone else think they're man enough to step up now?"

He turned around in slow circles, casting monstrous glances into the eyes of so many fearful kids around him. More people pushed themselves further and further into the shadows, trying to figure out ways to get out of here unscathed. It was useless, their attempts at escaping. Clay wasn't about to let anyone out of his sights, I just knew it.

I wished I knew where Marnie was, hoping she got out like the rest of the level-headed ones before us who had managed to get out before this happened. Instead, we chose to hide in corners and behind locker rows like they were the ultimate bulletproof armor.

"Where the hell is my sister at?" he bellowed, looking around at the scared faces of his former classmates once again. I immediately shrunk back against the wall, hoping he hadn't seen me yet. The fear coursing through my veins was making me feel on the verge of passing out then, everything around me blackening before he could make his way towards me.

"Come on out, Callie!" he taunted, his footsteps heavy against the ground as he walked back and forth down the hall.

I slunk towards the floor and crawled backwards towards a hidden corner where the teacher had locked the classroom door. I was wishing she hadn't, even though I knew it was in the rule books for events like this. She had to protect the kids inside and not let anyone else from the outside come in. Trying to find a shadow beneath all of the florescent lighting, I burrowed myself into a corner and prayed that he wouldn't come this way.

People around us knew I was Clay's sister, had grown up with us throughout elementary, middle and high school. We were inseparable as kids and still managed to make time for one another as we grew up. So I wasn't surprised when all of the eyes that were cast behind a shadow of the wall fell towards me as he spoke aloud. They knew what was about to happen, even if I was praying that it wasn't.

Clay's steps sounded closer the longer it took in the silence. I wished the floor would swallow not just me, but all of us up in that moment. It would be a safe haven, an escape from the chaos that was somehow unfolding in a small town, in a tiny school like Riverton. How could this be happening? How could my once admirable older brother be waving around a gun and ending lives like they hadn't meant a thing to him?

Someone screamed just before another gun shot went off, causing me to jump once again. My heart was now firmly planted in my throat, my bones shaking to the core and my heartbeat going a mile a minute. My palms were sweating as I dragged myself to a far corner against the floor. I had to keep moving, keep myself out of harm's way. I couldn't think about the other person he just hurt. I had to focus. I had to think of another way out.

"Wow, she's there to save the day every other time something goes wrong. Now all of the sudden she's too scared to show her face!" Clay kept on, his footsteps coming closer and closer as he inspected the crevices of the halls for my all too familiar face. "Come on, Cal! It's just me..."

I swallowed the lumps in my throat, biting back the sobs that begged to rack my body. Silent tears were already coating my face in a sheen of fear. I needed to get out. There had to be a way to get out.

"Ah, there she is," his voice bounced off of the walls in the tiny space I had managed to locate myself into. Now the four walls didn't seem so protective anymore, only making me feel a fearful sense of having nowhere else to go now.

I was quivering on the floor, my jaw shaking as I tried to think of something to say that would make him stop this madness. He was swinging the gun around his finger, watching me squirm with a teasing smile, like he knew he had me at a dead end with absolutely no way out.

"What happened? You didn't feel the need to save me anymore?" he asked, cocking his head to the side like a dog.

"I..." my voice shook. I hated that he could smell the fear on me. I showed no sign of bravery like I had those times I'd saved him from his own battles. I was so weak, so awfully unstable. "Cl-Clay. Please..."

"Please? Now why am I supposed to respond to your pleas when you never responded to mine? Every single fucking time I told you to back off...you just kept coming back," he mused, raising the gun slowly.

No matter how much he was scaring me, I couldn't take my eyes off of him. I kept thinking this was a bad dream, that I'd wake up soon before he took the final shot. People weren't dying, the kids at school were all fine. They were safe in their beds in their own homes, hidden way from danger like this. This couldn't be happening.

What I never expected next was the final raise of his gun, aimed directly at my head. I was so surprised at his skill with the deadly metal, how a boy who played Peter Pan in the school's winter production and full-hearted lover of people could possibly know how to work a thing like that. His hands didn't shake at all as he pointed it at me, his own flesh and blood, his baby sister.

All those times I had protected him, saved him and nursed him back to his former self, this was my repayment from him. This is how he thanked the girl who practically saved his life last night, by taking hers. I couldn't find air in that moment, could barely see the dense, icy look in his eyes through my clouded vision. He was actually going to do this. I had no one left to save me. He was going to kill me.

The one memory that kept replaying in my mind was the one that the picture in our living room captured, Clay pulling me around the front lawn in a red wagon, him only seven and me trailing behind thirteen months and about to turn six.

"Vroom, vroom," I blathered on as Clay drove me down the front walk. We careened through some shrubs and he almost had me buckling over at a sharp turn. My mom kept warning me that he was a boy and liked to play dirty. When boys got hurt, it didn't hurt them as much as girls. But I still loved playing with my older brother.

"Fast turn!" Clay shouted over the chirping of the birds above us in the tree he was about to hit. He turned me so fast that the wagon toppled over and sent me flying into the patch of missing grass, my face in the mud.

"Clay!" I whined, spitting dirt out of my mouth and wiping an already messy hand over my lips.

He came rushing over to me, dropping the handle to the wagon and looking somewhat worried. Although he played rough like most of the boys in my class, he always made sure he was looking out for me. He gently picked me up with his chubby hands, brushing more mud off of my kneecaps and dress.

"Mommy said to play nice!" I cried, rubbing my hand over a scrape on my elbow.

Clay looked sad as he examined my injury. Then, before I could blink, he was running into the house and leaving me outside all by myself. I pouted as I watched him go, upset that he would leave me alone while I was bleeding. Tears started pooling in my eyes, overdramatic traits spilling through, but they didn't have a chance to fall. He was already running back out with something closed in his tiny fist.

Walking up to me and picking up my arm, he opened the packaging around a band aid with his teeth and started placing it gently over the cut he made. Smiling to himself when the job was done, a tooth missing from his front set, he said, "Don't worry, little sis. I'll always keep you safe."

I wondered if he remembered his childhood promise in this moment. The statement that I kept close to my heart as we grew up...seemed so irrelevant now.

"This was my way of fixing it, Callie," he simply stated, before laying his pointer finger on the trigger and pressing it down.

On instinct, I squeezed my eyes shut, somehow trying to prepare my body for the blow of a single bullet. I was crying so hard that sobs were jostling my body, my fingernails digging into the fabric of my tights. All I could think was:

This is it.

Then two shots went off...but I didn't feel a thing.

8

CHAPTER 7

My ears were shot from the sound of the close range fire. I was afraid to open my eyes, still confused as to why I heard the shot but couldn't feel anything. Had he maybe hit a spot that had instantly paralyzed me? Did he miss and accidentally hit the wall right behind my head? I was pretty sure with a securely aimed shot like that I'd be dead upon impact.

My body was still violently shaking, the fear running cold in my veins. I was breaking out in a nervous sweat, but I couldn't stop shivering like I was suddenly in the southern part of Antarctica. My fingers had held a vice grip onto the legs of my tights, my nails digging holes into the seams. My heart was beating a mile a minute, thrashing against its tight confinements and reminding me that I was still...somehow alive.

Tears were drenching every inch of my face, all over my cheeks and over my lips and chin. Liquid was running down my neck and devouring my clothes beneath it. I wanted to stop shaking; I wanted to be able to breathe again. I needed to see what happened. If I didn't open my eyes and Clay had missed, I would miss my chance to escape as he reveled in the shock of missing my face much to his dismay. He had gotten Carter on the first shot, so why not me?

Was there a God watching over me in that moment? Had some rapid force of nature moved Clay's arm to aim the shot behind my head instead of in the middle of it?

Unsteadily, with my body still jostling and my eyes seemingly glued shut; I pried them open with force and took deep, uneven breaths. People were still screaming and crying, most sobbing and trying to make a run for it while Clay's back was turned to them. They all seemed so far away now, what with my lack of hearing and my mind zoned into this one moment. They were so close yet so far.

Looking up at Clay's shocked expression, his face was whiter than normal and now his limbs were unsteady. He was lowering his gun, the deadly metal dropping to the floor with a large clink against the linoleum tiles beneath his feet.

"What the hell! You weren't supposed to… You weren't supposed to do that!" he shouted, his voice uneven and breathy.

I noticed he wasn't even looking in my direction anymore. Now with the weapon out of his hand and the wild, insane streak in his eyes long gone, he was staring down at the floor in front of me. I followed his gaze, gasping and unlocking the door to another round of sobs as I saw who was lying in front of me. They were lying on my shoe, but I hadn't even noticed the heavy weight until I fully got a look at them.

The person lying on the floor in front of me was bleeding and panting heavily, a hand over the front part of their shoulder, Clay just missing a kill shot. As my eyes maneuvered all the way down their body, I noticed another hole in their leg, more bright red blood seeping through their pants and onto the floor. Some of it was seeping through my tights and covering the ankle of my leg, but I couldn't move. I couldn't breathe.

Clay put both hands to his head, gripping tightly to his hair. "This wasn't supposed to happen like this! Why did you do that?" he kept shouting, growling and screaming like he couldn't stop the thoughts running laps in his mind.

I couldn't take my eyes off the person in front of me, couldn't move or do a thing to help. What could I have done? I had nothing to stop the bleeding, maybe just a hand for the pressure. But there were two holes, two major wounds that were sucking the life right out of one of the students in this school that didn't deserve it at all.

"Oh my God, Carter!" I heard a shockingly familiar voice pipe up beneath all of the chaos erupting around us. "Carter!"

It was Marnie.

Her voice was laced with pain and reverberated against the walls around us, making others who didn't even know her shiver against the goosebumps that formed at her utterly saddened voice.

All those times we spoke about Carter, some good but most bad, I knew she felt the same way that I had when I saw the moment unfold. He had hurt her, crushed her heart and bruised her skin, but she couldn't even attempt to push down the feelings of regret and heartbreaking pain that coursed through her as she watched his still body drain from life the longer it lied there untouched and without help.

I couldn't see her from where I was situated in the corner, near a far off classroom, but I could picture her crumbling before him to her knees, not even aware that the gunman was still grazing these hallways. Her bright eyes were probably dimming by the second as she tentatively touched the captain's emblem above Carter's gunshot wound.

The odd thing was that Clay hadn't bothered to move an inch. Neither did I, but I had another issue to deal with and an older brother with his gun once aimed at my head. It was so easy...so effortless for him to aim the deadly weapon in my direction like he could care less whether I died or not. But when he heard Marnie's voice, I only saw his face flinch for a moment and then it disappeared. He replaced it with the shocked and angered expression, his skin paling again against the darkness of the bruise that was just forming beneath his one eye.

Marnie had helped him plenty of times as well. She had pushed herself into fights and beat up bullies with me when were younger. But Clay loved Marnie in a wholly other way, something I would never understand as he still trembled with the gun in hand in front of me.

I tried my hardest it ignore her pleas at Carter's silent face, my focus trained on the person bleeding in front of me, the one who had just saved my life. Clay was still standing there with the weapon as I attended to the person lying on the floor at my feet, but my heart was pounding against my chest as Clay's figure seemed to loom over me, still monstrous and so, so scary.

With trembling hands, I arched my body forward to run a hand over their hair, pushing it out of their eyes and away from their face. I hadn't realized my hand was covered in blood, probably from being near their open wounds. I furiously wiped my hand against my already ruined tights and tried to suppress the sobs.

"Grayson," I murmured breathily, tears freely streaming down my face. "Grayson, can you hear me?"

Grayson had jumped in front of the bullet. Both of the bullets. He risked his life to save me from my monstrous brother. We barely had spoken ten words to one another in the time that I knew him and he had used his body as my far from bullet proof armor. How could he do that for me? What in his right mind made him risk his life for someone like me?

He wasn't answering my pleas for his attention, a tight hand only gripping at the hole above his heart. His grey eyes were disappearing from view as they drifted further and further shut, closing out the world around him.

"Clay, what did you do?" I screamed, my throat sore from the sobs and thick with tears I couldn't seem to control.

"I didn't...He wasn't supposed to do that!" he shouted back at me, still running his hands through his disheveled locks and panting like he had just run a mile.

Only, he'd just wounded several undeserving human lives.

"I can't...I don't..." he muttered on, his arms and legs shaking as he tried to sift through the thousands of voices speaking to him at once. People were crying as they watched the blood surge further from each of their friend's bodies, sobs ricocheting against the thick walls.

Grayson and Clay had once been friends. They talked occasionally and Grayson even tried to get Clay a spot on one of his teams in the past few years that they'd known each other. True to Grayson's character, he was far from judgmental and just tried to get the best for Clay. They weren't best friends by any means, but I knew that Clay look to Grayson as someone he'd never come across in his years in school against the vicious kids who taunted him.

Then two of the school's largest football players came running towards Clay, pummeling him to the ground with a vicious force. Clay grunted then cried out as his head almost collided with the door to the stairwells I had just planned to go through not too long before this deadly stand off.

"Let go of me!" he shouted, trying and failing to flee from the scene. But both of the players combined weighed almost four of Clay so he wasn't going anywhere. One of them kicked away the gun so it was out of reach as they kept him pushed down and saved the others from harm.

"Callie! Callie, help me!" he screamed, the way he said my name now only making me flinch at the intensity.

He had raised a gun to his baby sister, planned to kill me all along with two far from simple shots to the head. He showed no remorse or regret for what he'd just done, not even for the other lives he either ended or harmed. All along, he complained about how annoying and embarrassing it was to have a little sister tag along in every fight and save him when he should have been saving himself. I had pushed him so much that he actually felt the need to kill me and push me over the cliff of his life.

And now he wanted me to help him?

"Callie!" he shrieked as the massive football players still pinned him to the ground with angry strength.

I tried to tune him out as I focused back on Grayson. The blood was still dripping and colliding with my skin and shoes. I blew all caution to the wind and pressed each one of my hands on both of his wounds, hoping the small pressure would do something in the long list of ways to save his precious life. He stupidly jumped in front of deadly bullets to save a girl he barely knew.

We only just had our first conversation this past week when we talked about a note for me from Carter.

I wasn't worth all of this. He was a boy with a heart of gold and smile to boot. He cared so much about everyone around him and strived so hard to be the guy that everyone at Riverton loved. In my mind, he was second in command to Carter's popularity, just with a better heart and conscious mind.

"Grayson, come on," I whispered, pressing down further on the wound and watching as the color drained from his skin slowly but surely. It killed me to watch this unfold, my heart breaking into millimeter pieces as that smile just seemed to fade from his lips.

"Callie!" Clay shouted over the chaos of jumbled screams and cries. "I need you, Callie!"

Shaking my head, I kept forcing myself to block him out of my mind. He wasn't the important one right now. He had become a fearful shadow of himself, going completely mad and mental. He didn't deserve an ounce of help. The people lying on these floors with bloody bodies and aching hearts needed help the most.

The rest of the scene came in a rush of actions. SWAT team members came barging into the school, gesturing for people to escape while the linebackers held down my crazy brother. They ran for their lives, all of them coming by my sight in whirlwinds and gusts of air. Most were holding onto one another with as much strength as they could, gripping each other's hands for dear life.

As I cradled Grayson's head on my knee, my hands still pushing down on the wounds and my heart still leaping into my throat, a few of the SWAT members gently pulled the linebackers from my brother's thrashing body. They were dressed in dark black attire, bulletproof vests and glass masks over their faces covering their precious parts. Each one of them was carrying an assault rifle, one bullet in one of those guns enough to end someone's life.

"Callie! Callie!" Clay kept calling, his arms and legs flailing as the members of the SWAT team banded together to get his arms behind his back and throw the handcuffs around his once feeble wrists. He was sweating profusely, shrieking my name like it was the answer to all questions.

After cuffing him properly, two of the department's men patted him down to make sure he wasn't armed with any other dangerous weapon. One of them stepped in front of me to pick up the lone gun, the one my own flesh and blood almost used to kill me.

I knew they had to secure the area before letting any type of medical personnel inside the school, but the time between cuffing my brother and them saving the innocent people's lives seemed to drag on for ages. The longer we all waited, the less life each one of them had left in them. They had to hurry. They needed to be quicker.

Right before they walked off with my brother's still thrashing self, he looked towards me with those same gentle eyes that I once remembered from our childhood. His bright eyes were back, almost teary-eyed as the SWAT members strived to push him out the doors and into captivity. He took a heavy breath before saying his last few words to me.

"Now I get to escape this mental prison, Callie," he said almost joyfully. His eyes were soft and sad, but his voice spoke volumes in the confinements of the halls. Before they fully had him out the door he smiled small at me, giving me the odd gift of one last look of peacefulness on my brother's face.

He had gone mental. Whatever he was doing in his room all those nights he spent locked away all led to his one, dreadful moment. Those horrid years of bullying, the punches and kicks, the swings and the blows, all of the dirty words and fights that ensued all rolled into this moment of a mental breakdown. I knew victims of abuse could only handle this pain for so long, but I never once thought he would end up like this.

Growing up with one another all our lives, I looked up to the man that Clay was becoming. He marched to the beat of his own drum and always wore a gentle smile on his face no matter the situation. He could have gotten the crap beat out of him at school that day or got called a 'faggot' again by some punk kid who probably didn't even know the dictionary definition of the term. But whenever those nights would arrive that he got to come home and spend time with his family, he would break out in a grin and the pain from the day seemed to slip away.

All this time I spent protecting him just seemed to make matters worse. It only embarrassed him further and pushed him to come to an end result that would save him from this life he no longer wanted to live. He was sick and tired of being sick and tired. He was done with the pain of the blows and the sting of the words like slaps across his face. As high school rounded the corner and Carter became the identity behind the fist always lying on him at all hours the school day.

There wasn't an option of switching schools for him because Riverton was a small town that only held so many jobs for my mother. She was making so much more in the city's hospital and my father was still enrolled in mandatory AA classes at the Rec Center just down the road from our house. They felt for Clay, as I watched some nights when I crept by Clay's door and my mother was running her hand across his back while he shoved his face in a pillow after another fist fight. My dad always tried to instill words of wisdom in Clay that would get him through the rough days.

Somehow, some way, Clay thought this was the answer to all of his problems. He didn't try therapy, didn't try to take some sort of self-defense class to learn to stick up for himself. He didn't go down to disciplinary or tattle to the Coach about Carter's vindictive ways. For some reason, he felt that this was his only option left to do. He had one more year left in this place and then he was off to NYU.

And he set out to ruin every other plan of his future.

"Miss...Miss..." a male voice coaxed me away from Grayson's still face. I snapped my head up, meeting eyes with a glass covered tanned face that was dressed in the proper uniform. "Are you hurt?"

I followed his gaze as he watched the pool of blood drift around Grayson and me. I shook my head fervently, my eyes still cast down to Grayson's closed ones.

"You have to come with me then. We need to secure the rest of this area," he stated, his voice seeming to boom in the small area.

I shook my head quickly. "No! I can't...I can't leave him here!"

Even if we had barely spoken a day in our lives, Grayson Foster saved my life and I couldn't just leave him behind like that. I was escaping unscathed and unharmed, yet here he was, full of holes and bleeding for a girl he barely knew.

"Miss, we have to get you out. I'm sorry," he said, picking me up gently by the arm and trying to avoid stepping in the blood puddles.

"No! Please, just let me stay with him!" I cried, but the SWAT guy wasn't budging, simply pulling me further and further away from him. Moving his head gently from my knee, I made sure he didn't bang his head once I was removed from the scene.

"I'm really sorry, Miss. We'll try to save your boyfriend," he said lowly, only soft enough so I could hear and he could maintain his tough exterior.

"He's not my boyfriend," I said softly as he pulled me away, my eyes never once leaving Grayson's limp frame. My hands felt so weird and slimy, covered in Grayson's blood. "He...he saved my life," I breathed.

Just as I got one last glance at Grayson's poor face, the SWAT guy pulled me one last time down the hall and through the double doors of the stairwell as he led me outside. Then he said, "Then all we can do is try to save his, too."

"What are you..." I stuttered, my teeth chattering against one another as he escorted me expertly down the hall like another gunman was on the loose. He was peering around corners and hastily making his way down the stairs and outside the main school doors. "What are you...going to do with him?"

"Medical personnel will make sure..." he went to say, but I shook my head at him, my eyes squinting against the bright sunlight outside.

It almost didn't seem right, the sun shining down on all of us and the wind blowing perfectly against our skin. This day had went down a path that seemed like thunder and lightning mixing as one, a possible hurricane to come. This day called for brighter days and feelings of hope.

There wasn't any hope left in the hearts of these kids anymore.

"No..." I breathed. "The...the gunman...what are you going to do with him?"

The man halted for only a small second before letting the main doors shut behind us, all of the scarred and wounded students still stuck in the bitter confinements inside. Right before he dropped me off at an ambulance to make sure I was okay, (the blood was still making him question my sanity), he turned to me and put a hand on my shoulder in a small effort of comfort.

"He's going to go away...for a long, long time," he said, squeezing my shoulder and moving off to join his team that had just cuffed my brother and taken his chances of any brighter future.

As I watched him walk off into the distance, his words swirled around in my head over and over.

A long, long time. My brother was going to officially be gone for a long, long time.

9

— ◆ —

CHAPTER 8

After getting checked out by the frantic EMT who swore I was delusional when I said I wasn't hurt, I was forced into talking to some of the detectives on the scene and chatting with a bunch of different business dressed men whose names I couldn't bother to remember. The amount of blood caked onto my skin through my tights and the spots stained on my clothes could have pointed in another direction, saying that I wasn't okay, but I was only hurting on the inside. Physically...I was okay. Mentally...I wasn't so sure.

The conversation I had with one of the detectives didn't last very long, for he told me that he would be in touch in the next few days for me to come in and give a statement and actually tell him what happened today. As I walked away from him, my heart was suddenly heavy with regret and an inkling of fear still running in my veins. Looking around me, people were crying, shouting, shivering against their nerves. I couldn't help but feel like I had caused this mess. Carter had pushed him, but I pushed him further.

I didn't know if I should apologize because I was his sister. I should have seen signs that he was going to do something so big like this. Maybe he had planted a path of small clues that I just stepped over and pretended I didn't see. But every time I passed another frightened figure in the schoo 's courtyard, I saw that I couldn't look them in the eyes. I felt respon sible, liable, and so fucking confused.

When I managed to make my way home, my father was the only one home, his car the only one in the driveway. I wondered where the hell my mom was, knowing full well that her daughter attended the school that just witnessed the first shooting in this city. My father's shrill voice picked up with the wind I brought in behind me, making me want to close the front door quietly and make my presence unknown. But I couldn't do that either.

I felt so outside of myself, like the person walking into this house and picking up their feet wasn't me. My heart wasn't the one that was beating; my eyes were the ones that were blinking rapidly to hide the incessant tears that just didn't seem to stop.

It hurt seeing all of the kids at school being reciprocated by their parents in the courtyard, mothers brushing back their daughter's hair and fathers not letting go of their broken down sons. Mine were nowhere to be seen in that moment, but I knew why. They were working hard or picking back up their broken pieces, so they must have missed the news of the shooting.

Until now.

As I slowly walked to the kitchen entryway, the squeak of my still somewhat slippery Doc Marten's must have pulled my dad's attention away from his conversation because he immediately dropped the phone, the pounding of plastic against the granite countertop making me jump, and he ran straight for me. Enveloping me in his arms, he kept squeezing me tighter, almost like he was trying to make sure that I was actually here.

"Jesus, Callie. Are you alright? Were you hit? How did you get home? Why didn't you wait for me?" he hurried on, his sentiment making the annoying tears spring back to life once more.

I hadn't answered after quite some time, so he pulled back and kept his hands clasped around my arms. "You're covered in blood! Are you hurt?" he cried, his dull green eyes wide with parental concern and relief that I was alive.

I shook my head abruptly, no longer keeping up with the job of pushing down the tears. I just kept shaking my head, my hair springing back and forth, and let the tears fall. My whole body seemed to break then, everything feeling weak and lifeless. Nothing seemed right. This school day didn't seem real. I half expected Clay to come through the door with that bouncy look in his eyes and greet everyone.

"Oh, Cal," he breathed, pulling me back into his arms and patting the top of my head in the most comforting way that he knew how.

This moment was odd for my father and I.

During my sophomore year, my dad was sent away to rehab after my mother had found him passed out drunk in the living room, too many beers littering the couch and a Jack Daniel's in his limp hand. He was barely breathing and before my mom had called an ambulance, she told us that this was the last straw. He had already been ditching work every other day to spend his days on the couch watching rerun episodes of Duck Dynasty and sipping from multiple selections of alcohol.

Ever since his stint in rehab last year, he seemed distant and un-heard of. He come home lifeless and pale, like rehab had physically and emotionally drained him to the core. He hadn't acted like a father for months. Most of the time when you asked him a question, he would just grunt in acceptance or pshaw in disagreement. His worried words were the first few I had heard in over a year.

I was panting in his arms, the sobs wracking my body and escaping when they finally got the chance. Digging my fingers into my dad's back, my knees felt weak and I started falling to the floor. He noticed straight away and dragged me to one of the wooden chairs that were dotted around the kitchen table. He sat me down gently and chose to kneel down on the floor in front of me instead of taking a seat himself.

"Sweetheart, who's...who's blood is this?" he stuttered, inching his fingers out to pull at it, but instead opting out and running it above the surface.

"It's...it's not...mine," I sobbed as I clenched my fists and pushed them in my eyes, trying to escape this stupid race of emotions.

"Then..."

I cut him off, still breathing heavily and barely able to catch my breath. "Gr-Grayson...It's Grayson's," I cried, my heart dropping to the pit of my stomach once again as I flashbacked to the moment when I opened my eyes and he was lying in front of me.

The distant sound of someone yelling cut into our own voices and my dad whipped his head around to the phone still lying on the counter. After squeezing my knee quickly, he jumped from his spot and placed the phone against his ear again.

"I'm sorry, Callie just came home," he said quietly this time. He wasn't yelling at the person on the other line, almost like his disbelief was now put to rest with me as proof. His fingers turned white as he grasped the phone tighter. "That can't be true! He's going to come home soon. They're probably just..."

The person on the other line must have started talking over to him because he shut up right away, his skin growing paler and his body was sagging. He ran his free hand through his thick mane of auburn hair, matching mine and Clay's, and tugged at the ends. Running it over the sweat on his face, he said, "I can't..." he shook his head. "I don't believe this," he said quietly and forced.

His voice seemed to crack at the end. The person said something else and he nodded along. "I have to...I have to go. Thank you for calling."

He slammed the phone onto the wall unit in front of him and let out a deep breath. Still shaking his head, he looked over to me with sorrow in his eyes. They were filled with so much life, so unlike the version of him he had been displaying the past few months. We just looked at each other in the horrible silence, both of us not sure how to handle this.

Then a single tear slipped down his cheek, the first tear I had ever seen my father shed. He was supposed to be the calm, cool and collected one. Father's were usually bread-winners for the family, did hard labor and bore, what seemed, like the whole world on their shoulders for their kids. And here he was, breaking down right in front of me.

"Dad," I cried, my heart breaking over and over as I watched him fall apart.

"Why did he do it?" he screamed, shattering the silence. "What possessed him to do this? He...he took lives. My son doesn't do things like this! He doesn't..." he shook his head, trying to get rid of the thoughts that must have been playing over and over in his head.

If only he knew what kept replaying in mine.

"I know," I sobbed, crossing my arms against the sudden chill in the room.

I hated this. I couldn't grasp onto reality. I couldn't come to terms with what was happening, what happened back there in what was once the safest place in town. My own brother turned so many lives upside down, tore so many hearts apart and scarred everyone forever. He unleashed a living, breathing, hell onto those individuals that thought their day was going to be like every other.

How could he do this? What did he become?

"Your mother called," he said randomly, making me pick my head up. "She's been called to help in the Emergency Room with the...victims," he gulped. "She doesn't know when she'll be home."

I nodded silently, swallowing down the sobs that threatened to come through again. The scenes just kept reeling over and over, I couldn't escape them. I wanted to rip my brain out so I could get rid of them. The images of everyone's scared faces, Clay's vicious streak in his once gentle eyes, Grayson's bloody body, the football players, Clay's voice.

Callie...Callie...Callie.

I placed my hands over my ears, like doing so would suddenly make it all go away. "Ah!" I screamed, squeezing my eyes shut as well to get rid of this. It wouldn't leave. It wouldn't stop. I just wanted it to stop.

I felt my dad's hands on my arms, pulling them from my ears. I tried to fight back, but he was stronger and succeeded before I could win. "Callie! Callie, what is it?" he yelled over my shouts.

"I can't..." I panted again. "I can't get rid of them! I can't stop seeing it all!"

When I opened my eyes, my dad was kneeling down in front of me again, his hands on my knees. "What happened back there?" he asked, quietly. "Why did he...?"

"I don't know! Everyone needs to stop looking to me like I know! I don't have a clue! Just because he's my brother doesn't mean I..." I shouted, throwing my hands in the air.

"Okay! Okay," he shushed me, bringing his hands up to my shoulders. "We don't have to talk about it. I'm just...I'm just happy that you're safe. You're here...and that's all that matters right now."

I threw myself up from the chair, almost knocking over my poor dad. "No! That's not all that matters! People back there...they're hurt! They were shot, Dad! And Clay, he...he did that to them!" I pointed behind me like I was back at school again.

My father went to say something in return, but I wouldn't let him. I ran as fast as I could from the house, right out the front door and into the open air. He was calling after me, screaming from the door and urging me to come back so I could be safe. But nothing felt safe anymore.

What was safe?

Home was supposed to be safe, but Clay tainted that. School was supposed to be the next safest place, but he tainted that, too. He ripped everything out from underneath all of us. We didn't stand a chance against him and his gun and he knew that. He woke this morning with a single thought in his mind that he was going to actually kill the people he went to school with. He was going to kill people with families and significant others and loved ones who would be shattered at the news of losing their closest person.

My own flesh and blood had conjured up a plan so foolishly and profoundly that it managed to scar the rest of us for eternity. No longer were we the happy little town of Riverton with a wrap around lake and a small population of about 3,000. We were no longer the cheery, gossipy type with an alliance on Sunday night football times. That tiny thread that connected each and every one of us just seemed to snap at the click of the trigger against Clay's finger.

I just kept running, not sure where my destination would be. I hadn't realized it started to rain outside until I managed to collapse on a park bench somewhere down the road. It was pounding against the pavement all around me, splashing up against the concrete and engulfing me. The clouds turned dark in the sky and the once bright, sunny day seemed to vanish all around me. All I could say for it was that it matched. It coincided with what the day had become...a dreary, dark and stormy time.

"Callie, you don't understand," he huffed, trying to walk away from me.

I grabbed him by the arm and pulled him back. "Then make me understand, Clay! I don't get why you're kissing these guys butts all the time. They're not nice."

I had just started sixth grade, Clay starting seventh and the second year the torture seemed to escalate. Now that he was in middle school, the bullies were harsher and Clay was interested in pursuing more of his interests. That is...until the biggest bully in school, Darren Taylor, told him that being a stage 'dork' would get him beat up.

"I just want to fit in!" he shouted, stomping his foot against the pavement while we talked outside at activities time during lunch.

"But you tried so hard to get that part in the play! Why are you going to throw it all away to be friends with that jerk?" I threw my dramatic hands up in frustration.

"Because!" he shouted back, making more eyes drift towards us as the kickball game seemed much less interesting than this fight.

"Because why?" I urged.

"I don't want to get beat up, alright?" he yelled. "Are you happy?"

My heart sunk as the brightness in his happy eyes seemed to dim. He was angry but his eyes spoke volumes in how he really felt, but was too embarrassed to admit. He was scared.

"Darren's all talk and no action," I shook my head, my voice becoming timid.

The eyes around us moved back to the kickball game as our words became less harsh and quieter. Clay hadn't responded to what I said, only looking at his dirty Converses and biting his lip. I knew he was hating this conversation, hating that he couldn't be 'tough' like the rest of the boys at school.

"I'm still giving up my part," he said quietly, pulling his backpack up his shoulder and preparing to leave. He was done showing his baby sister how scared he was. "It doesn't matter anymore."

"Clay..." I chastised, wanting to run after him and force him to think about this further. He worked so hard for his first ever part in the school's play. I didn't want him to give up something he loved for some boys who would never welcome him like he wanted.

"I just want to fit in, Callie. It's all that I want."

As I thought back to that moment, Clay still seemed the same to me...the scared, anxious boy he had always been. He was just so hell bent on fitting in with kids who would never accept him. He was different, out there and against what they all thought was 'normal.'

But to me, he was the older brother every girl would want. He was funny, caring and always accepted me for who I was. He was open-minded and so, so smart. He was charismatic. He had so much ahead of him after high school, no matter how small the world seemed to him from the inside of those walls. He tried to fix it.

But chose the worst way to escape it.

10

CHAPTER 9

School had been cancelled until further notice, as if this much wasn't obvious to everyone. There was still blood that needed to be mopped up from the once shiny floors and investigations that were still occurring. No matter what any one of us did, we couldn't seem to escape the confinements of that awful day.

It had been two days since the 'incident', which I had pushed myself to call it in an effort to push the memories out of my head. If I kept calling it what it was, a shooting, I just kept hearing gunshots and picturing people bleeding everywhere. Some nights, I woke up in a cold sweat, screaming at the top of my lungs and scaring my dad senseless. My hands would shake and the darkness seemed too much to look through. I wanted clarity, normality, things I could see in the distance without much effort.

I'd push myself out from underneath my now wet sheets and clamber over to the light switch at the other end of the room. When the single ceiling fan light clinked on, casting a soft glow in my once too scary room, I'd breathe a sigh of relief and slink back into my covers with the lights never seeming too bright to sleep through.

The same thing happened to me again last night, making me look like a jumbled mess when I'd managed to get out of bed this morning. Dark circles were underneath my eyes and when I first saw them in the mirror I was passing in the hallway, I paused. The faint, almost bruise-like, marks reminded me of Clay. The last time I had seen him he had a fresh bruise underneath his right eye, something that made him stand out even more underneath the fluorescent lights in school.

Not that he needed anything other than the silver pistol in his hand to stand out that day.

I tried to shake off the feeling of his eyes on mine, walking past the mirror and making a mental note to have my mom take it down for the time being. As I tip-toed down the stairs early that morning I heard the clinking of pots and pans, most likely my mother messing around to make breakfast and a pot of coffee for herself. I hadn't seen her since the morning that I left for school that day.

When I made my way to the kitchen entryway, large and somehow seeming overpowering above me, I just stood still as I watched her. She was hastily moving throughout the kitchen and occasionally pushing tuffs of blonde hair from her sweaty face. She almost spilled the hot coffee on her pristine white hospital sneakers, cursing to herself when it singed her arm.

She grabbed the end of her green scrub shirt and dabbed at the burning pain. It wasn't until she did this that I noticed the faint blood stains on her front, demanding to be looked at. I felt a shiver creep up my spine as to who the stains belonged to…Carter, Grayson, the girl who had been hit by a stray bullet?

"Jesus Christ," she cursed in vein, putting her arm underneath the faucet of the sink and running cold water over it.

"Mom," I whispered, the sound of the water running drowning out my voice. She didn't even flinch because she hadn't heard me. So I tried again. "Mom," I said a bit louder this time.

She jumped in place, slamming the faucet down to stop the water. Turning in place, her sneakers squeaking against the kitchen tiles, she looked at me wide-eyed. Her face was almost pale and her eyes were drained from the life that was always in them. She just kept blinking at me, not saying a word, and kept her arm hovering over the sink.

It was the first time either one of us had seen the other since the 'incident' and I wasn't sure where to start. Should she speak up first? Maybe ask me how I was doing? She was my mother after all. Or should I ask how she was doing? She was the one who was handling wounded teenagers who were shot by her own son.

We both had a lot on our plate to discuss.

"Callie," she cleared her throat. "How did you...how did you sleep, dear?"

I shrugged, walking over to the dining table but not taking my eyes off of her. She looked like she had so much to tell me, things she knew she couldn't discuss because of hospital policy. Behind those tired eyes were so many horror stories I wasn't so sure I was ready to hear.

"I haven't been sleeping very well," I mumbled, now casting my eyes down to my wearing nails. In the past few days, a nervous habit kicked in and I'd been chewing them to the bone without noticing. God, I was such a wreck.

She nodded quietly, measuring her next few words. "Yeah, try working a two day shift. Sleep seems like a gift to me right now."

I could tell she was trying to keep the conversation leveled, normal so I wouldn't start bursting into tears in front of her. She was too drained to deal with a broken daughter, let alone dealing with hurt teenagers and a jailbird son.

So I went along with her stalling and grinned while bearing my teeth. "I can imagine that those days must have been hard."

She stopped in her walk towards the fired up oven, her hand pausing before it touched the handle of one of the pots that I now noticed contained a few bits of scrambled eggs. Every time her shoes squeaked I kept wincing. I couldn't help it, everything made me jumpy these days.

All she did was nod her head silently, shoving all focus into cooking her meal and getting out of the stained clothes. I couldn't take my eyes off of the blood stains, wishing she would just open up and tell me what had happened down at the hospital with all of the kids I went to school with. How could it be against hospital policy when it involved people I saw every single day of my life? I grew up with these kids. One of whom saved my life. I had a right to know what happened, who was hurt, who was healing and who didn't have a chance.

"Mom…" I began wearily. I could see her raise her brow while she kept her eyes on the pan in front of her. "Whose…Whose blood is that?"

Her muscles froze again, but she quickly recovered. "What blood?"

So now she was playing stupid. Was this all just a coping mechanism? Or just a game to get me to stop reminding her of the past two days she spent with those kids?

"On the front of your shirt," I pointed at her.

"Sweetheart, why don't you pick out what you want for breakfast and I'll start making it for you?" she diverted, smiling grimly at me.

"Mom, whose is it?" I asked, my pulse now racing in my chest.

I kept making up scenarios in my head as to what exactly happened at the hospital. Clay had expertly hit Carter where he needed to in order to kill him. Had he died? Grayson was shot twice, once in the front shoulder and once in the leg. Had he died? All I kept seeing was blood and sad faces and scared eyes. I couldn't think about anything else, no matter how hard I tried.

"Callie..." she sighed heavily, stabbing at the eggs vigorously with her spatula. "It's against hospital policy to talk about..."

I cut her off, shaking my head. "I don't care if it's against codes or rules! What the hell happened back there, Mom!" I screamed.

My mother was pumping me with bullshit as she talked about hospital rules and regulations. Technically, she wasn't allowed to tell bystanders, even her family, what happened during the work day with patients. But she always came home with horror stories and creepy backlines about people we didn't have a clue about. However, now that it involved me, she had nothing to say.

"Why do you want to know, Callie?" she asked, throwing the spatula on the counter and placing her hand on the counter to lean her body. "Haven't you seen enough?!"

"I know those people! I was there! I saw it all happen! I have a right to know what happened to them," I shouted again, getting up from the chair this time. My legs were too jittery to sit still.

Her face went slack, all emotion draining from her face. The only person who knew that I was in the same room as the 'incident' was my dad. He must not have gotten to my mom yet because she looked too surprised to learn this new information. This was her first time home in two days and she didn't have a clue what was happening to her own kids.

"You were…" she gasped, placing a hand over her open mouth. "You were there?"

I nodded, rolling my lips into my mouth to stop myself from saying anything more yet. I wanted to let it all sink in, show her how scared I was for not just myself, but for all of those kids back at school. No matter how many times my dad kept telling me it wasn't true, I still couldn't stop myself from thinking that I was somewhat responsible for this mess.

He was my brother after all.

"Are you…" she trailed off, searching for the right things to ask me. What did you ask someone who's witnessed an 'incident' like this? What did you do to console them and comfort them?

"I'm not," my voice broke at my last word as I squeezed my eyes shut to stop the tears before I knew they would start. "I can't stop seeing everything and hearing all of those screams and the…" I stopped myself before I said the word that scared me the most.

As much as I hated the thought of it ever happening, I wished she was with me in that moment. She would be able to understand the things I just couldn't explain to her. She would see things through my eyes and not the eyes of a bystander who happened to help the wounded. Then she would be there to patch everyone up before the life drained out of their bodies like the SWAT team had allowed.

"Callie, I'm so sorry," she breathed as she raced across the kitchen to wrap me in her arms.

This hug was different than the one with my dad. His was based upon worry and anxiousness about me returning home safe. He was filled with shaky nerves about his now killer son and his mentally unstable daughter. Although it felt nice to be in his arms again and experience what it was like to have a father figure back in my house again, it wasn't like my mother's.

Hers was filled with sorrow and love. She was depicting to me all of the hurt she had been experiencing in the past two days and relieving herself of the burden of holding so many children's lives on her shoulders. This hug was for me as much as it was for her. Her hug was more heartfelt and caring rather than just concern.

We just stood there for a while, her releasing her burdens and me releasing mine. We didn't speak for what seemed like hours, just wrapped each other in hugs we hadn't known we needed. I wanted to tell her all about it, every detail, picture and sound. Maybe if I let it all out it would stop replaying constantly in my mind like a nightmare I couldn't get rid of. The words sat there on the tip of my tongue, practically panting in desperation to get out.

But I couldn't do it. She wouldn't understand. She would never be able to see it the way I saw it. No one would.

Except for those who were in the hall that day.

I pulled away after a long while, still wanting to know my answer. Her face was passive, her eyes telling me so many stories. The eggs started to smell like they were burning as she sniffed the air, immediately running back to the stove and shutting off the flame.

"Whose blood is it, Mom?" I asked again, my voice level and my eyes never leaving her.

She sighed heavily again, her lips in a tight line. "Are you sure you want to know all of this?"

I shook my head, my hair flying in front of my face. "I just want to know the answer to my question. I'm not...I'll let you know when I'm ready for the rest."

I wanted so badly to know about everyone else in that hospital. When I first walked in here and saw her hiding so many stories, I wanted to beg her to tell me everything that she knew, everything that she saw in the past forty-eight hours. But after mulling over my thoughts while she hugged me and realizing some of these stories may not have fairytale book endings…I wasn't sure I was ready to hear the outcomes.

She squeezed her eyes shut, her crows feet crinkling against her softly tanned skin. Taking a deep breath as she relived the moments in her head she said, "It's Grayson Foster's."

My heart dropped into my chest as I sucked in a shaky breath. I flashed back to the moment when I slammed my hands onto his wounds, pressuring myself against the pouring blood and trying my hardest to plug the holes so he would stay alive. I kept thinking about how he must have jumped in front of me. Why did he do this? What happened?

"Is he…" I breathed, panting heavily as I felt bricks land on my chest. This was the far from fairytale ending I was dreading.

"He's okay," she stated firmly, a hand cocked to her hip while she watched me unfold before her. "We managed to fish out the…" she paused and winced at the word she was about to utter. I knew why she couldn't say it. It was the same reason I couldn't utter the word 'shooting.'

"How is he? Can I see him?" I badgered, my nails digging into the wallpaper behind me as I breathed a sigh of relief.

Her eyes widened at my pleas. "I didn't know that you were close with Grayson."

"I-I'm not…" I stuttered. "He…"

She talked over me with hard eyes, like she was still keeping secrets from me. "He isn't allowed to have outside visitors just yet. He's still in Intensive Care Unit and regaining back strength. Why do you suddenly feel the urge to visit him?"

"Mom, Grayson was the one who…"

The sound of the doorbell ringing screamed throughout the house, promptly cutting me off before my jagged confession left my lips. My mother kept watching me with careful eyes like she was trying to read something I was sure I wasn't giving off. No matter how I looked, she would never be able to tell that Grayson Foster was the one who saved my life. She would never be able to read that from my body language.

I raised my brow at her, wondering who that could be there so early in the morning. My father hadn't even woken up yet and he was considered the early bird of the family. The sun was just starting to rise beneath the trees in the backyard behind my mother and most of the neighborhood never woke up at this time.

It didn't help that this was the residence that housed Riverton High's killer.

Who would want to visit us?

My mother walked past me and out into the family room, padding against the carpet in her too-white sneakers. I trailed behind her as she went, my mind wandering as I thought of who it could be. For a split second, I thought it was someone's family member getting revenge that my brother had condoned on their loved one.

When she finally opened the door, my stomach dropped once again this morning. Two men were dressed in long overcoats, shielding themselves against the bitter winter that was rounding the corner soon. Their faces were made of stone, the man in the front holding up a badge encased in a leather pouch.

"Mrs. Tollson, I'm Detective Warren. I'm here for your daughter," he stated, his voice business like and no nonsense. I found myself cowering behind my mother's shadow, grateful he hadn't seen me just yet.

But she was far from the protective mother I wanted her to be in that moment, pulling me by the elbow to stand in front of her and displaying me to the detective. "She's right here. Why do you need her?" she asked, an edge taking over her voice.

"We need to take her down to the station to ask her some questions about the shooting," he said, eyeing me quickly with no emotion in his eyes before looking back up at my mother.

"But she hasn't done anything."

"You're correct, Mrs. Tollson. We just need her to come down and answer some questions about her brother if that's alright. This incident is still under heavy investigation and she would be very helpful in this case," he continued, trying his hardest to lose the stony face and keep his voice light and level.

I looked up at her, practically begging her with my eyes to not let me go. She could come up with some excuse to keep me here. Hell, she could even slam the door in their faces for all I cared. I was already re-living the nightmare that was my brother's hurricane. I didn't want to talk about it all again like I knew the answers behind why he did this.

I didn't have a clue.

Just because we were related, everyone was under the assumption that I could read his every thought. We were so different from one another and I was out of tune with Clay's actions the moment he started locking himself in his room a few months ago. It wasn't like he sat me down the night before the 'incident' and told me detail by detail about his plans to take other people's lives because they had hurt him.

I almost wished he would have done that so I could have had the chance to stop him while he was ahead.

"I suppose she could answer some questions," my mother said.

I shot her a glare when the detectives weren't looking. "That's great. Thank you, Mrs. Tollson. Come on, Callie. Come with…"

My mom cut them off. "No! If it's alright, I'd like it if I could drive her down to the station myself."

The detectives looked stunned for a moment, but I was silently thanking my mother for offering up a bargain I was pretty sure they couldn't refuse. I was helping them. The least they could do was make me more comfortable by allowing my mother to drive me instead of being forced into a police cruiser.

Detective Warren cleared his throat. "Sure. We'll meet in fifteen minutes?"

My mother nodded before rightfully shutting the door in their faces. She turned to me with a worried expression, the frown seeming to overtake her. "Are you okay to do this?"

Was I was okay to do this? No. That much was obvious. I wished I didn't have to do this. I wasn't the one who had unleashed the hell upon the school. I hadn't hurt anyone. I hadn't become mad with rage like Clay had. Why was I suddenly the target for questions? There were so many other witnesses they could ask.

Just because we shared the same bloodline didn't mean that I had a front row seat to Clay's thoughts.

"No, I'm not. But I don't have a choice, do I?"

I didn't give her a chance to answer, just made my way up to my bedroom to change and making a conscious effort to avoid the wretched mirror in the hallway. After changing into something respectable enough for a police station interview, I realized I had yet to brush my teeth. As I made my way out of my room, I walked down the hall and froze in my steps. Clay's room was on the way to the bathroom and his bedroom door was open just enough to give me a glimpse into his once normal life.

His bed was unmade just like it had been the morning of the 'incident'. His hunter green comforter cast halfway down to the floor and his sheets crinkled from sleep. A worn white t-shirt was thrown on his desk chair, hanging from it by the collar of the v-neck. His old scripts from previous plays were piled high on his desk, some lying on the floor by the metal trash bin. And then my eyes met the simple, thick framed photo by his laptop that was still open.

It was the one we had taken the first day of his senior year and the first year of my junior, just a few months before this. We were all smiles, his arm thrown around my shoulder and me laughing like an idiot. His bright white teeth almost cast a glare from the flash of the camera, but we looked so...peaceful in that picture. He didn't look like a murderer. He was just my older brother, kind-hearted and open. Nothing about him screamed 'killer'.

He looked so...normal.

Everything he always wanted to be.

I choked back the threat of tears as I cast my eyes away from the photo and practically sprinted down the hall to get away from his bedroom. So many things in this house reminded of the person he used to be. His stuff was still strewn around here like he was planning on coming back in the next few days. So many pictures reminded me of the way things used to be. But I had to keep telling myself that that's exactly what they depicted, the 'used to be' moments.

Things would never be like that again.

CHAPTER 10

It was so cold and tiny.

The four walls around me seemed like they were about to close in around me, eating me whole before I had the chance to talk. It was weird to me, that I was a most so close to Clay here at the police station. The county prison was only about a mile or so away from here, so close that I could just run free from this place and demand to go and see him.

But did I really want to if I had the chance?

Shaking my head at myself, I needed to remember that he was not the person he once was all those years ago. Even just last week. It was like the moment at the party made him...snap. Everything he worked so hard for, all those times he persevered to the finish line, and he couldn't manage to make it the end. He got right before the final ribbon of the end and turned to the side instead of running straight through. Was the prize not great enough for him?

"So, Ms. Tollson," Detective Warren cleared his throat thoroughly as he said my name.

"J-Just call me Callie...Sir," I stuttered, figuring adding a term of respect would keep him on my side. If I broke down in this session, I wanted him to be okay with me leaving and not trying the good cop, bad cop routine that I heard about in so many FBI and CSI television shows.

He nodded. "Okay, Callie. Let's start by you telling me about your brother, Clay. What was he like...growing up?" He gestured for me to go with a wave of his pen in hand.

This question didn't need a well-thought out response. The Clay I was about to describe was the infamous big brother any girl would wish for. He was the poster child for the 'perfect son', despite what everyone around him batted into his mind.

"He was so kind. When we were little, he always let me play with him and his friends. My mom never approved of that type of thing, worried I'd mess up my dress or my hair. But I wasn't afraid to get a little dirt underneath my fingernails," I smirked slightly, the smile falling right away as I looked down at my bitten down nails and was reminded all over again what life was like now, not back then.

Detective Warren let a small smile peek through his stiff lips for only a moment. But it didn't last long, for it disappeared straight away as he looked down at a notepad in front of him. "So Clay had a lot of friends growing up?"

I looked past him and behind the window that was meant to be double-sided. I couldn't see the people on the other side, but they sure as hell could see me. It made me feel uncomfortable so I looked back down at my hands again.

"For a few years there he did. But then..." I coughed behind my hand. "He started to get into things like plays and reading books. People didn't...they didn't really approve of his life choices," I whispered.

The room was so tiny, but every word I said felt amplified. I could murmur a word and it was like a megaphone was preaching my words back at me. I found myself wincing at every word I said. Almost like I was betraying Clay for talking about him while he wasn't there. These people wanted to lock him up for a really long time.

And I was going to be the cause of this if I kept going.

I was ready to push myself up from the chair, declare myself a mute and run right out of that small office space. But then the images of the 'incident' came back to life in my mind and I abruptly locked my feet to the floor. I heard Marnie's screaming and saw Grayson's body. All of those people were hurt because of what my brother did. I couldn't just walk away to help give him an edge in court.

"These…people," Warren gestured with his pen again, almost mocking my words. "Did they bully Clay? Do you think that's why he ended up shooting them?"

I gulped at the verb. It was amazing how a seven letter word could pack such a punch as it was said. "Um…Well C-Carter beat him up a lot. He and my brother were always butting heads."

He nodded again, writing something down on the lined paper before him. "Now some eye witnesses mentioned a party of some sorts the night before the incident. Were you at the party that night?"

I only nodded. Pulling the sleeves of my jacket down my arms and cuffing them in between my clenched fingers. I was there again, standing before the fight and wincing as Clay got the life beat right out of him. All of the kicks were ringing in my ear, the cracks of hands against bone. I suddenly felt sick all over again.

"What happened at the party?"

I closed my eyes, taking in the scene of the front yard to Corey's house. My butt firmly planted in the grass where Corey had thrown me. Grayson pulling Carter off my brother's bleeding body. The way he pushed me away so easily and promised he would fix whatever had happened. Not even my worst doubts had me picturing him firing up at our high school and taking innocent lives.

I never knew he could pull off such a thing.

"C-Carter and some guys beat him up. But before things got…too bad…the guys were pulled off of him and Clay was bleeding a lot. He had a lot of bruises and cuts."

"Did Clay ever mention anything about doing…those things back to the guys who hurt him? Did he mention revenge of any kind?" he asked, eyeing me down for my answer. His bright green eyes were hard underneath the flickering lights.

I shook my head, positive that if he had said anything about bringing a gun to school and killing people for revenge, I would have remembered. And I would have tried to stop him. If only I had known…I would have been able to make all of this go away.

"He never mentioned doing…that. He just said he would…that he would fix it," I gulped, wincing at my own words.

My heart was beating on overdrive as Warren wrote down more of my testimony. I felt sick with guilt the more I kept talking to this detective. Clay was my blood, my older brother and the one who wouldn't be doing this to me if he was in my position and I was in his. I kept thinking of him in a jail cell, cold and alone. He was surrounded by people so unlike him. In county prison, there were rapists and robbers. There were con artists and murderers.

But Clay was now filed into a category of that sort. He was considered a murderer, attempted or fully committed. I wasn't sure of the answer to that yet, still not knowing how the girl was doing who he also hurt and how Carter was coming along. My mother still hadn't told me because I was afraid to ask.

So any feelings of guilt were swallowed down with the family pride that was no longer there. Every time I felt bad about talking to this cop and ratting my brother out, I kept picturing Grayson on my lap with a barely breathing rhythm coming from his chest. He deserved some sort of solace.

Even if that did mean sending my brother away for good.

"I see…" Detective Warren said, writing what seemed to be a novel in that tiny book of his. His letters were chicken scratch, making it hard for me to read over the table. A chill ran through me as I thought up all of the things he would be saying about my brother. In one breath, I was retelling childhood memories. In the next, I was speaking of a completely different life.

"Are we done here?" I asked, frantic to get out of here and go back home in my bed where I felt the safest at the moment.

Now realizing how close Clay really was to me, it scared me, sending shivers deep to the bone. It was hard to understand why I kept forgetting what he had done to all of these kids at school, yet always being reminded of the images and the sounds of that day. I wasn't putting two and two together, lining him up with the shadow that was playing in my mind that was holding the gun in his hand. It didn't seem real that he was the one who caused all of this.

I still wasn't ready to come to terms with it.

Holding up one finger he said, "One final question, Callie." Reading from his notes, he repeated a question scrawled in his hard to see handwriting. "Do you think that's why he did it? Do you think that's why he shot those kids…because they bullied him?"

The all important question to this session left me filled with rage. He thought he had the whole situation figured out with a few simple questions from someone who still didn't even know the answers herself. He was watching me with a glint in his eyes, almost like he was rubbing it in my face that he knew the answers and I didn't. He didn't have a damn clue about the person my brother was. He didn't know the first thing about what happened that day, only reading reports and seeing blood splatters and hearing 'eye witness accounts'.

"Tell me, Detective Warren. If you think you have it all figured out now, explain to me why I was the final one he pointed the gun at when I was the one saving him all his life?" I spat, slamming the palms of my hands onto the table top and picking myself up from the chair.

Warren watched me with wide eyes, dumbfounded that he didn't know this crucial piece of news. He thought he had the motive down to a T. That all-knowing look in his eyes ceased as he watched me walk out of the room, slamming the door behind me as I went.

My mother was waiting on a plastic chair in the room outside, stunned when she saw me storm out the way that I had. "Are you alright? What did he say?"

"Take me to see Grayson," I said, bypassing her questions and eyeing her down like I was somehow overpowering her.

Her eyes were wide with confusion. "Why would you want...Honey, I really think we should talk about everything that has happened before you go off and see him. Plus, I don't think they'll allow you to visit him. He's under strict..."

I cut her off. "I want to see him. Take me to see him, Mom."

"But I just don't understand. Why are you so interested in-"

"Because he was the one that saved my life," I stated.

My mother slammed her hand against the steering wheel as she made her way towards the city hospital. I felt somewhat bad for forcing her to take me back to the place that had swallowed her up for the past two days, but being in that small room and talking about my brother's 'incident' all over again made me that much more determined to see the boy who had saved my life.

"Why won't you tell me what you meant back there, Callie!" she yelled at me, slicing up the eerie silence in the car that ensued during the long drive to the city.

After finally telling someone else that Grayson Foster had been the one who had saved me, I felt that it wasn't right to relay the entire story just yet. All of it felt unfinished, like Grayson held the reigns to that piece of news. I still hadn't known why he did it, or if he just did it because he felt like being a hero for the day. He could have done it because he cared about me. Or he could have done because he was tired of seeing everyone hurt by my brother. I could have meant nothing to him.

I just felt like I needed answers.

And I couldn't give my mom any more if I didn't know them myself. I still hadn't worked up the nerve to tell her that her son was the one who pointed his final bullet in my direction. It was too hard to say, stuck somewhere deep down in my throat with no way out. All I kept seeing were his eyes on me, pointing the gun in my face with a look that was fiery with determination to kill his baby sister. It was the face that woke me up every night, screaming for a brighter vision.

All of it seemed like a recurring nightmare, one that I knew my mom would never understand. I was too scared to let her know the real reason behind the hero that was Grayson. She was already eaten up alive with the fact of knowing her son was never coming home again, branded as the city's murderer with a vengeance. He hurt people, mangled people's hearts. She already had too much going on and telling her that he was aiming at me too would just...consume her.

"I just...I just can't, Mom. You have to understand that," I whispered, my fingers begging to push the radio button to give the air a lighter feeling somehow. This stuffy silence was becoming frustrating and too much to handle.

"No, I don't have to 'understand' that! What I need to understand is how Grayson saved your life like you said. Did someone else come after you? Was there another person with a gun?" she listed off, never once going near the question of her son doing it to his own sister.

I wasn't sure if she was avoiding it because the thought itself was horrifying or because she hadn't even thought to ask. For years, she held Clay up on the highest pedestal, showering him with so much love it was like he could burst with it. She paraded him around to her friends as her 'star son' and always found the opportunity to brag about him at family parties and brunches with her girlfriends. Instead of feeding him some trashy line on how to stand up for himself against the jerks at school, she just held him while he cried to her or nursed him back to health if the bruises and cuts became too much. She never understood why people picked on him that way that they did, always saying that they were jealous because he was just that amazing.

"Stop asking, Mom. I'm just...I don't want to talk about it right now," I huffed, propping my feet onto the dashboard and keeping my eyes trained out of the window. My heart was racing with anticipation and anxiety at the thought of seeing Grayson. I wasn't sure what I would say, how I would act, or if he was even awake from surgeries yet.

She sighed heavily and I looked over at her. Her eyes were glassy with incoming tears, ones I knew she had been holding since the day of the 'incident' when she found out that her son was the reason behind all of this.

"Mom...are you..."

"Do you know the women at work won't even look at me when I come in the room?" she cried, her voice strangled with sobs. "Even those women I had known for years, the ones who always come to family parties, they won't say a word to me when I'm there. It's like they're blaming me for what he's done. Because I was the one that raised him. I didn't...I never expected him to become this..."

"I know," I whispered, placing my hand over hers that was on the gear switch. "I didn't either."

"Why did he do it, Callie?" she breathed, trying to wipe tears from her cheeks with the sleeve of her blouse. She had finally changed out of those rancid scrubs that were covered with blood. "Why would he do this to those innocent people?"

I shook my head, tears springing up in my eyes now. For the first time since we had talked, it almost seemed like we understood one another in that moment. Neither one of us knew the answers behind his behavior. Bullying made people do such drastic things, even going as far as killing themselves. But never in a million years did I pin my brother as the one to kill people. Revenge, to me, would be a punch or two to Carter's face. Or maybe getting Lily back for faking the date he was so excited for.

Why did he choose a bullet instead?

"I don't know, Mom. I wish I did," I whispered.

She swallowed back the sobs and tried to keep her eyes trained to the road before her. When we got a red light, she turned a bit in her seat to look at me. "I feel like I'm responsible for this, somehow. Maybe that's why the people at work refuse to look at me. I'm the one who raised him and taught him right from wrong. He was...he was my baby boy. I should have known when something wasn't right. I should have...I should have sensed that he was going to do something like this," she shook her head, jumping in her seat when a car beeped behind her as the light turned green.

We rounded the corner to the hospital, the tall white building blocks coming into view behind the immense trees. A large M glinted against the sunlight, initialing St. Mary's with one metal symbol. I gulped as we pulled past the lift that allowed us into the parking lot. My mom's hands were turning white around the steering wheel, her muscles shaking the closer we got the entrance.

I felt so much worse about forcing her to take me here. If I had known what she was going through, how people were treating her at work, I would have just taken myself here. I could have found a bus route or maybe even walked to the hospital on my own. She looked so shaken up and sad, something I had rarely seen on my mom. She didn't even look this sad when we dropped my dad off at rehab.

She pulled up at the front entrance, revolving doors opening and closing as visitors, patients and nurses came in and out. I kept my eyes on the door and tried to take a deep breath before getting out of the car and leaving myself stranded here. I was waiting for this moment, the time I would get to thank Grayson for everything that he'd done for me. But I wasn't sure how to go about this or if he would even remember me as the girl that he saved.

"Is it alright if I drop you off?" my mom sniffed, wiping underneath her eyes with a tissue she must have found in her purse. "I don't want...I can't go in there right now. Not like this."

I nodded frantically, more than okay with her going home and getting some rest. I just now noticed the bags under her eyes and how much heavier they seemed from earlier in the morning. Her eyes were bloodshot and she looked like she needed a few good hours of sleep before figuring out how to sort this all out.

"That's fine!" I breathed. Stepping out of the passenger seat, I held the door open while I looked at the moving doors. So many people kept coming in and out, not realizing the luxury of being able to leave this place once you've gotten there. I gripped the door tightly, wondering if I still had the chance to back out and go home with my mom.

Suddenly rest seemed like the better option.

"When you get to the front desk, ask Maureen for his room number. She'll remember you from the times I brought you in. I'm sure she'll be nicer about visitors than the other nurses would be," my mom said, eyeing her reflection in the mirror above her.

"Maureen's the uh...one with the dark red hair right? Kind of heavy set?" I stalled, even though I knew exactly who the lady was. I had seen her at every Christmas party and family gathering since I was eight years old. I didn't want to let go of the car door or even leave my mom alone in the state that she was in. But I was here, where the boy who saved my life was. I owed him...something. I wouldn't be standing here without him.

But he wouldn't be here without me either, which was worse.

She only nodded her head, giving me a questioning glance when I had yet to move from my spot by the door. My hand was still gripping it, a silent plea to hop back in and just forget about this stupid, hasty idea.

"Okay honey," she said. "Just call me when you're finished and I'll come pick you up."

I nodded, swallowing down the will to leave. I was already here and Grayson was on one of those floors of this building, writhing in pain because of me. I at least owed him a thank you or...something to show how grateful I was for him jumping in front of me like that.

"Okay..." I trailed off, looking behind me again at the scary building. What was going to happen after I got in there? Were those kids still in there with Grayson? Were they okay? "Mom?"

"Yes?" she asked, her face so preciously spent.

"It wasn't your fault. There was no way any of us could have predicted this. You raised him with love just like he needed. You taught him right from wrong. He just...broke down. There was nothing you could have done to stop it," I whispered my last sentence, keeping my eyes on her the whole time.

Her face fell once more, the tears welling up in her eyes again. She sniffed quietly and looked ahead of her for a moment. When she turned back to me she said, "Thank you, Callie," smiling small.

I smiled back at her, the first genuine one I had held since the 'incident'.

"Well..." she sighed. "Good luck. Be safe. And call me when you're done."

I nodded one last time before deciding to quickly shut the door before I backed out of my idea again. My mom needed her space to grieve and to break down without me there to hold her hand. She had things she needed to sort out that she didn't want me included in, I was sure. She needed her time just like we all needed ours.

She drove off, the car zooming past me and leaving me in the dust. I took my steps one by one, so filled with mixed emotions on how to handle this and how this would go. Did he even want to see anybody right now?

I got up to the front desk of the floor my mother told me Grayson was on and slowed even further when I saw Maureen, bright locks and all, sitting at the first chair behind the desk. She was shuffling between some paperwork and pulling a pen from behind her ear as I approached her. When she saw a shadow cast across her papers, she jumped slightly.

"Oh!" she yelped. "Callie Tollson...is that you?" she asked, stunned by my presence and the fact that I hadn't been around this area since I was almost twelve. My mom used to take me around the hospital with her while my dad was working and she had no one else to baby sit me.

"Yeah, hi Maureen," I smiled slightly through beared teeth. "Um, I'm here to see Grayson Foster?"

Her face fell a bit at the name, her eyes giving me a disapproving vibe. "I'm afraid Grayson isn't allowed to have visitors at the moment. He's in a lot of pain and he's still healing from surgery."

"Please?" I begged, my hands gripping the tacky white desk. "It's...it's important. Just a couple of minutes. That's all I'm asking."

She sighed heavily, still eyeing me with that disapproving stare. She flipped through a stack of papers in front of her for a moment and then said, "I'm not supposed to do this but...he's in Room 355, right down the hall down there," she pointed to the right of me.

I let out a breath I hadn't known I'd been holding. "Thank you!"

"A couple of minutes!" she called after me as I paced down the hall she'd directed me to. "I'll send someone to come and get you in a few if you're not out soon!"

I waved her off as I kept shuffling down the hall, my moccasins sliding against the freshly waxed floor. The lights above me seemed so bright in this big expansion of wounded victims. Everything around me was so plain and boring, the walls a simple beige color and lacking any paintings or pictures. My fingers skimmed against the smooth walls, my nails on my other hand gripping at my pant leg while I got closer and closer to his room number. Room 349...351...353...

"355," I breathed, my chest suddenly feeling tight. The urge to turn around and run back home came over me once more and I was feeling the fear running through my veins as my hand inched towards the door.

I pushed it open with a shaky hand, stalling for a moment when I heard a gravelly voice. "What do you mean he's dead?" he yelled, and my heart sank in my chest when I realized who he could be talking about.

Oh no.

"No! That can't be...But I thought...!" he kept shouting over and over in the silence. He must have been on the phone.

"That's bullshit!" he growled. And my instincts rang true when I saw a phone fly across the room and onto the floor, past the curtain that was blocking him from view. I felt close to tears at the thought of that person actually being dead. There was no way. Isn't that what hospitals were for? They had saved Grayson. So why not him?

I took the silence as a last bit of motivation to move forward. I let the door shut quietly behind me as I slowly walked around the curtain and into view. My fingers played against the light pink curtain, looking for something to hold onto that could keep me standing tall.

"This is such…" he uttered, pausing when I came into view.

He was in the midst of shaking his head before he paused. His all too familiar striking grey eyes met mine, wide with shock and something else I couldn't quite place. He didn't say a word, just sat there in his bed and watched me with even breathing. The breathing, I found, being the one thing that gave me solace. His chest was moving at a smooth pace, unlike how it was when I last saw him on the hallway floor. I wanted to rush over there and wrap him in my arms, thank him for being so brave and doing what he did. But I fought the urge, gripping the curtain even tighter with one hand.

"C-Callie," he stuttered, his Adam's apple bobbing after he murmured my name.

I swallowed back all of the fear and anxiety I'd been writhing in since I figured out he was alive. I had so many questions, so many things I wanted to know. But most of all, I'd just wanted to be in this room with him, spend time with him and figure out someway to repay him for my life.

"Hi, Grayson."

12

CHAPTER 11

"What are you doing here?" Grayson asked.

His tone was moderate, not high pitched or angry. I couldn't read into his words and whether or not he was happy to see me here. After all, I was interrupting his recovery time. And after that phone call with whoever was on the other line, he seemed like he needed time to himself to grieve over the loss of his captain.

I bent down to pick up his now slightly damaged cell phone and palmed it as I walked closer into the room. "You know, I think it's against hospital policy to be using cell phones around all of these machines," I joked, gesturing towards his immense amount of machines that must have been responsible for keeping him alive.

He blushed a bit, the rosy color pooling at the tops of his cheeks. "Yeah, I know. Maureen would kill me if she knew I was on the phone."

I laughed lightly, handing him back his phone. He was careful not to let our fingers touch, something I felt a bit deflated about. I don't know why I was upset about no spark being able to fire up between us, considering I barely knew the guy. I shouldn't have been expecting this grand gesture of love and heartfelt secrets. He flipped his phone back and forth in his hands, jostling the IV that was hooked up in his left wrist. I felt wary about seeing all of these machines beeping and buzzing around us.

"But it was pretty important," he whispered in the eerie silence, swallowing audibly as he looked up at me. "I just...I just found out that Carter..."

I cut him off, hoping it would make it easier on him. "I overheard as I was coming in. I can't believe it..." I shook my head.

"That guy was like my older brother," his voice shook slightly. "I can't fucking believe he's gone," he said somewhat viciously, the venom in his voice slipping through on his curse.

My heart dropped at his confession. I knew Carter was the leader on most of Grayson's teams and they had practically grown up together while they played sports. They always seemed like they were together, whenever Grayson wasn't pushing his head in his sketchbooks. A physical aching in my chest occurred as I, yet again, realized my brother was causing all of this mess. I still couldn't wrap my brain around it. He was now a murderer. A ward of the state. He was never getting out now.

And I wasn't sure how I felt about that.

Nothing more was said between us for a quite a long time. I didn't know where to start. What do you even say in thanks to the person who literally saved your life by helping you dodge a bullet? He could have picked anyone else to save, my money highly bet on Carter if he was there to see it all happen. Why did he choose me?

"What made you want to stop by and see me?" he urged again, looking up at me with anxious eyes. I almost felt swept up by those charcoal grey, glassy eyes.

I gulped. "Well, uh...my mom...she, um told me that you were in here and that you'd just had surgery. I wanted to...to make sure that you were doing well," I stuttered like a mad woman, cursing myself for not being able to form one coherent sentence with him in the room.

What had gotten over me? He was just a boy and I was just a girl who barely knew him. He barely knew me, hadn't spoken to me once until the day that Carter forced him to hand me the threatening note. My palms were sweating with nerves and my head was spinning with different ways this conversation could possibly go. All I kept seeing on his end was the movement of his phone from hand to hand and his emotional eyes.

Looking up at me once more, he nodded slowly. "So this doesn't have anything to do with the fact that I jumped in front of the gun for you?" he deadpanned.

I stood on the side of his bed, several feet between us, with my jaw literally hanging open. I was gaping like a fish with wide eyes filled with surprise. All those years before, I remembered Grayson Foster as the shy and quiet type. Even though he was enrolled in so many different sports teams, he was always immersing himself in his sketchbooks with his hand flying against the paper. I'd had at least one or two conversations with every single person in that school, but never him until that one day.

Now he was hitting the nail on the head without a single stalling pause. What had gotten into him?

"I...uh. I...um, what?" I kept muttering, tripping over every syllable in my sentence and blushing so hard I felt like my cheeks were on fire.

Now it was his turn to blush. He must have noticed his straight to the point attitude. "I didn't mean to sound cocky! I just...I was wondering if you'd even notice who the person was that did...that," he mumbled off, looking out at the window behind me and not into my eyes anymore.

I felt my heart squeeze for a moment. I couldn't imagine what he was going through right now. Sure, my mom was getting shunned by her coworkers and my dad was still trying to come to terms with that fact that his one and only son was the city's brand named murderer. I hadn't even talked to anyone else other than my parents since the day of the 'incident' so I wasn't sure how things at school were going to be when they finally made us come back. Grayson was probably suffering from terrible pain and constantly reliving similar images that neither of us could get out of our heads.

"Of course I noticed!" I spluttered, my voice squeaking a bit and making me blush once more. I must have sounded like such an idiot to him right now. "When I..." I trailed off. "When I finally opened my eyes, you were just..."

He shook his head quickly. "Don't tell me. I'm already having trouble getting it all out of my head," he whispered.

I nodded silently, not sure what to say. The main reason I came here was to thank him for saving my life and have him answer my burning questions. He didn't want to talk about that day or why he did it or even how it happened. How was I supposed to get answers from someone who didn't want to give them out?

Looking behind me, out the window and over the tops of the trees to the bright sun, I bit my thumbnail and didn't even bother to try to stop myself from the recurring bad habit. "Me too," I whispered.

"What?" he piped up, and I heard him shift in bed, crinkling the sheets beneath him. It was so awkward seeing him in a hospital gown and frazzled like this. Most of the girls at school would have killed to be in my position, in a room alone with a half naked Grayson Foster lying in bed.

But probably under different circumstances.

I turned back to him and took a deep breath. "I can't stop picturing it all either," I murmured.

His face dropped and his eyes softened ever more than they already had. I had to keep fighting the urge to run over and just wrap my arms around him, mumbling thank you's over and over in his ear. I didn't like maneuvering around the subject like this, like we were tip-toeing around a sleeping monster that would arise with a vengeance.

I heard him breath out a heavy sigh. "That look in his eyes, right?" he asked.

My heart started up again, quicker and quicker as the silence around us floated on. I thought I was the only one who kept picturing his eyes. Everyone else, I was sure, was most likely picturing the shootings and the blood, hearing all of the screams and gunshots. But no matter how many times I thought about it and heard it all in my head, it all dwindled down to that horrid look in his eyes, like he had turned into a whole new person.

"He just seemed like a completely different person," I breathed, not thinking twice about it as I sat down on a couch that was propped up against the wall across from Grayson's bed. There was enough space between us to make it somewhat comfortable, but not enough to make my heart stop hammering in my chest and my nerves from making me shake.

"I know!" he agreed. "All those times he and I had talked before then...he was so nice to everybody and always smiling like nothing could beat him down. I knew what was going on but every time I tried to stop it or steer the guys in a different direction when he came down the hall, they never listened to me. That day…God, it was like he turned into a nasty version of himself."

My eyes started welling up at Grayson described the change that I envisioned all too well. I sniffed what I thought was quietly, but his bright eyes snapped to mine at the sound. This room was seriously too small. You couldn't hide a thing.

"Are you…?"

"Okay? Jesus, I'm really starting to hate that question," I breathed, trying to push down the tears that were coating my throat and making me sound scratchy.

A side smirk graced his lips at my words for just a moment. "Don't I know it. I don't know why I was going to ask that. I'm getting quite tired of it myself."

As soon as I opened my mouth, it was like word vomit had taken over me and I couldn't stop myself. Normally, I'd measure my words and think about the outcomes of such things leaving my brain, but I just let it all out right after he paused at the end of his statement.

"It's ridiculous, isn't it?" I said, my voice rising slightly as the anger of the past few days started coursing through my veins. "I mean, of course we're not okay! This is the first time something like this happened in the history of this town. We were known for being those quiet city people with no bad news on the television stations. Now we're like the poster kids for violence!"

I managed to be standing up and flailing my arms around in the midst of my rant. The room felt oddly quiet as I finished, making me that much more embarrassed that I was basically complaining to a kid who was full of holes while I was physically fine. He was sitting in a hospital bed with pain meds and a surgery in his book without a complaint to utter.

He started to chuckle. This turned into a full-on belly laugh, causing him to bend over slightly in his upright position, putting a hand over his stomach. My face was on fire by now, making me wish the floor would open up and swallow me whole. This was why I kept my mouth shut. Just because he understood one thing about this situation, didn't mean that he was going to get the entirety of my anger and fear. He was getting a seriously good laugh out of my emotional breakdown.

Pacing towards the entrance of his room, I mumbled a quick, "Um…I think I'm going to go. I'm sorry for…ranting like that."

Before I got behind the curtain he called out for me. "Callie, wait!" his voice was still breathy as little chuckles released themselves, making me wish I could just shrink against the wall with shame. But I still froze in my place, waiting for his next words. "I'm sorry. I'd blame the meds they have me on for making me hysterical, but you were just so…funny with your waving arms and shouting."

I was certain my face was similar to a tomato right about now, making me want to hide it behind the light pink curtain that blocked the view of his bed from the room door. "Sorry. I don't know what got over me there," I said, trying to shield my face from view.

"Come out from behind there," he said, waving me over with the hand that was hooked up to the IV bag. "Pull over a chair."

"I can't…" I muttered, cursing Maureen in my head for ordering me my limited amount of minutes to visit Grayson. I still had so much I wanted to say, so much I wanted to talk about with him. If anyone would understand what I was going through, it was him.

"Maureen gave me strict orders to leave in a couple of minutes. I think I've passed my designated limit."

"Screw Maureen!" he boasted, grinning a bit and showing his bright teeth. "You came all this way. Just...sit."

I slowly made my way over towards the chair that was next to the couch, pulling it over to his bedside but leaving enough room to make this a somewhat comfortable atmosphere. He didn't fiddle with his phone anymore, I noticed. And his eyes weren't filled with nerves as he watched me. He just seemed...calm. I pushed a piece of hair behind my ear as I lifted my eyes up to face him when I finally managed to sit down.

The silence overtook us and I felt like he was waiting for me to continue this halted conversation. "I feel bad. I was standing there complaining about all of this stuff when you're the one who's cooped up in here. I hadn't even asked how you were doing. How are you doing?"

His eyes dropped from mine to look down at his patched up shoulder and his right leg that was wrapped in a cast. His dark brown hair was disheveled, like he'd just woken up before he was on the phone with that person who told him the bad news. His slightly tanned skin seemed to glow beneath the bright florescent lights.

Huffing a stifled sigh with his chin near his neck he said, "I'm alright, I guess, physically. They fished the bullets out during the surgery and gave me this medication that's supposed to stop the pain. Whatever it is, it's working pretty well. I'm not digging the cast though."

My eyes fell towards his leg just like his did, wincing when I realized that my own brother was the cause of his discomfort. The guilt crept up in my stomach, making me feel sick again. I don't know why I kept feeling responsible for all of these kids' misfortunes when I wasn't the one holding the gun. But he was still my brother and I always sensed something was wrong with him. I couldn't help but feel like I'd purposefully stepped over the warning signs and left them in a pile behind me that I'd see to later.

I should have picked up on them sooner.

"How about your shoulder?" I whispered. "If that had been any lower down, you could have..." I trailed off, so scared to finish that sentence. Even thinking about Grayson dying at my expense made shivers run down my spine and tears form in a puddle at the base of my lids. I would never be able to forgive myself if that happened.

He winced a bit. "Don't remind me. The nurse and doctors keep telling me that. It's hard enough thinking about the day itself. Let alone..."

"Grayson," I breathed, not too sure where I wanted my next sentence to go. I had a jumbled mess of 'I'm sorry' and 'Thank you' tangling up in my throat that was trying to force itself out. What one seemed more appropriate in that moment? Which one was more important to get out in my limited time with him?

"Don't you dare apologize for what he did," he said, a mixture of anger and sadness seeping through his tone. His eyes finally fell back to mine and they were hard with emotion.

"But if you hadn't jumped in front of me like that and if I just picked on his signs-"

He cut me off. "That has nothing to do with you!" he shouted, his lips in a tight line. "It was my choice. I don't-"

Maureen came rushing in at the sound of a fight forming, throwing open the thick, grey door and giving me another disapproving stare. "What's going on in here?" she asked, her hands on her wide hips.

"Nothing," he sighed angrily, running a hand through his messy bed head.

"Callie, didn't I tell you that you only had a few minutes? It's been a half hour already. I think it's time for you to get going," she chastised, pointing a finger behind her in forceful manner.

"B-But…" I stammered, looking to Grayson for some sort of help. He was watching his wounds with careful, hard eyes. But he didn't say anything for what seemed like a while.

"Maybe we can talk another time, Callie," he muttered, still not looking at me like he was afraid I'd hate him for saying it.

A little stunned and a little heartbroken that this conversation had not gone the way that I had planned, I cleared my throat from the mess of words I'd wanted to say and dragged the chair back to its rightful place. Maureen watched me for a moment to make sure I was really getting up to leave before she let the door bang shut behind her and returned to her desk.

I didn't look at Grayson as I started to walk out of the room. He didn't want to talk anymore, at east at the moment. I knew I should have just come in here, said thank you and left without another word. What good could come out of a personal relationship like this? We clearly didn't know anything about one another, including knowing one another's boundaries.

Right as I was about to walk past his bed, his hand shot out and grabbed mine. My hand tingled at the feeling of his warmth in mine, but I forced myself not to read anything into it. I froze in my place just as he grabbed me, stuck in the trance of those strikingly bright grey eyes.

"I don't regret taking the bullets. At all," he whispered to me, watching me closely for a moment before releasing my hand and giving me a small glimpse of a half smile. "I'll see you around?"

I grinned back at him as I walked towards the door, my hand still tingling with the feeling of his skin on mine. What the hell had gotten into me? And why hadn't I noticed this feeling before all of this happened?

"Yeah, see you around Grayson," I whispered back, pushing a piece of hair behind my ear again shyly and walking out of the room.

As I made my way out of the room, a wave of emotions washed over me. I was still scared about the outcomes of Clay's actions, wondering how he was feeling at this very time. He was probably locked behind metal bars, on the floor of some cold jail cell. I kept thinking of Carter and his family, how horrible they must be feeling. And I couldn't stop thinking of Grayson.

It amazed me how he was actually laughing and smiling at a time like this. He was cooped up in some hospital room with limited entertainment and wrapped up in two different places. Who knew if he'd even be able to walk on his leg once he got out? Yet he was still giving out a small sense of positivity under his circumstances.

"I assume you attended to that important matter during your visit?" Maureen piped up, making me jump as I realized I was now standing in front of her desk once again.

I shrugged. "Somewhat."

"Next time, try not to rile him up when he's hooked up to all of those machines, you hear? It's not good for someone in his condition," she smirked at me.

I nodded, waving at her as I exited the floor and got into the elevator. I liked the idea of a 'next time'. A lot was still left unsaid.

There were so many more things that we needed to talk about, more things I wanted to know.

But I still liked the prospect of a 'next time.'

13

CHAPTER 12

As the days progressed in my house, it seemed like my parents were finally able to talk to one another about the situation that involved Clay and admit their feelings to one another. While I was still cooped up in my bedroom most nights, my parents stayed up talking in the living room while they sipped on coffee and shared tissues.

I still was having a hard time communicating what I was feeling and the thoughts I was fighting within me. The secret of what actually happened between me and Clay before he was towed away by the police ate away at me every single day. The more my parents watched me with worried eyes, the more I felt like I was going to be sick if I didn't spill the scene soon. Everyday my mom would ask what I had meant inside the car on the way to see Grayson, and every time I would shake my head and tell her it meant nothing.

Grayson and I had started talking a bit more in the following weeks, text conversations and casual hospital visits happening on a semi-daily basis. I was learning so much about him while we talked and he was making it effortless to have even the biggest of conversations whenever I was with him. I hated that an 'incident' like this was bringing us together somehow, but I liked being able to talk to someone who understood the pain and the anguish from witnessing something like that.

Although he was opening up to me about his life and his personal issues, he always made sure to bypass the subject of why he jumped in front of the bullets for me. Often I would try to bring it up in casual talks, making it out to be like I wasn't constantly mulling over the reason behind his actions. But whenever I managed to slip it in, he'd shake his head or sigh heavily and continue with a different topic. It was so frustrating and made me over think on too many occasions, but I was still sticking around for some reason.

Maybe I just felt like I needed a friend to lean on.

I hadn't heard from Marnie since the day of the 'incident' and she was making it so hard to get in contact with her. I tried texting her, leaving voicemails for her to hopefully get to later and even tried going to her house once, only to have the door slammed in my face by her little brother who told me she was busy and 'couldn't talk.'

Today had been a particularly harder day because the school had called the students, with automatic voice-overs of course, leaving messages for them all to say that school was about to be back in session the following week. It had only been two weeks since the 'incident' and I didn't think it was long enough to grieve over a thing like this. People had lost loved ones, were scarred from the images they saw that day, and I was the sister of the boy who pulled out a gun on school grounds and killed their star athlete.

So instead of keeping myself cooped up in my room and thinking about the many different ways Monday morning could go, I sprinted down the stairs and made a move to grab my bag. Grayson was still stuck in his hospital room for another week at least and I figured paying him a visit would be better than worrying myself to the bone like this.

But just as I slipped my fingers around the strap to my bag that was hanging off of the dining room chair, the house phone rang and a mess of shuffling was heard in the kitchen. No one had called the house lately, considering our family relations, so hearing it go off was odd to all of us.

I let my bag drop to the chair again and slowly walked to the kitchen, making sure my footsteps didn't squeak on the creaky floorboards. Slinking behind the wall to keep myself out of sight, I peeked around the entryway as my eyes landed on my mom with the kitchen phone pressed to her ear.

"Oh my God, are you okay? How are you doing?" she cried, her fingers clenching around the phone and turning the skin around it as white as a sheet.

Fresh tears were pooling up in her eyes as she paced the kitchen back and forth, only pausing briefly to shoot my dad a worried look. Who could she possibly be talking to? It couldn't be…could it?

"I tried to! It's hard to find you someone who's willing to work for you. I mean…you…" she trailed off, probably cut off by the person on the other line.

I couldn't take not knowing who it was, especially when I had a clue as to who it could be. Tiptoeing across the floor and getting back to the living room, I picked up the other landline phone slowly and quietly placed it to my ear.

"But I need someone to help me get out of here! I can't be in here forever, Mom!"

My breathing hitched, my lungs suddenly feeling too tight to hold anymore air. How was he even able to call here? He sounded so distressed, his voice high pitched and anxious. I only noticed a slight change in his voice, gravelly and oddly enough, more mature.

"Clay, I'm trying! Okay? But you did a terrible thing that you cannot take back," she cried softly into the phone.

He scoffed into the phone. "No I didn't..."

My mother and I both took in sharp breaths at the same time, lucky enough for me not to get caught listening in. I couldn't believe him. He killed someone, shot two others and mentally scarred the kids he used to go to school with for life. Everyone was scared to leave their homes, petrified at the thought of even going back to the scene of the crime and grieving over the people who were hurt and lost during his breakdown. I thought if we ever got the chance to look back and talk about it with him that he'd at least feel an ounce of sympathy for his actions...but he was the complete opposite.

"Sweetheart, how c-could you n-not think that..." she sobbed. I pictured her putting her hand over her mouth in utter shock, appalled that her son who used to have a heart of gold was acting so out of character.

He cut her off before she could finish. "I don't regret a single thing I did that day. They deserved it," he simply stated.

Before I realized what was happening, I was sobbing as well, joining my mother's wracked breaths and sniffling as he continued. He was turning into such a monster. I had never seen this side of him before, so nonchalant about others and cocky. He spent his life in the hands of people just like he was acting like now, and you would think that those types of things that happened to him would steer him from this type of behavior. He took a life and could care less about it.

"What have you become, son?" my father's voice popped in, probably just taking the phone away from my mother when she told him what he said. His voice was clipped and dry; like he was trying to choke back sobs himself. But he sounded angry, most of all, that his son was acting this way.

A maniacal laugh sifted through the line, making fear boil in my blood. "I've become a version of myself I should have become a long time ago, Dad. Maybe if I did this sooner, I'd be out of that hell a lot quicker than this."

"You killed someone, Clay! That's nothing to laugh about!" my dad shouted, causing me to wince at every heightened syllable.

"I'm not laughing about that! I'm laughing because of how pissed off you guys are making me by talking to me like I didn't know what I was doing back there! You don't think I thought about my actions every single day? You don't think that I prepared for something like this to happen? It's not my fault that it happened! They shouldn't have done those things to me. If they weren't such assholes I wouldn't have pulled the fucking trigger!" he screamed, my heartbeat quickening as he continued.

Was I one of the people he was referring to? Was I that horrible of a sister to him that he actually planned out a plot to shoot and kill me in front of the whole school? I thought I saved him when he was growing up. I thought I was doing such a good job of protecting his heart and keeping him here with me.

And he actually planned to shoot me?

"Clay," I sobbed, my breathing long gone and my tears seeming never ending.

There was a long pause on his end, something that was making my heart beat faster and faster. My parents had hung up the phone and came rushing into the living room, standing before me with guarded expressions. My mother's fallen face was making my heart break further.

He snickered. "How did I know you'd be listening?"

"You planned that? You set out to..." I couldn't even finish my sentence. The fact that I would ever have to ask such a question to my once admirable older brother seemed so unfathomable.

"Of course I did," he breathed, his tone dropping just a bit at my cries. "You thought I just woke up that morning and decided on a whim to do it? I had to know exactly what I was going to do before I actually did it."

This angered me more than it hurt me, I discovered. "Then what about me, huh? You actually..."

He cut me off. "You were a last minute decision!"

"A what?!" I shrieked. "What the hell did-"

"Listen, Callie, I have to go. Next time...don't listen in on something you're not so sure you want to hear," he stated, hanging up before I could even find the words to respond with.

"Ah!" I screamed, throwing the phone onto the couch with vigorous force and hating the tears that were continuing to fall down my cheeks.

"Callie? What did he say?" my dad asked, coming over to me and placing a hand on my shoulder while I sobbed.

So many mixed emotions were ripping through my heart, tearing it into pieces. I felt like I couldn't hold myself together, the tears and the sobs wracking my body without my permission. My hands clenched into tight fists as his words kept replaying over and over in my head.

You were a last minute decision.

What the hell caused him to come at me in the end? Did he have an epiphany that caused him to make the best of situations turn me into some sort of monster?

"Sweetheart, what did he…" my mom went to say, but I cut her off by shaking my head and walking into the dining room to grab my bag.

"I'm going to the hospital," I stated, slinging my bag over my shoulder and letting the front door slam shut behind me as I went.

None of this made sense to me. I hadn't gotten one bit of a clue as to why Clay would do such a thing, choose the people that he chose to hit, and act the way he was acting. He was turning into the nastiest form of a human being, laughing in the face of his mistakes and not carrying that caring heart that I admired so much in the past.

Why had he chosen me to use his last two bullets on? Why did he have to kill Carter that way he had? What justified his decision to end lives and create havoc on the Riverton population?

No matter how many times I asked myself the same questions, looked back on his actions from the past, tried to come up with options that made sense in my head…nothing ever resulted in an ending that made sense to me or to anyone. I was so scared of my only brother, the one person who was supposed to save me, not choose to end my life.

And I couldn't stop the tears as I made my way down the street and to the only person who seemed to get it.

"Is he awake?" I asked Maureen at the front desk, wringing my hands until they were rubbed raw and turning pink. My voice was cracked and the tears were still brimming in my eyes.

She looked up at me from her paperwork and then back down quickly to Grayson's sheets. "Looks like he was just given breakfast. I'm sure he'd be happy to see you," she smiled softly; her smile falling slightly as she finally got a good look at me. "Is everything alright, dear?"

I gulped. "Everything's fine. I'll just go see him then. Thanks, Maureen," I whispered, giving her a matching soft smile that was the hardest form to fake, and made my way down the hall to Grayson's now familiar room number.

I could practically feel Maureen's eyes on me as I paced down the hall and breathed a sigh of relief as I got into his room and shut the door behind me, leaving her in the dust. The curtain was brought around Grayson's bed, blocking his view of me, so he called out to the silence.

"Callie, is that you?" he asked, his voice sounding light and somewhat excited.

I probably looked horrid, red rimmed eyes and pale skin from all of the crying. It almost made me want to run back and forget about doing this. I could see him a different day. Why had I even chosen to come and see him when I was this distraught anyway? He hadn't even seen me yet, so if I really wanted to, I could escape without any harm being done.

But that nagging feeling deep within me that always made me want to stick around when I was with Grayson pushed me to step away from the door and peek around the curtain so he could see me. The smile on his lips almost made me weak in the knees, pulling up his skin and creating a small dimple on the right side of his lips.

"Hey you," he beamed. It only lasted a fraction of a moment though because it didn't take him long to see how much of a mess I looked. "What's wrong?"

Both of us discussed the annoyance we felt with being asked the same, dumb questions like: 'Is everything alright?' 'Are you okay?'

So we agreed that if either one of us felt that the other was upset or needed help that we would come up with a statement that wouldn't sound like the others that we were asked too often. Grayson, with his blunt character, always chose the immediate and too-the-point route.

I sniffed lightly and ran a finger underneath my eyes to fix my smudged liner. "Nothing," I batted him away nonchalantly. "It's just cold outside. The wind's atrocious today."

I moved across the room to drag the chair over to his bedside, like usual. His eyes were burrowing holes into my back, never once leaving me as I shuffled around the room and made myself at home.

"The wind?" he asked, sounding far from convinced. When I finally had the chair next to his bed and sat next to it, I dropped my bag to the floor and tried to smile at him. He was raising a brow at me, shifting in the bed so he was sitting up further and giving me his full attention. "That's all?"

I nodded. "Yup. So how's your day been so far? Did you ever get to that movie last night that I brought?"

I looked around for the remote to the room's television that was hung up on the wall and out of reach. I tried to keep my eyes busy so I wouldn't have to keep looking at his deciphering expression. His eyes wouldn't leave mine, almost like he was contemplating his next few words.

"I didn't actually. Want to watch it with me while you're here?" he asked, his voice leveled and his eyes still assessing me.

I nodded again, too enthusiastically. He grinned at me like he was trying to lighten the mood. Wrenching the remote from behind his back, he powered on the television set and pressed play. I had placed the DVD in the player right before I left last night, figuring he'd get to it on his own before he went to bed.

Leaning back in my plastic chair, I put a hand underneath my chin and gave the movie my full attention as the opening credits started to pop up on the screen. I could still feel Grayson's eyes on me, silently begging him to knock it off and watch the movie instead.

"You look uncomfortable. Come up here with me," he stated, sliding over to the farthest side of his bed, bringing the pillow his hurt leg was propped up on with him and patting the open space.

My eyes bugged out of my head, wide with surprise. "N-no, I'm alright here."

He grinned knowingly at me. "C'mon, Callie. I won't bite, I promise."

I could feel my cheeks heating up, praying that the blush that usually graced my face decided against it today. My hands were practically shaking as I got up from the chair and lifted myself on to the side of the bed that was unoccupied. The sheets beneath me were warm from his body heat. I tried to keep as far away from his body as possible, which was almost undoable in this tiny bed made for one.

As the movie rolled on, out of the corner of my eye I kept seeing Grayson look at me every so often. Forcing myself to keep my attention on the movie, and the movie only, I crossed my arms over my chest and kept my eyes glued to the small screen.

Then suddenly, I felt an arm bring itself across the pillow I was lying on and scooting underneath my head. For a moment, I worried that he was hurting his shoulder. But if he was hurting it, he didn't show an ounce of pain. I allowed it to go behind my head, feeling a mess of butterflies sprout in flight in my stomach. The warmth of his skin near mine was like a fire you couldn't put out. By doing so, he had brought his body closer to mine and slightly pulled my face to lie in the crook of his arm and against his chest. I was thankful for the fact that the hospital was allowing him to wear a normal set of clothes in his time of recovery because a hospital gown would have made this situation a hundred times more awkward.

He cleared his throat momentarily. "You can tell me, you know?"

I felt my heartbeat pick up as his soft voice made his chest reverberate underneath my ear. "Tell you what?" I whispered back.

"What's been going on...it's rough. You don't have to hide it from me. I know how it feels to constantly be forced to think about what happened. You can tell when things get too hard," he whispered, his breath hitting the top of my hair.

I let out a breath I didn't know I'd been holding. "Nothing's wrong," I shook my head against his chest, his sweater rubbing smoothly against my cheek.

"I'm not so sure I believe you," he replied.

It was clear that neither one of us was going to be paying attention to the movie anymore. I knew he wouldn't quit unless I told him what happened before I got here. Just the thought of talking about my brother to someone again caused so much anxiety and fear to run through me. I loved talking about him in past tense, the way he was before. I hated talking about the horror movie character he turned into.

Swallowing audibly I said, "I talked to him today."

I couldn't say his name, feeling like I would curse this room if I said it. He was already following me everywhere in my dreams and in my thoughts. This room was the only place I felt safe anymore and I couldn't let him ruin that.

Grayson let out a breath. "What did he say?"

The tears started pooling in my eyes again and I was even more thankful that we weren't being forced to look at each other. My vision was blurring as I kept my eyes on the screen, wondering where to even start.

"He acts like he doesn't even care about what he's done," I said, wincing when my voice went against me and cracked at every syllable.

"Did you expect him to say sorry for all of that?" he whispered. "Don't you remember the way he…"

"I can't stop thinking about the way that he looked at me," I cried, the tears hitting Grayson's sweater and leaving a soaked spot on his grey attire.

"Callie…" he breathed, trying to pull away from me. I kept my head against his arm and wouldn't let him move so he could see me like this.

"He told me he planned everything out. He knew exactly what he was doing. And when I asked about…about m-me…he said I was…" I trembled, my hands shaking uncontrollably and my heart pounding against my chest. "That I was a last minute decision. It's like he thought about me and suddenly felt the need to kill me. What does that make me?" I sobbed. "Why did he think of me and decide that he needed to…that he…"

Grayson's arms came around me in an instant. I relished in his warmth, pressing my face into his chest as he rubbed soothing circles at the bottom of my back and just held me. He didn't say much; just let me cry into his shirt for one elongated moment. I no longer worried about being embarrassed about crying in front of him. The only thing I could think about was that he was the only one who understood, who allowed me to fall apart like this. He hadn't judged me, pushed me away because of my family relations. He just let me in.

And that was more than I could say for anyone else.

"That doesn't make you anything. Just because he broke down mentally doesn't mean you did anything wrong. Stop blaming yourself. Stop thinking that because your brother decided to do this, that you're somehow different than what you used to think. Stop thinking so much. He isn't worth this. He doesn't deserve to make you feel small," Grayson whispered into my ear.

And somehow it was what I needed to hear in that instance. I didn't know that I needed to hear those things in order to make myself feel better. But Grayson was always coming up with ways to surprise me in how well he understood this.

But I still had to keep telling myself to force down those feelings of intimacy in my heart, feelings that willed me to pull away and just kiss him like I really knew who he was. He was being a friend, someone to lean on, a shoulder to cry on. I wasn't about to ruin that with my inner, frantically romantic emotions.

So I just let him hold me while I simmered down, whispering encouragement into my ear as he did so. I let myself break down for Grayson, opening myself up in ways that I had never done before. I felt that I owed him that much, showing him my true colors.

In a small and not nearly enough way in exchange for what he did and was still doing for a girl like me.

14

— ◦ —

CHAPTER 13

I woke up Monday morning with a sickening feeling in my gut. It was enough to make me want to run to the bathroom and wretch into the toilet. My fingers were trembling and my body was sweating at just the mere thoughts of what today held. How would people look at me? What would they say to me? Would they say anything at all?

When I mentioned the idea of changing schools to my mom, the conversation just seemed to be one-sided. I kept giving her options that would allow me to go off to a different school, maybe move away to a new city and start fresh. But she would just wave me off with a flick of her hand and go back to reading her latest romance novel that she was invested in on her off nights from the hospital. The only thing I could get out of her in formal words was, 'I can't leave my job at the hospital, Callie.'

So then, as a proper child birthed from two level-headed parents, I ran straight for my dad's office space. He was a far better listener than she was, actually keeping his eyes on me while I spoke my side of this argument and nodded along to my options that I listed off on each finger while I went. I was almost excited at the prospect of getting someone on my side of this until he gave me a tight smile when I finished my speech.

"Cal, I'm still documented at the Rec Center. If I leave the meetings, I'll get in trouble. If it was a different situation..." he grimaced.

"But you don't understand! You and Mom get to hide out at home while I get pushed back into the place that Clay unleashed all of his...crap! I can't go back there, Dad! I can't do it," I shook my head furiously with my arms crossed at my chest.

He sighed heavily, turning in his chair to fully face me. "We can't do it, honey. As much as I wish I could take you away from all of this...it's just not a good time."

It was safe to say that I wasn't going anywhere for the time being. The mere thought of stepping foot back into that school scared me beyond belief. It wasn't fair that Clay had chosen his own actions and now everyone had to pay for them. He was away, paying for his mistakes on the city's terms, but he wasn't stuck going back to the place that he ruined.

If I had someone to tag along with me and hold my hand then this day might have seemed a tad bit better. But Marnie had been MIA since the day of the 'incident' and Grayson was still strapped to his hospital bed until at least the middle of this week. I had to shake off the nerves and start the day off by myself, much to my dismay. I carefully pulled a sweater from a hanger in my closet and slipped on a pair of skinny jeans before I slowly made my way out of my room and downstairs to join my parents at the table for breakfast.

My mom was making blueberry pancakes, which she knew were my favorite, causing the griddle to sizzle against thick batter. The smell overtook my senses, making my stomach churn once more. I couldn't fathom touching food right now with the weary feeling going on in my stomach. Placing a hand over my middle, I slid into the seat and slacked my body.

"I'm making your favorite, Cal," she grinned slightly, obviously doing this to make up for the fact that she couldn't take me out of school and relocate the family because of her job.

"I'm not hungry," I grumbled.

She placed a plate of small pancakes in front of me, along with a glass of orange juice. I decided against the food and sipped lightly at the drink, hoping it wouldn't react badly with the anxiety bubbling in my stomach.

"C'mon. You have to eat something," she prodded, flipping another pancake still on the griddle.

"Well I can't," I snapped, slamming the glass of juice onto the table and causing a few stray puddles to form.

She placed the spatula down gently and turned down the burner. "You can't be mad at me for something I can't control, Callie. If the circumstances had been different then maybe..."

I cut her off with an eye-roll. "If things had been different we could have moved. I know! Dad's told me enough times already. But neither one of you seem to understand how hard this is going to be for me! I'm the sister of the kid who shot up the school, Mom!" I shouted, throwing my hands up in angry gestures.

"I know better than anyone!" she yelled back, slapping her hand on the counter. "The women at work still treat me like I'm the cause of this mess!"

"But at least you don't work at the school, Mom! That's the place that he unleashed everything. He hurt all of those people in those hallways. And now I have to go back and there and act like everything's normal!"

She sighed heavily. "Callie, you're being unreasonable. I doubt it will be…"

I scoffed. "Forget it, Mom. You don't understand. You never will," I mumbled the last part before taking a final sip of my drink and grabbing my bag off of the back of the chair. I rightfully slammed the door behind me for dramatic effect and went down the street to my car.

Every time I imagined walking through the first set of double doors, all I could see were multiple pairs of eyes watching my every move. I thought about wide eyes and scowls on everyone's faces. I wondered if the teachers would even treat me normally. But all I knew was that no matter how today went, along with my thoughts or not, it wouldn't end well.

There wasn't a positive hope to hang onto.

As soon as I stepped through the doors at Riverton High, it was exactly as I had expected it. The moment the doors slammed shut behind me, it was like they were all waiting for me to arrive. Every pair of eyes in the main hallway snapped to mine and widened with shock and a small tinge of anger. People clutched their books tighter to their chests and some of the girls looked too scared to even be standing a few feet away from me.

I wasn't sure if people were running off as soon as I walked down the hall because they were scared of my family tie or because they were scared that I'd somehow snap too. Most of them were probably picturing me with a hidden gun in my bag and a revenge to seek out for putting my brother into prison.

But little did they know, I was actually happy that he was locked away.

The eyes that were on me were burning holes into my back, sidestepping my every move and making sure I wouldn't suddenly turn on them all. I swore that when I unzipped my bag at my locker that some of them who were watching had taken in a breath.

A noise a few lockers down from mine startled me, reminding me instantly that Marnie had the locker on the same floor as mine, not too far down. She couldn't avoid me forever, especially with her current location, and I knew if I ran up to her now it would scare her too easily.

So I pretended that I hadn't heard her, picking up textbooks I needed for my next few classes of the day and putting away homework that I didn't need until later. Every so often, I'd sneak a peek around the edge of my locker door, wondering if she'd noticed me yet.

Everyone else seemed to have.

I shut my locker door with as little force as possible, trying to not look like such a freak to the people who were already scared of me. Marnie was still fiddling inside of hers, grumbling underneath her breath as she tried to find something in that mess of hers. Swallowing harshly and pushing my shoulders back in a small bout of bravery, I pulled the strap of my bag up my shoulder and made my way towards her.

"Marn," I whispered gently, wincing when she jumped at the sound of my voice.

Normally, if the situations had been different and the 'incident' hadn't happened, she would have practically jumped in my arms as a greeting. Her bubbly personality was what drawled me to her when we were little, as it did with almost everyone she came into contact with. She always knew how to keep up a conversation and she was never one to keep silent.

"Jesus Christ, Callie," she breathed heavily, putting a hand to her chest as she heaved. "Did you really have to sneak up on me like that?"

"I'm sorry," I mumbled. "I was trying to do the opposite actually."

Finally locating what she was having such a hard time finding, she slammed her locker door shut and let out another breath as she stuffed a book into her bag. "What's up?"

Clearing my throat I said, "Well I haven't talked to you since…" I trailed off, not wanting to bring up the thing that seemed to be following me everywhere. The last thing I wanted to do was remind her of the fact that I was related to the thing she was most scared of. "Anyway, I was wondering how you were doing."

She looked up at me beneath her millions of lashes, brushing a stray strand of short blonde hair behind her ear. "How do you think I'm doing?" she asked, her voice sounding strained and painful.

I winced again, hating how this was going. It's not the direction I was aiming for at all. "I just…I missed you, Marn."

Her eyes softened just a bit as she watched my face fall. "I missed you, too," she whispered, looking around her as people walked by our conversation, eyeing her down like she was insane for talking to me. Didn't she know who I was? Who I was related to?

"Then how come every time I tried to talk to you, you ignored my calls and your brother slammed the door in my face when I came to visit?" I asked, my heart dropping as I watched her face configure at my words.

"It's just…" she huffed. "It's complicated, Callie. Things aren't the same anymore. Not after…"

"I know that!" I shouted, cursing myself when some of the kids walking by halted in their steps and widened their eyes at me again. God, it was like I was a ticking time bomb. "I know that," I said softer this time. "But I didn't do anything, Marn."

"No one said that you did. But your...brother was the one who caused all of this. He was the reason Carter..." she choked up, tears brimming at her lids. She sniffed quickly and shook her head. "I promised myself I wouldn't cry today. I've had enough of that."

"You don't think that thought makes me sick?" I countered. "It's all I can think about. All I keep seeing is blood and his eyes...the way that they..."

She cut me off. "Stop! Just stop it, okay? I've had enough of picturing it all and going over it a thousand times in my head. You didn't find him. I did. You have no idea how I-"

It was my turn to talk over her this time. "Bullshit! While you were tending to Carter, I was stuck in the hallway with Grayson Foster on my lap and Clay pointing the gun in my face. Don't you dare say that I have no idea how you felt or how it all turned out!"

Tears were filling in my eyes now, matching hers from earlier. Her jaw slacked as she turned my words over in her head, realizing what I had meant. The silence that followed my confession seemed to stretch on for hours, just her watching me with bugged eyes and a hand gently placed over her mouth. The bell rang around us, signaling the start of the first class of the day.

"I have to go," I shook my head and made my way around her to my class. I half expected her to not say anything else to me, too surprised to even have a response for something like that. She was the first person I told about that day, aside from Grayson who already knew because of what he had done for me.

This was why I didn't tell anyone about it. They would never be able to understand the thought of it. Marnie may have seen Carter covered in blood and dying right in front of her, but she didn't have a gun aimed at her head from someone who shared the same DNA. She didn't have someone jump in to save her life. She'd never be able to understand the immensity of this type of situation, never be able to see things through my eyes.

"Callie, wait!" she called to me, making me freeze. I didn't turn around to look at her, just waited for her to come to me. She came into view, biting her thumbnail and looking as worried as I felt.

The halls around were clearing little by little as the final warning bell went off, telling us that Marnie and I were officially late on our first day back. On the way, people kept bypassing glances in my direction, the farthest from entertained but their eyes glued to my every action. I hated the way they all looked at me like I was about to implode with rage or cry at the drop of a hat.

I was nothing like him. I never wanted to amount to anything like him. For years as a kid, I looked up to him and hoped to one day carry the pride that he did. I wanted to be kind-hearted like he was and open with everyone around me. I wanted to be able to wear my heart on my sleeve for the world to see and walk around with my head held high, no matter the situation.

But what he did those weeks ago, aiming a weapon in the face of everyone who had hurt him and his baby sister who only tried to help him, I pushed myself to be everything but him. Who would want to be like a killer? Who would want to be similar to a monster that was slowly falling apart mentally?

He disgusted me and the thought of even amounting to anything like him was appalling and hard to even think about.

"Why didn't you tell me what happened to you?" she whispered, glaring at the rest of the people who couldn't stand to look away from me.

"You were pretty hard to get a hold of," I said, blinking back the tears that had yet to fall at the memory of that day.

"But that day...why didn't you come to my house or something? Why didn't you come and find me before you went home?" she questioned, her eyes never leaving mine.

I gulped, hating that we were rehashing the memories I so badly wanted to get rid of. "I heard you...before Clay came back to me. I heard you screaming for Carter. I couldn't stand the thought of seeing you that hurt over something that my brother did," I cried, the tears now freely falling down my cheeks.

She immediately wrapped me in her arms, patting my hair as my tears hit the shoulder of her jacket. "But I'd never be able to blame you for that, Callie. If anything, I'd want you there to comfort me. You're my best friend," she whispered as I continued to cry.

I squeezed her tightly before sniffling and pulling back. "I know," I sobbed, my voice sounding pathetically painful. "I just...I can't help feeling like I'm somehow to blame for some of this," I gestured around me. "You saw how close we were. I should have known. I should have been able too-"

"Enough of that!" she scolded, shaking her head and putting a hand on my shoulder. "Clay's actions had nothing to do with you, despite what he decided to do that day. There was no way you could have known he was going to bring a gun," she whispered the last word harshly as she looked around us. "To school. No one could have known. There's no use blaming yourself over something you had no idea about, Cal."

"But now Carter's d-dead," I sobbed. "And Grayson's in the hospital with a hurt shoulder and leg. And I'm partly to blame for that!"

"No you're not!"

"But I am! Grayson would have never gotten shot if it weren't for me!"

"Callie," she shook her head at me again, like she couldn't take having to repeat herself. "It's not like you were holding the damn weapon in his face!"

"He jumped in front of the bu lets for me, Marn. When I closed my eyes..." I breathed shakily, squeezing my eyes shut at the memory. "I expected it to all be over. But then I heard it go off and I didn't feel anything. When I opened my eyes...he...he was just lying there, bleeding. He took them for me, Marn," I said softly.

She gasped. "You mean...Grayson saved your life, then?"

Nodding silently, I watched her face unfold in a mess of different emotions. She went from shocked to appalled and then to a lighter mood I couldn't place.

"Damn, that boy really did have it bad..." she mumbled off, not even looking at me.

Now I was the one surprised. "What?"

"He took shots for you, Callie. He risked his life to save you..." she listed off, like I wasn't sure of what was obvious.

I nodded frantically. "I know all of this already. That's what I've been trying to explain all along."

She smiled small at me, the first bout of happiness I'd seen from her since the 'incident.' "You never noticed, did you?"

The look on her face read something like, 'I know something you don't know.' The taunting on her end was making me want to slap her. Now wasn't a time for childish secrets and keeping things from me. What was she aiming at?

"Noticed what?"

She grinned knowingly at me once again before looking down the hall. "I think we're late," she responded, stating the obvious. "We'd better get going."

She went to walk down the hall, smirking still as she decided she would keep to herself whatever she was hiding. I paced after her, grabbing a hold of her arm and twirling her around. "What was I supposed to notice?"

Marnie opened her mouth to say something, but was cut off by the beeping of my phone. I held up a finger for her to pause and fished for my phone in my bag. When I'd finally gotten it out, I flicked my finger across the screen to unlock it and a text came into view from the familiar grey-eyed boy in question.

Hey, how's the first day going so far?

I smiled unknowingly at the text, grateful that he remembered my worries I'd relayed to him back at the hospital the other day when we talked about school starting again and everything being different with the kids at school. He could have been using his time by catching up on school work or sleeping for that matter, but he made sure to check up on me.

"Is that him?" she piped up, making me jump for a moment.

I cast my eyes up at her, raising an eyebrow. "How did you know?"

She laughed and waved me off like I was too naïve to understand what she was already thinking. I ignored her for a moment, typing back a reply to Grayson before I went off to class.

Everyone's just waiting for me to crash and burn. Tell you about it tonight?

My phone beeped again quickly.

Can't wait :)

I was pretty sure my cheeks were on fire after reading those two simple words. When I put my phone back and met eyes with Marnie, she was still grinning at me with her knowing look gleaming.

"What?" I asked, acting like I wasn't blushing and smiling like a bumbling idiot.

"I still can't believe you haven't noticed it before," she breathed, still shocked at the fact I still wasn't clued into.

"My God, can you just tell me what it is you're talking about already?" I begged, rolling my eyes at her immaturity.

She turned and walked away without saying anything else. Waving a hand behind her, jiggling her fingers in a fancy gesture, she ignored me as I called after her.

"C'mon! Just tell me what you meant!"

She only turned her head to smile back at me, waving her fingers again. "Tell Grayson hi for me, will you?"

As she clicked down the hall in her expensive Jeffrey Campbells, far from the scared and depressive girl she'd been when I first approached her; I found myself still standing and all smiles. I thought she would still be too scared to even speak to me, let alone taunt me about a boy like we were in the fourth grade again.

Okay, so the kids at school were still waiting for me to fail and unleash a temperament onto the students like Clay once had. I was the most watched in the halls and probably wouldn't be able to even eat a sandwich at lunch without being accounted for every move that I made. This was going to be hard and frustrating. It wouldn't take a day to get over.

But now I had Grayson and my best friend back in my corner, which was enough for me to get through this day little by little, despite the circumstances.

15

CHAPTER 14

Somehow I had managed to get through the first two days back at school, but just by the skin of my teeth. The stares hadn't faltered and the whispers always seemed so loud as I walked down the hall. People weren't even trying to hide the fact that they were blatantly talking about me. Sometimes they would even point directly at me when I walked towards them on my way to class.

The whole thing was quite ridiculous, if you asked me.

Just because I was related to a boy who made his mistakes didn't mean that I was suddenly the runner up. He and I were far different from one another and I surely didn't plan on committing his actions in my lifetime.

But today was going to get a bit better because Grayson was going to be by my side. While his walk was slightly crippled by his massive crutches and he wasn't the happiest about finally being on his feet once again, it still felt good to have him walking along side me as I took on the eyes and the gestures. It was almost like Grayson was my armor for the day, shielding me from any further damage that they all dished out.

So when we finally made it through the double doors, everyone ready to deal out my well overdue punishments, my breathing wasn't as harsh with him by my side. He was a lot slower than I was, hopping on one foot and leaning forward to throw his body with each swing just to get down the hall. They school had given him an elevator pass considering his handicap, which meant we'd have to part ways sooner than I would have liked.

"Wow..." he gasped. "You really weren't kidding."

I watched as he glanced all around the halls, pausing in his movements. He was taking everyone in; casting angry looks towards some of the girls who wouldn't stop looking at me like Santa Claus had just appeared. When I looked down to the place where his hand rested on his crutches, his knuckles were turning white as he gripped it forcefully.

I scoffed. "This is nothing. You should see how it is in class."

As I paced myself to stay next to him, he gave me a surprised side glance. "You mean it's worse than this?" he gestured around us with a crutch.

"The teachers are somehow under the assumption that I'm stuck in his deep depression because my brother did what he did. They keep treating me like I'm going to just implode in the middle of class or something," I waved it off as we continued our walk.

He shook his head, some of his dark locks fraying and falling into his eyes. I had the strong impulse to just reach over and push them back out of his view, but clenched my fingers in a small fist instead.

In the past two weeks that I had gotten to know Grayson, the feelings that were brewing in my heart were becoming faster and more intense than anything I was used to. I had dated casually before, all of which didn't work out after just a few months. But being around Grayson was something so new to me. We seemed so connected, much more than I had with any other guy before.

He understood me before I even finished my sentences and always seemed to know what I was thinking.

I was beginning to get to know his little quirks, the way he would side-smirk at me when he was in on a secret that I didn't know about. He would run his hand from his shoulder down his arm when he was nervous; sometimes running it through his hair and pulling at the ends, making it stick up everywhere. He told me about his family and how much he loved baseball and hockey.

But the two things he seemed to always stray away from were his pieces and why he saved me the day of the 'incident'. When the topic always came up about his artwork, he would always smile so wide, almost convincing me that he wanted to show me his work. But then he'd just shake his head and wave me off when I asked about them. And whenever I asked about that day, tried to sneak in a simple way to bring it up, he'd completely sidetrack me and throw us into another conversation about movies or his little sister's cute habits.

At first, I allowed him to run us off the topic and leave me in the dark when it came to knowing about that day. I thought, maybe he hadn't been ready or he was scared to tell me what he was feeling. There were more things that I didn't know, things he probably thought I wouldn't be able to handle. But now I was just becoming more frustrated. I was opening up to him on every level, letting him know my deepest secrets when it came to Clay and how I was feeling all of the time. Where as, he was just kept throwing me for a loop and bypassing any topic that even came close to the day of the 'incident'.

And I really didn't know what to believe anymore.

"Well this is me..." Grayson trailed off, shrugging towards the elevator doors.

Immediately, I felt my once sturdy shoulders slump and things suddenly seeming heavier than they were when we first walked in. It was nice having someone there for me who wasn't trying to label me as the freak that'd drop soon. I wasn't going to be able to see him until Algebra later on in the afternoon, which seemed too far away for me.

He must have noticed my sluggish and sad appearance because he said, "Come here," as he smirked at me.

Opening his arms slightly, which was hard for someone in his condition, he waited for me to come towards him. "Grayson, I can't. You can barely keep your balance on those things as it is."

He took both of his crutches from underneath his arms and placed them against the wall where the elevators were behind him. Balancing on his sturdy foot and letting the booted one hang back, he grinned wildly at me, winking at me as he expertly stood there waiting for me to just hug him.

Shaking my head but matching his contagious grin, I walked into his open embrace and relished in his overwhelming warmth. He tightly held onto me, one of his arms hanging lightly against my back and near the base of my spin where my shirt had ridden up a bit. I tried to suppress the shivers as I wrapped my arms around his middle, letting my cheek lie against his chest. I could practically hear his heart thumping outside of his shirt and I smiled.

"Now you listen to me," he whispered in my ear, just loud enough to be heard over the incessant chatter around us. "You're stronger than anyone I know. If you could get through the past two days, you can get through today and every one after that. Don't let these idiots get to you. The only person who knows almost everything is you and only you. You know that you won't break like they're expecting you to. Just breathe and you'll get thought this. I'll see you in Algebra, okay?" he finished, reluctantly pulling back and casting his eyes down to mine.

His eyes were shining with something I couldn't quite place, but his hands still laid on my hips, a most like he didn't want to let go. Not that I was complaining. Biting my lip a bit unsurely, I nodded my head in agreement. His eyes fell down to my lips for just a moment, so quickly I thought I'd just imagined it. But just as quickly, they flickered back up to my eyes once more and met me with a smile.

"Thank you," I whispered, rightfully ignoring all of the stares our way.

"Eh, just reminding you of what you already know," he grinned again.

I just laughed at him, rolling my eyes as I turned to make my way to homeroom. I heard him chuckling behind me, ignoring those stupid goosebumps at the sound of his laugh and continued walking without turning back. I was almost mad at myself for feeling this way towards him. If he ever found out that what I felt for him was stronger than what we ever talked about, he'd probably run for the hills. We established this connection that not many got the pleasure of feeling. I was getting to know one of the golden boys in a way that no one else got to. We were just close friends who understood one another, who were there for one another.

I couldn't ruin that for some silly crush.

When I got into homeroom, of course met with multiple gazes as I found my seat, the intercom flickered overhead and everyone paused momentarily. Conversations died out and most of the eyes that were on me, traveled up towards the ceiling. It was odd hearing the intercom go off, considering it was barely used and the home-room teachers usually led the morning's announcements on their own time.

"Pardon the interruption students and faculty. In the light of…recent events," Principal Ortiz coughed awkwardly. "We will be canceling this morning's classes and having an assembly in the auditorium. Please make your way quietly downstairs and in an orderly fashion. Thank you."

The intercom fizzled as it clicked off and the eyes suddenly fell back down to me. We all knew what this was about, even though Ortiz only hinted towards the topic that would be discussed. This would be about my brother and what he did. This would be about Carter and the girl who got hit by stray bullets. This would be about Grayson.

And somehow this would be about me too.

Shit.

"Good morning all," Principal Ortiz greeted us as the student population filed in the auditorium, group by group, all grabbing seats near their designated friends and cliques. "I know this isn't the best circumstances to be meeting under, but I felt that we all needed to band together this week."

My eyes fell towards a banner behind Principal Ortiz, bearing Carter's now retired jersey number and hundreds of condolences and memories printed in different fonts and colors from the students. I didn't find it odd that no one told me about this, figuring that I didn't quite care about Carter's well-being because if my brother hated him than I hated him too…right?

Ortiz took a handkerchief from the breast pocket of his suit jacket and dabbed at his sweaty forehead. "What has been done in this school is nothing short of a tragedy. My condolences go out towards Carter Wayland's family and loved ones. He was one of the brightest, hardworking individuals I'd ever had the pleasure of knowing." Ortiz coughed subtly behind his handkerchief, looking like he was trying to choke down a cry that begged to get out. "He was kindhearted and ambitious. His parents even tell me that he was planning on attending University in the fall on an immense football scholarship."

People around me started sniffling and crying on one another's shoulders. I'd secured a seat in the very back; figuring people would be too entranced by the assembly and wouldn't be able to keep looking back at me where I was seated. And if they did, this gave me a perfect view of who instead of wondering if I had sat in the front.

A small piece of my heart went out to Carter and all of his friends and family. As much as I used to say that I hated him and how horrible he was to my brother, Marnie and I, he was still a human being with goals and ambitions just like the rest of us. He was a person who loved life, loved football more than any guy I knew, and who would do anything for his friends. I didn't know the reason why he picked on my brother or why he chose the Tollson family to hold such a grudge against. I'd probably never know.

But I did know that he didn't deserve the fate that my brother gave him.

A girl choked back a sob a few rows ahead of me, laying her head against the shoulder of a boy next to her. Tissues were handed around by the staff, the school's guidance counselor watching all of us from the front of the room with a small frown on her thin lips.

Everyone here seemed so sure how to portray their feelings. If someone wasn't crying, they were shaking their heads and crossing their arms against their chests in anger. Some were even talking in hushed tones about how strongly they felt about this incident. I wondered if they were talking about my brother or even me, my ears waiting to perk at the sound of familiar names.

I subconsciously slunk further into the plastic chair, trying and failing to go unnoticed. My eyes kept roaming around the room, hoping to meet Grayson's but not meeting any such luck. I saw many familiar dark haired boys with their heads facing away from me, but not one matching his.

"Yvette is on hand for anyone who feels like they need a bit of time to grieve," he continued, gesturing towards the guidance counselor next to him who practically begged us to call her by her first name, insisting that it 'added to the building relationship' we would all form with her.

Yvette took the microphone Principal Ortiz was speaking into and nodded her head to his words before speaking again. "What's been done here..." she trailed off. "Is not something that will ever be forgotten. No one is asking you to move on right away from this. It will take time and understanding from many of those around us. If any of you ever feel the need to talk or maybe just sit with your thoughts for a while, my office is open all throughout the day. You can come by anytime. And your teachers were notified that you may leave class and do so if you need to."

I gulped, feeling a fresh round of tears start to overcome my body. It kept coming in shockwaves, hard and fast, sometimes so quickly I couldn't catch the tears before they fell against my cheek. I felt my insides twisting as I listened to this and watched it all unfold before me. People were hurt and confused, some angry and wanting revenge, for something someone related to me had done. Carter had died because of my brother. He wouldn't be able to continue on with his goals and with his life because my brother felt that the best revenge was something you couldn't ever take back.

I'd spent so long pushing all of these emotions and events out of my heart and mind. Days were spent pretending like this hadn't happened, forcing myself to forget that my brother was the behind the hand that held the gun. No matter how many times I thought about that day, I still couldn't make the right connection to this. I couldn't help but wonder if it was because he was a completely different person that day. Maybe that's why I couldn't put two and two together.

Or maybe it was because I was still too scared to believe that my own flesh and blood had done this to so many lives.

"The banner behind me," Yvette pointed. "Is there for those who have messages for Carter or for his family. You can write personal memories down or send your condolences to his family. After all is said and done, we'll be handing it to his family along with his retired jersey. We encourage all of you to come and at least write down your thoughts or feelings. If you don't feel comfortable doing so in front of everyone, we have index cards you can bring with you today if you find you have something to say later on. There will be a box in my office where you can drop off your cards when you're finished."

As the tears fell freely down my face, feeling far from cleansing at this point, my eyes immediately flicked towards a boy standing up in his chair. "What about graduation? Will his name be read then? Will he get recognition?" he asked, his face like stone.

Yvette and Principal Ortiz looked put off for a moment, surprise washing over their faces. But Ortiz didn't take long to regain his composure. "That is the plan. But graduation is so many months away, that we still have much to talk about."

"Because I don't think it would be fair that he doesn't get his name read at graduation because he couldn't live long enough to see it. I mean, he didn't choose to get shot by that imbecile," the boy continued. I couldn't even remember his name, too zeroed in the fact that they were blatantly talking about my brother without saying his name. It was like they were too disgusted and he didn't earn the right to be acknowledged. I just kept sliding further and further from view.

"Yeah! Just because that idiot brought a gun to school and took his crap out on everyone else..." someone else chimed in.

"No one deserved that! I don't care what was going on with him. He shouldn't have..."

"Carter deserved to live! He deserves to graduate with the seniors!"

The auditorium erupted in angered voices, some people standing up and making their point as clearly as they could. Teachers around them tried to settle everyone down, quieting them before it all became too much. Principal Ortiz took the microphone from Yvette and cleared his throat.

"Excuse me! Settle down, please! Please quiet down!" he shouted, earning a dimming silence from the student body. Teachers were helping some of the kids sit down while others took crying students out into the hall for some air.

"Now students," he began again, his voice somewhat smaller than before. "There is much to think about before graduation even comes into our minds. But we also need think about the fact that Clay was bullied. He was picked on by some of the students in this school. This is also the reason why we're here. Now, I am not stating in any way that he should have surmounted to an act like he had, but bullying is also a situation we need to resolve this year. I don't want someone to..."

That same boy, who stood his ground before, took the floor once more and pointed a finger at me, making my heart sink into my stomach. I was about to be sick. "What, did she tell you that?"

And just like that, hundreds of eyes turned and fell on me. I felt like an experiment being scrutinized underneath a microscope. A lot of the girls had red rimmed lids and running mascara, while some of the football guys looked like they were about to throw all etiquette out the window and beat me up for even being related to a guy like Clay.

"Mr. Samson, please take your seat! This has nothing to do with Ms. Tollson!" he ordered, his face burning red as the anger bubbled in his blood.

"But she's part of the reason why we're here, isn't she?" he barked back, not even caring anymore that he was back talking the one man who could kick him out of school.

"Nathan, I highly advise you to take your seat and be quiet," Yvette whispered into the microphone as the other eyes stayed glued to me.

I looked a state, my face probably red with embarrassment and from crying so much. I could feel them judging me for crying over something like this. How dare I be sad about this when my brother killed him? My hands were gripping the underside of the plastic chair as I tried to find one pair of kind eyes in that sea of hate. I couldn't find Marnie's or Grayson's, making me feel much smaller than I had this morning when I thought I could count on them.

I just needed someone.

"She's his sister. She should have warned us or something! You're telling me she didn't know a damn thing about what was going to happen that day?" Nathan rambled on, his fists shaking at his sides.

The impulse to run was growing by the second, the more I felt myself getting smaller in this suddenly too-small room. I just wanted to hop up from my seat and shout that I didn't have a clue as to why he'd done this. I wanted to clear my name and say that no matter how close they all thought we were that he never once mentioned something like this. Did they all think so little of me that they believed I would keep something like this from everyone in school so he could actually go through with this?

"Mr. Samson! I will not tell you again!" Ortiz shouted again.

"She could have helped! She could have saved his life!" he kept thrusting his finger at me from across the room, causing more rambling from everyone around us.

And then I just ran. I ran as fast as my feet could carry me. Tears were soaking my cheeks and my shirt, my nails already digging permanent holes in the palms of my hand. My shoes were smacking against the linoleum floor with such force, I thought I'd fall through the imitation tiles.

I couldn't stop replaying Nathan's words.

She could have helped.

She could have saved his life.

She's the reason why we're here.

Could that have been it? Did I really step over every crumb that led me to Clay's downfall? We were such close siblings after all. There had to be some sign that I chose to miss along the way. How does someone plan all of this without leaving some sort of clue behind in their wake?

My breathing was becoming harsher as I kept going; the silence around me engulfing me and sending over the brink I hadn't known Clay had created for me. Why did he have to do this? Why did he think this was the ultimate decision he had to make?

Just as I was about to round the corner and make my way towards the school's exit doors, a familiar voice caused me to freeze in my tracks.

"Callie, wait!"

16

CHAPTER 15

I don't know why I stopped, really. I should have just kept on running, just like they wanted me to. Maybe running just made me look a coward. It could have automatically pinned me as guilty for knowing something I didn't feel the need to tell anyone else. They all probably thought that I was the one who knew about Clay and his ideas. They were most likely chattering about me right now, stating that this was proof of what I'd kept to myself. Principal Ortiz was trying to settle everyone down as the voices just seemed to grow...and grow, swallowing my being whole.

Running was what made everything easier, wasn't it?

People ran for their lives every single day. Running was how you admitted you had a problem. People ditched their responsibilities because they were too much to handle. They either weren't capable enough or felt that there was nothing else they could do but bolt. It was the easiest route to take, one that would ensure that you'd never have to deal with that problem again.

But that was the thing about running from your issues. Now matter how fast or how far you ran away from that haunting problem, it would always come back to hit you eventually. You didn't get rid of things by leaving them behind in the dust. If you didn't face things head on, they would still be there when you got back.

Or even worse, follow you all the way to your next destination.

That was why I stayed where I was, my feet stuck to the floor and my heart still racing from the exertion. The doors were right there, just begging for me to throw them open and leave. It was a way out after all. I wouldn't have to deal with anything or anyone if I just left. But I knew that I couldn't run forever.

Even if it wasn't my own issue to run from.

"Have you ever thought of joining the track team?" he breathed as he approached me. The impatience of watching him slowly make his way towards me on his crutches was enough to make me want to bolt again. It's not like he could catch up to me if I decided to go along with the idea.

I stayed quiet. Instead of thinking up some witty reply, I started biting at my thumbnail. At least what was left of it anyway. After a few, mind-numbing and long moments, he was finally in front of me and panting heavily.

"Can't give the crippled kid a break, huh?" he asked, a small grin playing at his lips.

I'd be lying if I said I wasn't surprised that he was even here right now. What happened back there was nothing short of appalling. I had never been more embarrassed and ashamed of myself in my entire life. After they said all of those things about me, you'd think that Grayson wouldn't want a damn thing to do with me.

Yet here he was, in all his glory, once again surprising me with his efforts I still hadn't quite caught on to.

He nudged me with the toe of his crutch. "C'mon. Not even a smile?"

I kept my eyes trained to the floor after that, still biting rapidly at my nail and creating a sour nub at the end of my thumb. I could feel his eyes on me, studying my every motion to see if he could read me. He was becoming so awfully good at it that it was beginning to scare me a bit.

I felt like I couldn't hide a thing from him anymore.

"Callie, what happened back there was not your fault. What they said about you wasn't true. You know that, right?" he whispered.

My tears betrayed me for the hundredth time this week, coming over the edge as I finally gained the courage to look up at him. "But it is! Can't you see that?" I cried, my shouts reverberating against the walls. "He was my brother, Grayson! He used to tell me everything about his life. I knew his inner most thoughts and feelings about every little detail. I was his confidant. If anyone was able to know what he was about to do...it was me!"

"So?" he replied, his voice now high-pitched and angry. "Just because he told you things about his life doesn't mean that he didn't hide things from you, too."

I swallowed back the sobs that were wracking my throat, shaking my head at him. "You don't get it. You'll never understand!"

"I'll never understand?" he stepped back a beat from me, shouting this time. "I was fucking shot, Callie. I think I understand than most of those idiots back there!"

The guilt that been laced within my bones for the past two weeks had reared its ugly head once again. It fizzled in my stomach and made me ill to even think about it anymore. Whenever I looked at Grayson anymore, talked about the issue that was haunting all of us, it always fell back down to this point. He had jumped in front of a gun for me, took two bullets in his precious body for me.

And what had I done? All I had done for him was tell him a few bits and pieces about myself and visited him when he was holed up in a too-quiet hospital room with no one to keep him company.

I wasn't worth all of this. I should have taken the bullet myself. It's what Clay wanted after all. He wanted me to pay for the events I'd subjected him to. I was the last minute decision that had gone completely and terribly wrong from the start. If Grayson hadn't jumped in front of me, I wouldn't be here right now. There wouldn't be fingers pointing at me and blame cast upon the girl who didn't have a freaking clue as to why her once admirable brother did this.

Squeezing my eyes shut at the pictures colliding in my brain, I swallowed back the guilt once more. "You didn't deserve that. I don't know why you jumped in front of those bullets for me, but you shouldn't have."

"Callie..." he urged.

"And I don't know why Carter always chose my brother to pick on, but no matter how much I wanted to hit him back for what he did to Clay, he didn't deserve that either. Neither did that girl who was only trying to help. If anyone deserved what happened that day, it was me. I was the one who embarrassed him so much growing up. I was too overprotective and too clingy. I didn't let him live his life the way that he wanted to."

"Can you just..." he begged once more.

Opening my eyes to face his weary ones, I took in a deep breath. "I deserved what Clay wanted. Not you. Not Carter. No one but me."

Grayson's face contorted as he took in my words. His eyes were somewhat glassy, looking like he was about to cry himself if I didn't shut up this instant. He looked so pained and at fault, something I'd wanted to rid him of since the day of the 'incident.'

I wasn't sure what I wanted after I let go of that thought. It was the first time I was admitting that I knew that I was to blame for this mess. So many hours I had spent held up in my room, hiding underneath the covers and constantly replaying the day's timeline like every moment was mapped out for me to see over and over. Deep down, I knew the guilt kept coming back because I knew that I was the cause of this. He wouldn't have broken down the way that he had if I had just picked up on the clues he left behind.

A part of me wanted Grayson to just say, 'I'm done' and leave me be with my own devices. I wanted him to realize that I wasn't worth saving. If it wasn't for me ignoring all of Clay's signs, than the school wouldn't have had to pay for the mistakes I had made. Someone needed to be there to protect my older brother and get him the help that he needed. My parents were always too busy to notice how badly he was handling things.

I should have noticed.

I expected so many things from that confession. Most of which led to Grayson leaving and realizing that he was wrong for what he did, no matter how heroic he seemed. I envisioned having to face the world without him holding my hand against it any longer. That's what was supposed to happen in a situation like this.

But what I wasn't expecting was Grayson to say his next few words.

"There's a lot you need to know. Can we go somewhere to talk?"

After helping Grayson into the passenger side of my car and throwing his crutches into the backseat, all the while ignoring the fact that it was only second block and someone would undoubtedly noticed we hadn't shown up for class, I was somehow making my way towards the docks by the lakeside.

Riverton was famous for its expansive lake that wrapped around the city like a blanket. It surrounded us, leaving us divided from the town across the bridge and a boat ride over. The water was always flowing heavily, sunrays bouncing off the waves and creating a bright glow. A row of planks and support beams spread out from the wide expansion of grass and trees, creating a walkway towards and over the water as an exclusive spot.

The whole ride to the lake's edge was silent, save for the low volume of some catchy pop song on the radio while I drove. I kept looking over at Grayson at stop signs and red lights, hoping he'd catch my eye and smile at me to reassure me that what he was about to tell wasn't going to change my view of him, of us. But he just kept his eyes trained out the window and the only movement was of his chest rising and falling gently beneath his green sweater.

As I parked the car a few feet away from the dock, I bit my lip as I made eye contact with the prison across the lake. It was large and haunting, barbed wire wrapping around the prison walls and creating a blockade between the criminals and normals. I thought of Clay in a cell, seated on a recreation mattress with a snaky smile on his lips. He was dressed in an orange jumpsuit with the Anatoga town name printed in large block letters across his back.

The thought alone gave me shivers as I willed myself to hold it together for the sake of this conversation. I wanted to know what Grayson was hiding, the secrets behind that all-knowing smile of his that he always seemed to showcase whenever we were with one another. The only thing keeping me afloat right now was finding out his secrets and figuring out why he chose me to protect of all people that day.

Anatoga's prison walls were hard to ignore, bright red bricks and smoke tangling with the air above it from the kitchen's chimney. It made me think of criminals working slave labor as their punishment instead of just being held up in their cells all day. But I had to keep my eyes on the stake at hand.

I retrieved Grayson's crutches from the backseat of the car and helped him hop out of his seat. He wouldn't meet my eyes as he took the crutches from me and heaved his body towards the dock. On the walk to the water's edge, I kept wringing my hands and trying to keep my thoughts at bay, the many ways I thought this conversation could go. What would he tell me? Would it change how I felt?

Uneasily, Grayson managed to sit down at the edge of the docks, his booted foot curled in front of him and his other hanging over the wooden planks and skimming the water. I sat down in front of him, turning my body slightly away from the prison that was practically screaming for me to look its way. Grayson kept his eyes trained on the water's brimming, small waves as he cleared his throat to begin.

"I feel awful," he started, his voice scratchy and laced with pain.

"What in the world could you have to feel awful about?" I whispered, crossing my legs in front of me and leaning forward.

"There's so much you and Clay didn't know. So much I should have told you both before this all happened. Maybe then..." he trailed off, his eyes briefly looking across the water at the building that seemed to be taunting us both. It was almost like Clay was eavesdropping on our conversation. "Maybe then he would have thought twice before doing this."

What in the world did he know? "Grayson, what...?"

He cut me off by flickering his eyes towards mine. The bright grey glistened against the sun behind me, making me wish I could just read behind them instead of sitting in agony like this. "There were things you guys didn't know about Carter. Reasons why he chose to pick on Clay."

I raised an eyebrow, my heart beating rapidly against my chest. My fingers felt fidgety, like they needed something to grab onto or busy themselves with. I settled with picking at the toe of my Doc Marten's, my eyes never once leaving Grayson's.

"Your brother was always so...eccentric, you know?" I nodded in agreement. "He wore weird tights in those plays and was bubbly whenever he talked to someone. He had that somewhat high-pitched voice and never seemed to have a girlfriend. His whole life, he was...out there, I guess you could say."

My blood boiled at the characteristics he was giving my brother. I knew exactly what he was getting at. Grayson was going to give my brother the label he'd been running from his entire life. Ever since the day the kids at school found out that the term 'faggot' didn't just mean a pile of sticks anymore, it seemed to chase him wherever he went. That label, I believed, was part of the reason why he tried so hard to fit in. He must have thought that if he fit in before the term was permanently labeled on his back, that he wouldn't have worry about it if people already loved him.

Bearing my teeth I said, "What the hell are you getting at?"

His eyes widened at my rapid anger, surprised that I'd switched moods so quickly. He shook his head straight away, raising a hand in a silent surrender to give him a moment. "I'm not trying to label him! That's not what I'm getting at here. Give me a chance to explain."

I just stared at him, waiting for him to make up for what he just said.

"You know what everyone always used to say about him behind his back," he sighed. "Because your brother wasn't like every other guy on the football team or something...they just assumed that he was gay. Now I never judged him. I was still his friend despite what everyone else said about him. I didn't care whether he was gay or not. None of that mattered to me. But Carter...Carter was having a hard time with it."

"I don't understand..." I butted in.

Grayson looked out into the water again. "God, he'd kill me for telling you any of this. I was the only one he told. He trusted me to keep this a secret."

"Grayson," I urged.

He started playing with his boot, ripping at the Velcro and biting his lip with his two front teeth nervously. He did that thing that always meant he was anxious, running a hand from his injured shoulder down the length of his arm without looking at me. "You know that Carter was like an older brother to me."

"You mentioned it once. I never knew that you guys were so close," I whispered, my voice crashing loudly with the subtle sounds of the waves beneath us.

Taking a deep breath he said, "Carter had a secret that no one else knew about but me. He wasn't the lady's man and player that everyone pegged him to be. I mean...he was acting that way, but that's not who he was."

If Grayson didn't stop beating around the bush like this, I was sure I'd push him backwards so he'd land butt first into the lake underneath us. My heart kept racing as the anxiety whirled through me, halting any other thought I'd had about today. If Grayson wanted to keep me on the edge of my seat, this was definitely the way to do it.

"Carter was gay," he gulped.

And just like that, every understanding I ever thought I'd had, shattered all around me like glass hitting the pavement. Each shard was a secret I thought I knew, each piece of a part of me that believed I knew it all when it came to this topic of conversation.

I always thought that I knew everything there was to know about Carter. I was under the impression that he just hated my brother because he was an annoyance in his life, something to keep him entertained when his life got boring. Carter Wayland strutted around school like God's gift to humanity, with a smile and a swagger to melt any girl that walked his way. From what I heard around the rumor mill, he slept with over twenty different girls in his high school career already. He was always one for random hookups and never girlfriends, until...Marnie.

"What?" I spluttered, my mouth gaping like a fish.

He just nodded. "He never told anyone because he hated himself for it. He wanted to be straight. He knew that if the secret ever got out...no one would look at him the same anymore. He had a life and the team, the guys he was friends with would never accept him for that. So that's why he slept with so many different girls. He let them fall at his feet so he could prove to everyone that he wasn't what he truly was."

All I could do was shake my head and keep my jaw hanging like an idiot. None of this made sense. So many secrets were being dug from their closets, skeletons on display for the world to see. Why did it take such a tragedy for things like this to come out? Why couldn't Carter just take his inner-hate and channel it into something else?

"Then why did he choose to pick on Clay?"

"Carter didn't want to be gay. He tried everything in his power to fix that. He thought if he slept with a bunch of different girls every night that it would somehow alter him. He fought so hard to remain the only thing he knew. I guess he thought that if he beat up Clay enough that he'd…fix him too before it was too late," he trailed off, his voice becoming nothing but a slight murmur against the wind.

It was so hard to wrap my brain around. Carter Wayland was gay. He was in the closet for so many years, simply because he was scared of what other people would think of him. My brother spent years trying to become one with people like him, for the same reasons Carter never showed his true colors. While none of it still made sense to me, it somehow brought me full circle.

Part of this did make sense.

Clay was bullied because of how flamboyant and different he acted than most of the guys at our school. He wasn't normal to the others around him. He should have been working out, playing for sports teams and dating multiple girls at once. He shouldn't have been acting in plays, wearing tights for costume and acting so eccentric around people all of the time.

To most of those around him, Clay always seemed like he played for the other team. I'd never judge my brother for his life choices, but I never once stopped to question if what people said about him was really true. Was he hiding out like Carter once had?

"I can't believe this…" I murmured, my voice catching in my throat. I looked across the lake at the prison again, wondering so many things about my brother I once thought I knew. His true colors were now starting to bloom, exhibit A being the day of the 'incident.' I wondered what would have happened if someone had told him about Carter and why he was getting beat up everyday.

Would he have still brought the gun to school that day?

I wanted to be mad at Grayson for keeping something like this from me. All this time, I kept straying the blame from Carter and putting it on myself. I spent so many nights, lying awake in fear and in guilt because I thought I was the reason behind this mess. I never once thought that secrets and misleading stories would be in the background, hiding behind a curtain and shaded from the world as I once knew it.

Grayson's Adam's apple bobbed in his neck, my eyes hanging on his every movement. "There's something else."

My eyes almost fell out of their sockets. "What else could you be keeping from me?" I gasped.

"Callie, I..."

My phone rang, the sound making us both jump. We were both so stuck in this small conversation, our own little moment we'd surrounded ourselves in that we almost forgot that there was an outside world that still seemed to exist. I didn't know who could have been calling me at this hour, making me wonder if this was an emergency.

Clicking the answer button with a finger as I saw that it read my mother's name, I released a breath I didn't know I'd been holding. "Hello?"

"Callie," she breathed. "I was hoping you'd answer."

"What's wrong, Mom? Why are you calling me at this hour?"

"It's your brother," she said shakily, her voice cracking like it killed her to label him as my brother with his previous vicious background. "He's being insistent." She took another breath before saying, "Clay wants to see you."

17

—— • ——

CHAPTER 16

"**I** can't believe you," he shook his head at me.

I couldn't believe myself either. After the amount of emotional turmoil I've been through, I shouldn't want anything to do with my brother any longer. He was the reason someone died, two others got hurt. He was to blame for putting me up against the entire school in the auditorium two weeks ago. Clay was the reason that I felt like I couldn't pick up all of the pieces of myself that he'd shattered and left on the ground.

Today was the day I was going to see my older brother in prison. When my mother asked me to reconsider my answer to this question he posed for me, I wasn't quite sure why I was so dead set on my answer. I thought I would want more time to think about the consequences of this. After all, seeing him for the first time in almost a month scared me more than I was willing to admit. As soon as the question left her lips, I immediately knew what I had to do. I didn't over-think the situation, didn't allow myself time to talk about what could and could not happen during this visit.

I just said yes.

"Sweetheart, you have to think about this," my mom huffed a few days before. She kept pacing the kitchen back and forth, a hand planted on her hip and the other over her mouth. She was appalled that I wasn't considering my answer.

Standing my ground I said, "Mom, I don't need to think about this. I have to see him. It's what he wants."

"And who's to say he's allowed to even ask for what he wants?" she shouted, stomping her foot on the kitchen tiles and facing me with an expression of anger and confusion.

I sighed heavily. "He's still my brother. Maybe he wants to see me to apologize or something..."

I knew I was acting irrationally. I was being naïve if I even thought for a second that Clay would want to apologize for the things he had done to me and to everyone that day of the 'incident'. The way he acted on the phone the last time we spoke was enough proof to me that he wasn't about to change his view on the situation at hand that was keeping him in prison.

But no matter how much my mother tried to drill it into my head, I couldn't allow her to change my mind. A small part of me believed that somewhere, deep down in his heart, he was going to be the same boy I'd grown up with. There was absolutely no way, in my mind really, that he could change this quickly. Those memories I had of us at the park, on our front lawn in the red wagon, and growing up with him by my side were suddenly starting to seem like mirages. I was almost convinced that I was making them up along the way.

I wanted to do this to find a way to prove that he was there somewhere. The part of him that I admired so much and the part that I loved so dearly couldn't have disappeared with the snap of his fingers like that.

My mom rolled her eyes at my response. "Stop acting like a child, Callie. You were there when he did those things to those children. He does not deserve your appearance or anything else he plans on asking you for. He's probably only asking for you because I refuse to go and see him until he realizes that what he's done to this town is wrong."

"And that may be it, Mom. He might just want to see me so he can spite you for not going to see him. He might want to grill me for information. He might even tell me that he's still not sorry for what he's done. But that's why I want to go; because all of these maybes are really starting to mess with my head. I need to know."

She sighed once more at my lack of acceptance for her wishes. "I just don't want you to go there and have him hurt you more than he already has."

I watched as her previous angry expression crumbled before me, replaced by softer eyes and a kinder face. "Just let me do this. Let me go and talk to him."

She let her body fall against the counter, wiping a hand against the fraying hairs in her face. "I'm not going to stop you. I'm just warning you…that you might not like what he has to tell you, Callie."

So that's how I ended up at today. I was running around my bedroom, shoving odds and ends into my bag after getting ready for my meeting with Clay. Grayson was perched against the edge of my computer desk, arms folded across his chest. He was finally rid of the pesky crutches, but his step was still reduced to a jagged limp.

I was rushing around, hoping that if I occupied myself with busy things that I wouldn't be over-thinking this visit. The more I let myself be alone and ponder my thoughts, the more I kept thinking of different outcomes for this meeting. What would he say to me?

Would he be happy to see me? Would he be the furthest thing from what I was hoping I'd see?

"You're crazy. I can't believe you," Grayson said again, his voice still full of shock.

"Say that one more time, why don't you, Grayson?" I mocked, throwing a small pack of tissues into my bag for a 'just in case' find. I didn't know how today was going to go, but I was sure I'd need them by the end, no matter the outcome.

He pushed himself from my desk and limped over to where I was standing near my closet. "I just don't understand why you feel the need to see him. He almost shot you, Callie," he said softly.

I ignored the way he said my name, how it seemed to pleasantly roll around his tongue before he let it out. The longer we were spending time together, the more I kept chasing away those annoying feelings for him. Ever since the day we sat at the docks and he made his confession about Carter, he was starting to slowly open up to me more and more.

Still leaving out what he was going to tell me before my mother interrupted with her phone call and why he saved me from the shooting.

I stopped in my trek around my room and looked up at him. He was watching me with worried eyes, his dark hair playing at his lashes as he looked down at me. We were so close that if I stepped just once more, we'd be nose to nose. Close enough to kiss him if I had the courage. But I just shook my head, trying to rid the feelings from my tingling skin.

"I know," I whispered, never moving my eyes from his. "But he's still my brother. There's so much I want to know, things only he can tell me. You understand that, don't you?"

He let out a breath. "I guess I get that. I'd want to know everything, too." He looked away from me while he said this, a look on his face that I couldn't quite place.

Every time we brought up the subject of finding out the secrets behind that day, he always acted like there was still more that I needed to know. Never once did he manage to open his mouth and spill what he was hiding, but he always looked almost guilty in a sense. I didn't push it, knowing if I did it would only drive us both crazy.

The more time I was spending with Grayson, the more I was realizing that he wasn't one to keep his mouth shut for too long. It took him a while, but once you let him slowly break down his walls, he'd give you the world if you asked for it. It just took him a bit longer than most.

"How's the shoulder?" I asked, placing my palm on the warmest part of his body. I could feel the bullet hole through the thin material of his shirt and almost cringed at the feeling of it between my fingers. I remembered him complaining about it last week, saying that the pain meds they prescribed him weren't doing him any good.

He finally looked back up at me, his eyes still swimming with secrets. "Better," he whispered, his breath so close to me. I squeezed at the material of his shirt in an effort to forget about these idiotic, romantic thoughts that kept coming to light in my head whenever he was near.

His eyes dropped down to where my hand was gripping his shirt and then fell back down to me. Those bright grey eyes that I sometimes couldn't get out of my head were shining in the light of my bedroom, drawing me in and drowning me in their waters. While he watched me, I swore I wouldn't be able to keep my head bobbing above the waters much longer.

Licking his lips momentarily he whispered my name. "Callie."

"Yeah?" I breathed.

He gulped as his face seemed to inch closer and closer. I thought I was imagining it all. "You..."

His lips were now just millimeters away from my own, begging me to budge and attach mine to his. He was so warm, inviting even. My fingers just clenched stronger onto his t-shirt, my knuckles brushing against the bumpy pieces of skin where he was injured...for me. I could feel his breath against my cheek, making me close my eyes momentarily.

"You..." he tried once more, but failed as he fumbled with his words. I opened my eyes again to find him staring into me, his hands inching towards me and trying to grasp onto my hips, something to bring us closer together. The moment probably took seconds, but it all felt like years, so slow and insanely addictive.

When his hands found both sides of my hips, it was like his confidence filled him to the brim. His fingers curled into my skin, his skin brushing against the skin not covered by my shirt near the base of my back. He pulled me to him roughly once he took hold, clashing our bodies together.

"Grayson," I gasped.

And then I was drowning at sea without a life raft to keep me up. He quickly kissed me, placing his lips roughly but sweetly all at the same time against mine. My hand was still at his shoulder, slowly letting go of the fabric of his shirt and running up to the base of his hair. The kiss was so intense and mind-numbing, something I wasn't used to at all. My fingers started to play at the ends of his hair, twisting them every which way as we practically devoured one another. My skin tingled where his fingers were playing near the waistband of my leggings.

Just as he was about to part my lips and create a sea far deeper than I could imagine, a voice broke us apart.

"Callie? Visiting hours are almost over. You need to get going!" My dad knocked on the door before I heard his steps retreat down the hall and away from us.

The surprise made us both jump apart from one another, leaving me panting as the distance seemed too far away from what it once was. Grayson's eyes were heady with emotion I couldn't place, clouded with the actions of what we'd just done. His lips were plump from the kiss, making me just want to kiss him again.

Clearing my throat as I ran a hand through my hair I said, "Um...we should really get going."

His eyes widened. "You..." he stuttered. "You want me to go with you?"

I looked at him like he'd just said the dumbest thing imaginable. "Of course. Who else would I ask?"

He quickly nodded his head, running his hand from his shoulder and down the length of his arm. I almost wanted to smile at that, knowing that it only meant that he was nervous.

I made him nervous.

"Yeah, I-let's go," he said.

The doors to the visitor's area buzzed as the prison guard scanned his ID card to allow us through. The walls were a creamy white, pale enough to lack any depiction of emotion or fun. In the hallway in front of us there were plastic chairs with soft bottoms, sturdy enough to hold someone waiting but uncomfortable enough to make you wish even more that you were anywhere but here. It all smelled like disinfectant and scary stories.

I couldn't help but think of the hundreds, maybe thousands of people locked up behind steel bars for things they either wished they hadn't done or weren't sorry for. There were murderers, rapists, thieves and down right delusional human beings locked up behind these cells every single day. It didn't seem right that my own flesh and blood was labeled as the same as these daily criminals.

"I'll uh...just wait out here," Grayson murmured, his voice seeming to bounce in the tiny hallway. He gave me one last side smirk, one that sort of look forced, before sitting down in the chair that was meant for those who weren't ready to face the person behind the metal door.

The whole drive here, Grayson barely missed a beat. He talked me through the day ahead, let me complain to him and reassured me that I wanted to do this for a reason. He always kept adding, 'Even though I don't agree with this...' before everything he said, but he was still helping me calm down while my nerves rattled my bones. I thought, with the way that he acted after we were forced to jump apart back in my bedroom, that he'd avoid any talking and refuse to look at me.

But he was Grayson Foster after all, known for his surprises.

I nodded at him, giving him my best reassuring smile before jerking my head at the prison guard that was blocking my access to the room that housed my brother. They were letting us meet in a room that would be watched by two guards and someone behind one of those two-way mirrors (standard for people who committed crimes like him).

The prison guard was dressed in navy blue clothes, stone-faced and lacking any type of sympathy. He probably did things like this everyday, witnessed the crying and the swearing from any person imaginable. Jobs like these, where you worked with the criminally insane, were meant for people with cold hearts and strong shoulders.

I gulped as the door buzzed open, seeing the guard nod his head as a sign for me head on in. I crossed my arms in front of me, my leather jacket squeaking as I pulled myself tighter in. The room was believably small, almost reminding me of the room where I was questioned the two days after the 'incident'. There was a square table parked in the middle of the room, a metal chair on either side of table. I looked up at the two-way mirror, wondering who was watching me right now while I waited for Clay.

I took my seat slowly. My hands gripped the edges of the table as the clock above me seemed to tick on and on while I waited. It was only five minutes later that two guards opened the door that was next to the mirror, dragging in my brother. I gasped when his eyes flickered to mine, noticing how dull and hard they looked. He was dressed in an orange jumpsuit, those Anatoga letters I imagined scrolled in thick font on the back and front of his clothing. His light brown hair was sticking up every which way, slight facial hair growing in on his upper lip and chin.

He was handcuffed as the guards brought him in, only briefly being released as they attached him to a bar on the opposite side of the table and kept him hooked with no place to go. A snaky smile was playing at his lips while he watched me squirm beneath the florescent lights.

"Callie," he stated, my name sounding horrid on his tongue. It wasn't pleasant like the way Grayson made it sound. It almost wrapped itself in malice and disdain.

"C-Clay," I murmured, keeping my eyes trained on him in a desperate attempt to seem somewhat strong in front of him.

He licked his slightly chapped lips. "I can't believe you actually showed up. Mom won't even bother to take the time out to come and see me herself."

I subconsciously picked at my bitten nails underneath the table. "She's been pretty busy with work," I lied through my teeth.

He let out a rumble of a laugh. "Bullshit," he spat, his eyes becoming hard once more. "I know she's avoiding me. She doesn't want to see me."

I shook my head, my hair falling in my eyes. "That's not true-"

"Stop fucking lying to me!" he growled, slamming the table with two strong hands. The guards placed behind him started to make a move for him, but he gave one of them a bored look. "Oh stop. I'm not going to jump over the table and fucking kill her or something."

I watched him maneuver his way around the guard's weary expression, shell-shocked that this was my older brother. The boy I remembered barely uttered a curse unless he was truly angry with someone. He didn't slam things or take things too far when they didn't need to be. He was watching the guards like he could read them like the back of his hand. That dirty look still filled his eyes, making me want to shrink in my seat.

Slowly, he whirled his head back around to face me. "So why did you come anyway?" he asked.

"I-I think the better question is, w-why did you want me come here?" I stuttered beneath his gaze. I was suddenly grateful for the fact that Grayson was outside right now. I wasn't sure I'd be able to stand on my own two feet after this.

He sat back in his chair, his hands straining against the cuffs. "You wanted an explanation on the phone last time we talked. I wanted to give you one."

I gulped. "And what's that?"

He studied me like a bug beneath a microscope. I was sure he could smell the fear coming from me as I let him watch me. My mind that was usually wandering with different ideas as to what he would say was suddenly drawing a blank. I couldn't think of anything but his hard eyes and how much he had changed from the boy I once thought I knew so well.

What had happened to him?

"You know what happened with Carter and the guys before him when I grew up," he stated, running his calloused finger against the edge of the metal table. "I was tired of them thinking they could fuck with me the way that they had. It was the only way I knew I could have the upper hand."

"But you killed him, Clay," I spluttered, not able to wrap my brain around his words. How could he possibly think that acting that way was a good thing? Was shooting someone who picked on you really the answer? Was escaping the bullying really worth sitting in prison for the rest of his life?

"That was the point," he snapped, barely blinking as he sliced his words straight through my heart. I never would have imagined my brother thinking up someone's murder in his mind. All those nights in his room, quiet and untouched, were spent plotting the death of a boy who didn't deserve it in the slightest.

My jaw dropped. "Clay, you can't honestly be telling me that you planned to kill him the way that you had?"

"Why is that so shocking to everyone?" his voice boomed in the small expansion of the room. The guards around him barely flinched while I jumped at his every word. "He beat the shit out of me for years. Years, Callie. You think what he did was right?"

"No! But..."

He cut me off. "How else was I going to get rid of him, huh? Now he can't bother anyone else..." he trailed off, looking down at his nail beds like this conversation meant absolutely nothing to him.

I was entirely and completely appalled. The words I wanted to say sort of jumbled up into something I couldn't admit out loud. Nothing made sense to me. I couldn't comprehend why he would think that what he did was the answer for his problems. He had such a life ahead of him, away from Carter and the kids that would pick on him. He'd meet new people, be able to create a proper life for himself that wouldn't make him change who he was.

But he just threw it all away for a boy who he could have easily escaped.

"Clay," I breathed. "You were going to go to college. You were getting out of the city and about to live on your own. You had just one year left. That's all!"

"That's all?" he shouted back at me. "That's all, really? You try stepping into my shoes for one moment," he held up a finger. "One fucking moment. Being me was like living in hell every single day. I couldn't bear to get out of bed in the morning. Walking around school was like subjecting myself to a disapproving audience. I'd been at this game of theirs for years, Callie. I couldn't waste another day like that."

"And sitting in here is so much better?" I yelled back this time, the fear slipping away as his words just seemed more and more unrealistic. This wasn't my brother. He was nothing close to the guy who used to help me bandage my cuts as a kid. This wasn't him.

He laughed snidely. "You'll never understand," he shook his head.

And there it was, the words I'd been throwing at people left and right since the day of the shooting. Every time someone tried to talk me out of my high jumps or made a move to talk to me about what happened that day, I just kept telling them all the same things. Grayson got shot for me and I still told him he'd never get it. I hated that he uttered the same words that I once had. I hated that we had a small similarity.

I wanted to be everything but him.

I smirked angrily. "You know what? I won't ever understand why you did what you did. I've spent nights lying awake wondering what in the hell caused you do such a thing to so many innocent people. You're right; Carter was a horrible person to you. But you don't know what he went through, either. Just like you're telling me right now, how I won't ever understand what you went through, you'll never understand what anyone else went through either," I pointed a shaky finger in his direction. "You won't know what Carter went through, what his family and friends went through, what Grayson went through...what I went through. You'll never begin to fathom how we feel, at all. So you can sit there with your snide smirk and act like you're better than everyone now because you found the secret to escaping that hell you went through everyday. You can pretend like you know it all now. You can act like this whole ordeal has made you some tougher version of yourself. Act like you've won, Clay. Do it. But you didn't win. Not even close," I shook my head at him, murmuring my last sentence before pushing myself up from my chair.

His face still didn't change, h s eyes only somewhat softening as he took in my words. He watched me get up, begging me to turn back around and look at him so he could be the bigger person here and make me quiver in fear once more. But now I'd had more than enough confirmation that this wasn't my brother any longer. Who Clay was now, was the furthest from the boy I once thought I knew. The Clay sitting in that chair with the smug smirk on his face, strong shouldered and cocky like he'd just won the game of all games, was some monster created long before I could even imagine.

"I still have more to say!" he boomed, making me pause before the door and causing the guard to look down at me a bit quizzically, like he wasn't sure how I would react to this. I don't even think Clay was sure how I'd react. I believed he thought I'd just sit back down, go with his orders and listen to him.

"Save it for the judge," I stated, nodding at the guard as he buzzed me out and slamming the door behind me, severing any tie to that man in the metal chair that was ever created between us.

18

CHAPTER 17

The night after visiting Clay, all I could do was toss and turn. The constant rewind of his eyes hard and cold on mine was keeping me awake and making me curse myself for turning out the lights fully before coming back into bed. I wrapped myself tight into my covers, almost squeezing the life out of my middle with the tightness. Nothing was helping me overcome this.

Huffing, I threw the covers off of me and raked my hands through the hairs fraying out of my messy bun. My room was just too quiet, silent enough for me to be able to replay the scenes of today over and over in my mind.

A normal teenage girl would be going over the events of one of the best kisses of her life that happened just earlier today. If I was able to function like a proper girl, I'd be squealing and feeling little butterflies in my stomach as I thought about the way Grayson's lips moved against mine, the way he held me so close to him like I'd run if he didn't. Instead of going over the nightmare time and time again, I should have been thinking about Grayson.

But no matter how hard I tried to think about something…anything other than Clay's words and his eyes on me, it was becoming futile. Not only was Clay insisting on making me cower beneath him when he was in the same room as me, but also when he was across the bridge and almost thirty mi es away. I couldn't catch a break, barely even a breath if I tried.

After realizing that sleeping tonight wouldn't be an option, I wrapped a sheet around my body and proceeded to slink out of my room and downstairs to get myself a drink of water. Every step I made seemed to creak even louder the longer I walked. Right before I reached the stairs, a movement in the mirror on the wall beside the banister made me pause. It was only me, tired and sick looking as always.

With one hand still securing the sheet around me, I reached up with the other and pulled at the bags beneath my eyes. I hadn't gotten more than an hour of sleep each night, and that was only right before the sun rose and beamed in through my bedroom window. If I wasn't having nightmares about Clay's actions during the day of the shooting, it was his eyes on me and the way he watched me like he knew the littlest things that would make me crack.

Clay was supposed to know those things about me. He was programmed to know the smaller things that made me tick and how I handled frustrating and awkward situations. He would know better than anyone how I was when I was angry and what would set me off. I shouldn't have been surprised when he looked at me like he could see within me and not just at me.

The feeling that seemed to be eating away at me whenever I thought about us in the room together was that he did know the things that made me tick. He watched me like he could read me like an open book, on display for everyone to read. I hated that he could easily see right through me. It disgusted me that I was even related to such a vulgar monster, one who felt like the world owed him a favor now that he killed the one person who pretended like the world didn't.

The thought alone was making me sick to my stomach once more. I bit my lip as I watched my face disappear from the mirror and glide down the stairs. So much was changing that I couldn't stop. I couldn't sleep at night. Walking around school was hard enough with the constant stares and whispers, now only amplified by random Nathan's speech in the auditorium. My parents were such polar opposites on the subject of Clay and his prison sentence that it was sometimes so hard to even talk to them about it if I really wanted to.

Nothing was going the way I wanted it to, simply because my brother made the wrong decision.

Wincing as I stepped on another loose floorboard at the bottom of the stairs, I paced to the kitchen quickly afterwards and grabbed myself a bottle of water from the fridge. The kitchen windows were open and a slight cool breeze was blowing in, whipping lightly at my hair. I decided it was nice enough out to spend my sleepless night on the front porch instead of tip-toeing around my house.

While trying to make as less noise as possible, I made it back across the living room and out the front door in one piece. As soon as I turned to sit down on the porch swing, a shadowed figure made me jump in my place, sending the water bottle flying.

"Jesus Christ," I cursed, my heartbeat bouncing against my chest.

"Sorry, I didn't mean to scare you," he whispered, bringing his face into the small sliver of light coming from the street lamp. He leaned down from his seat on the swing to pick up my abandoned water bottle, holding it out for me to take.

Slowly, I took it from his hand as I eyed him warily. "What the hell are you doing here at three o'clock in the morning?"

He shrugged, his jacket loosening around his shoulders. "I got here about an hour ago because I couldn't sleep. I was hoping you couldn't either, because I remembered you telling me about that. I tried to knock, but then I realized that your parents might be sleeping and I didn't want to piss them off. So I..."

I cut him off. "Grays," I smirked lightly. "The point?"

He released a heavy breath. "Right. I came here because I couldn't sleep because I needed to talk to you."

"And this couldn't wait until tomorrow morning?" I mocked, noticing his nervous quirk again.

He just shook his head, a sheepish smile forming on his lips.

I nodded uneasily before taking a seat next to him, careful to leave a little bit of room between us. We still hadn't spoken about that kiss in my bedroom earlier in the day, and I wasn't sure how he was handling it or how he even felt about it. Tightening the sheet around myself, I tried not to make my squirm evident in front of him.

Clay could already read me without a problem; I didn't need Grayson finding out that trick too.

My eyes dropped down his hands where he was wringing them over and over. That look of guilt and uncertainty crossed his features for the hundredth time, only making me more nervous. I just wanted to ask so many questions, receive the answers I thought I deserved. How could someone save my life and then leave out the reason why?

"Grayson..."

"I'm sorry..." he talked right over me, our words jumbling together in a gigantic mess.

I smirked at him at first, only having it falter when I realized he was apologizing. Those two potent words could be related to a number of things. Was he apologizing for kissing me? Was he apologizing for keeping secrets from me?

Or could he possibly be apologizing for saving my life?

I gulped as the tears started to make their way towards my eyes once more, uncontrollably. Taking a deep breath to calm myself down, assuring myself that it couldn't be the final one, I made sure my voice was sturdy before I continued.

"Sorry for what?"

I watched his Adam's apple bob beneath the collar of his jacket. "There's so much I've left out these past few weeks…things I should have told you from the start. I've spent all this time trying to bring it up in random conversations, hoping you would somehow understand. But every time we were together…I just sort of forgot to mention it. We were either having so much fun or just talking about your life and how you were feeling. It felt wrong to bring things up then."

If my heart was beating rapidly when he scared me, it was going a hundred times faster now. As much as I wanted to know what he was hiding from me, I was also pleasantly unaware for a really long time.

Although we all search for honesty from the people we care about the most, there's something simply sweet about being blissfully ignorant to the obvious. Sometimes the truths we wanted to hear didn't always come wrapped up in goodie bags and tied with bright colored ribbon. They were ugly and defiant. They made you change the way you thought about others, how you thought about yourself.

But most of all, they could leave you with a change of heart. That of which I didn't think I was ready for.

I'd already experienced so much change in the past month and a half, enough change to leave me on my hands and knees, begging for something to remain the same. My school had changed, my friends changed, my family changed...my own brother changed right before my eyes. I was really counting on Grayson to leave me with some type of normalcy.

"What brought this on?"

He shook his head, pieces of dark chocolate hair falling into his eyes. Without thinking about it for the first time in my life, I reached forward and gently brushed them away from his eyes. My fingertips skimmed against the skin of forehead, making him hold his breath.

He grabbed onto my wrist to stop me from moving away. "This," he whispered, as his face became a lot closer to mine than I realized.

"What do you...what do you mean?" I asked breathlessly.

His other hand reached up to stroke the fly away pieces of hair from my face, just like I'd done to him. He was watching his hand move for a moment, just until he was finished and satisfied with his handy work. Then his eyes flickered back down to mine, making me drown in his graying waters for the second time.

"I don't think you realize how long I've waited for you to notice who I was," he whispered, his voice being carried away by the wind picking up around us.

"I've always known who you were," I said.

He smiled at me for a brief moment before shaking his head at me again. "No you didn't. You knew about me. But you never bothered to get to know me."

"Grayson..."

"Right after the shooting, you came to visit me. You didn't act like I was some pariah or something. My own family was tip-toeing around me like I'd drop at any moment. But you treated me like I was the same kid before I got shot. At first, I shamelessly thought you were there because you actually wanted to be. But then after thinking about it...I realized you were really only there because you thought you owed it to me for saving your life," he finished, releasing his grip on me and dropping his hands into his lap.

My eyes widened considerably. "No! I didn't..."

He cut me off. "But I was being selfish. I kept you around thinking that you'd somehow begin to fall for me just like I had for you. I thought maybe if we really got to know each other that it would be different. It wouldn't always be about you feeling like you needed to give me gratitude or something."

"But I..."

"I realize now that I was wrong. I was wrong about all of it. You'll only ever see me as the kid who saved your life that day. If it wasn't for the shooting...you would have never taken the time to get to know me," he ranted on.

He tried to talk over me when I butted in again, but I grabbed his face with both of my hands, causing him to pause. "Stop! Grayson, will you let me talk?"

He winced. "Just let me finish. I have to get this out."

I dropped my hands from his face and nodded. While he was still reeling over what he had to say, I was doing the same. I had so much I wanted to tell him, all of the feelings I'd developed over the course of the weeks I'd gotten to know him. Sure, in the beginning, I visited him because I felt like I owed him and wanted to check up on him to make sure that he was okay.

But the longer we got to spend time together and the more we began to open to one another, the closer I felt to him. I hated the circumstances that surrounded us finally connecting, but I couldn't help the situation we were thrown into. For all I knew, it was fate's stupid, twisted ways that brought us into this mess together. I still wanted to be with him, whether he was the boy who saved me from the bullet or not.

He sighed again. "And then that kiss today. I don't think you know how long I've been waiting for that," he laughed forcefully, running a hand through his hair. I blushed at his words, grateful that the street lights didn't create much exposure. "You kissed me back, which I never expected. When I realized that there was even a slight chance that you could have the same feelings for me that I did for you...I knew I had to tell you everything. I couldn't hide all of this anymore. You deserved to know the truth, no matter how much it'll make you hate me in the end."

As much as I hated the way his speech was making me feel ill, I was realizing that this was the first time Grayson was truly opening up to me. He was breaking down his walls and showing me the heart beneath it all. I never once expected him to admit his feelings like that. The entire time we were together I was under the assumption that an 'us' would never work. But as he kept raving on about his feelings, I couldn't help the small flutter in my stomach as he confessed the things I never thought I'd hear.

"Grays, you're making me nervous over here," I laughed anxiously. "Can you just get on with it a ready?"

He looked away from me, looking up at the moon above and wringing his hands again. I watched as he ran a hand over his injured shoulder and rubbed it carefully. "There is a chance though, right?"

he quickly averted his eyes back to mine. "There's a chance that you could feel the same way?"

My heart was racing and my palms were beginning to sweat. Although it was moderately cool outside and I had a sheet to shield my body from the colder weather, my whole body felt warm. I knew my cheeks were probably matching the colors of ripened tomatoes, but was lucky to be sitting in the dark with him.

I wasn't sure why I was so nervous to just say it out loud, make a gesture to show him that I was agreeing to everything that he just said. He already admitted that he had feelings for me. He already took the leap. All I had to was follow his lead. Why was this so nerve-wracking to admit?

Biting my lip, I nodded quickly. I paused as I watched his murky grey eyes light up at my motions. He didn't smile like I'd expected him to. I wasn't really expecting him to bring me into his arms and kiss the life out of me either. But the look in his eyes was enough confirmation that my truth telling wasn't a bad thing. There was nothing to be scared of anymore. It was out in the open and we were admitting our most hidden secrets.

Except, I'd forgotten that he still had much more to let go of.

"Fuck, this is going to be so much harder to say now," he breathed, looking the vision of anxiousness.

A part of me just wanted to tell him to forget all about it. We'd already done enough letting go tonight. We released a lot of feelings neither one of us expected to have to admit. That in itself was a big accomplishment, at least to me, and something that shouldn't have been taken as lightly as it had. If this was a normal situation, we would be talking about a relationship or working something out that would allow us to act on these spoken feelings.

But again, we were the furthest from normal and Grayson was still full of surprises.

"Before you tell me these…things you've been hiding, could you at least answer some questions of mine first?" I piped up, going against my better wishes and avoiding the inevitable.

He jerked his head, nodding quickly. "Anything."

"That day…" I trailed off, my mind already wandering. "So many people were getting hurt. Most of the kids in that hallway ran for the lives instead of sticking around for the finale. Carter was the first one shot. How did you find me?"

He looked to be reciting my words over and over again in his head. Out of all of his secrets and hidden agendas, this was the one I wanted to know most of all. Well, that and:

"Why did you choose to save me?"

He sat back in the swing, pushing on his feet gently and sending us back and forth at a slowed pace. Grayson didn't bother to look at me, keeping his eyes trained at something across the street on my neighbor's front lawn.

Placing his hands on his knees, he said, "I was on my way to Bio. I normally took the West Wing to get there, but I…I decided to go a different way because there were too many kids in the stairwells and I knew I'd be late if I stuck around to wait out the herd. No one in the West Wing knew about the shooting yet. Everyone was so damn unaware that I almost wished I'd gone back there before I opened the door to South Wing," he gulped, clutching his knee caps briefly as he looked back on the dreaded day. "I saw some people running past me, but I didn't really think anything of it, you know? I barely looked at their faces so it was hard to tell that they were scared. I just figured that people were late and they were in a hurry," he shrugged.

I squeezed my eyes shut as I thought of all those kids running from my brother. I remembered a whirlwind of so many faces and scared eyes. People were screaming and running for the lives. It was so odd watching the event unfold, how everyone went from happy-go-lucky and counting on a good day, to completely shell-shocked and frightened beyond belief.

"When I got to the end of the right hallway, I saw that people were hiding behind this row of lockers. People were clutching onto each other and crying. They were watching me like they couldn't believe I was still standing in open range. Why wasn't I hiding like the rest of them? That's when I saw Clay's back to me. I saw his hand out in front of him and heard him saying those things to you. People had their eyes glued to his every move. I just kept walking closer, trying so hard to ignore everyone's calls for me and pleads for me to just seek shelter. I happened to look down at the other end of the hall and I saw the blood around Carter's body. I never thought..."

He shook his head furiously, bringing his head in his hands. His voice was muffled as he continued. "Then Clay moved, just two or so steps over and I saw it. I saw you in the corner on the ground. I saw the gun aimed at your head. And that was it. I didn't think about it. I just...jumped."

Tears were starting to stream down my eyes now, with me only making a lame attempt at using the sheet as a tissue. "Grayson," I cried, my voice almost breathless.

"Don't you dare tell me I shouldn't have done it," he picked up his head and eyed me sternly. "I already told you that I didn't regret jumping in front of those bullets for you."

"But you were on crutches for weeks! You were held up in a hospital bed for weeks before that! You have permanent scars in two different places because of me!"

He laughed angrily. "It's not because of you, Callie! Jesus, when will you ever get that through your head? I jumped because of my own decisions, my own feelings. Sure, maybe I did it because I've been in love with you for as long as I can remember. But I believe that even it wasn't you on that floor, I probably would have done the same thing. It just so happened that the girl I loved was about to die right in front of my eyes, so I acted as quickly as I could."

My heart almost stopped as the words left his lips. He was in love with me. Grayson Foster just admitted that he was in love with me for...years. For the past few weeks, I'd been afraid I was too hasty with my feelings and thought it was too soon to admit such things, while he's been hiding this for years.

I didn't think twice before bringing my hand behind his neck and inching us closer together. All I wanted to do was kiss him and show him that everything would be alright soon enough. I wanted to instill some type of hope into this boy who was so hell bent on ruining the normalcy he'd created for me. But just as I was about to place my lips on his, he shook his head out of my grasp and pulled back with a sorrowful look in his eyes.

"Don't...don't do that. You can't...We can't..." he stuttered on, becoming frustrated with himself.

"Why not?" I asked, appalled that he'd just denied me. A sinking feeling made its way to the pit of my stomach as I rolled over his face in my head.

"Because you're going to hate me after I say what I have to say! I can't sit here and pretend like things are better, when there's so much I kept from you."

My face fell, my heart shattering moment coming to light on my face. He noticed before I had the chance to hide it, his face falling as well.

"Callie," he groaned. "I want to kiss you. Believe me, it's the only thing I want to do right now. But I can't do that when I know how this is going to turn out. I came here to tell you the truth and I'm not finished yet."

"Grayson, whatever you have to tell me isn't going to change how I feel about you. You've been there for me through the toughest moments in my life. You picked me up when I thought I wasn't able to put myself back together. You stood up for me and you listened to me. That's more than I can say for even my own family."

"I wouldn't be so sure about that…" he bit his lip nervously, his eyes heady with a fear I'd never seen in him before.

"I don't think…"

"Callie, I knew about the shooting before it happened."

19

CHAPTER 18

"So you just let him leave?" Marnie asked, shutting her locker and leaning against it with a weary expression.

I tugged my books closer to me and nodded my head bravely.

It had been two days since I last seen Grayson, my words to him the farthest from kind. He looked so ashamed and so far from proud when he uttered his final sentence to me. As soon as he said it, I couldn't think about anything other than Clay. How we could have gotten him help. How Grayson could have told someone before this all happened.

In the beginning, I was practically begging Grayson to just keep it to himself and save us both the misery. God knows we had both been through enough as it was. Now, I didn't care that I went against my adamant wishes and allowed him to finally tell me what he had been hiding from me since the first day we started talking to each other.

All I could think to say after he uttered those words was:

"Leave."

I pointed my finger away from us and kept a stone face until he was far from view. He knew I was going to be upset about this. He knew the power behind his secret and how much that small detail held. But he wasn't allowing me to push him away just yet.

"You have to let me explain. Please," he begged, interlacing his fingers together in a pleading gesture.

The tears were starting to flood in my eyes again but I didn't want to let it show. I couldn't let him know that he hurt me. I'd spent too long allowing other people read me and letting others in only to be pushed over the edge.

"Get off of my porch, Grayson," I seethed, venom dripping from my words.

He watched me with sorry eyes, looking almost like he was about to cry himself. All I could think was that he deserved to feel like this. Carter died. He got shot. Another girl was hurt. I almost died at the hands of my own brother. This entire time everyone in the school was pointing fingers at me and at Clay for what happened that day.

Although Clay was the one who pulled the trigger, scarring those kids for life, Grayson Foster was the one who knew his plan before it even happened. If he just told someone about the idea, made it known before we all entered school that day, then this would have never happened. There would be no emotional turmoil, no scars, and no deaths. Everyone would be able to go on without even thinking of a day that would go down in history. My brother wouldn't be in jail and serving a life sentence.

Grayson pushed himself up from the porch swing, making it rock back and forth unsteadily. I didn't even watch him go, instead just avoiding his movements and allowing the door to slam behind me. It was almost four in the morning and my parents would probably curse me for waking them up at this hour, but I didn't care. It was like one last slap in Grayson's face. He'd allowed all of this to happen.

How could someone hold ontc a secret like that?

This wasn't a string of gossipy rumors. It wasn't like he knew someone was cheating or a girl at school was pregnant. Those types of rumors, while still able to sting when they were heard, weren't even close to the value of a human life.

Many human lives.

"I can't believe you just made him leave without explaining himself," Marnie shook her head at me before turning to walk down the hall. I followed behind her, keeping on her heels.

"You can't believe me?" I practically shrieked. "What about him? He knew Clay was going to do this and didn't bother to let anyone else know about it. Do you understand how much could have been avoided if this was known to everyone else?"

She stopped in her tracks, her face hard. "I understand," she said firmly. "I was the one who had to drive home with Carter Wayland's blood on my clothes, Callie. I wish more than anyone that we all could have somehow avoided this mess. Carter would still be here. Your brother wouldn't be in jail. We could have helped him before he decided to make this decision."

I cut her off. "Then why are you acting like I'm the bad person in this situation?"

"Because Grayson Foster isn't a bad guy, Callie. I figured you would know that more than anyone. All that time you guys spent together, didn't you realize that he didn't have a bad bone in his body? I mean, the guy jumped in front of a bullet for you. And you're acting like he planned this out with Clay or something."

As I approached my locker, gathering my books for the end of the day, I tried my best to turn her words over in my head. She leaned against the locker next to mine and eyed me carefully. But I just shook my head.

"It doesn't excuse the fact that he hid this from everyone," I stated.

She sighed agitatedly. "God, Callie! You don't know that! You didn't even give the poor guy a chance to explain himself. There's so much more behind this story that you don't know. He could have tried to talk Clay out of it. He could have told someone else and they either didn't know how to handle it or didn't get to Clay in time. Why can't you give him a break?"

After throwing my textbook into my locker, I slammed it shut and faced her. "Because my brother's in jail, Marnie! He's not getting out for the rest of his life because he took someone else's. If Grayson would have even told me, I could have gotten him help before it was too late. All along, I've been pointing fingers at Clay when..."

She cut me off with a raised hand. "Whoa!" she yelled. "Just because Grayson may have known something before it happened, doesn't switch the blame! Your brother was still the one who pulled the trigger and took someone's life. You have no right to put the blame on Grayson like that."

I rolled my eyes. "Stop protecting him, Marn."

She stomped the floor in her skinny heels. "Stop protecting your brother! You've spent your whole life protecting him from the bad things and look where that got you. A gun raised to your head with him holding the trigger. Or have you forgotten that?" she whispered off before stomping her way down the hall and out the front doors.

I flinched when the doors slammed shut behind her. Deep down in my heart, I knew that Grayson wasn't totally to blame for what happened that day. Clay was the one who brought the gun to school and he was also the one who threw all love for me out the window by pointing it at me last. But I couldn't shake the 'what if's' that came along with Grayson's full fledged secret. How would things have differed? Would Clay still be here, healthy and better than ever?

Maybe it was just a part of me that was still ticked off that I shared so much with Grayson since the day of the shooting and he hid this from me. Every time we spoke about that day, about Clay's past and how surprised I was at his behavior, those would have been good moments to speak up and let me know. He told me that no time seemed like the right time.

But then again, would I have handled it any differently if he told me sooner?

Sliding my bag up my shoulder, I finished my trek down the hall with my head down. I felt like I couldn't catch a break in any situation anymore. I was just finding a piece of normalcy in my whirlwind life, and this was how it broke down. I wasn't even sure I could look at Grayson the same again, no matter what else lied behind his confession. Whatever he said could not justify the fact that he missed the window of opportunity that secured my brother's future. I spent so long thinking that this idea of his was sudden and not well thought out. Meanwhile, he had told someone before he made any further decisions.

And Grayson could live with himself after hiding something like that?

I was so caught up in my own thoughts that I didn't see the pair of feet that came into view, causing me to bump right into someone holding a long sleeve of poster paper in their freshly manicured hands. Startled, I quickly looked up and immediately dropped my jaw like a gaping fish.

"Oh…" she gasped. "Dear, I apologize. I didn't see you there."

When I looked down at the sheet of paper in her hands, I realized it was the school's banner for Carter, the one filled with memories and well wishes for the family. The woman holding it was dressed like a soccer mom with track pants and a white v-neck. She had maroon colored acrylic nails and her dark hair was cut into a short style, just a little bit longer than Marnie's.

This must have been Carter's mom.

Her eyes widened as we both took each other in. "No…" she trailed off, disagreeing with her assumptions. "Callie Tollson, that's not you, is it?

I gulped. How in the world did she know my name? "Yeah…" I said gingerly.

She looked on the brink of tears as she realized who I was. She brought a hand to her mouth, covering it in astonishment. The paper dropped from her hands and I quickly bent down to pick it up but taking caution, feeling like it would burn me if I laid a hand on it. I felt like I wasn't allowed to touch such a sentimental piece of property.

"Do you mind if I ask how you know who I am?" I asked suspiciously, trying to ignore the depressing look on her face.

She blinked back the tears, wiping away the stray ones with the back of her hand. After sniffling heavily, she said, "I'm sorry. I've been so rude. I'm Carter's mother, Mary Wayland." Mary stuck her hand out to shake mine and I took it gently, handing her back the poster afterwards. "I've seen your photo on the news, dear."

My heart dropped into the pit of my stomach. I had been avoiding any type of city news channels for that exact purpose. I knew they would somehow find the family photos and use them against us, showing the world that we were related to Riverton High's killer. My face burned at the realization that she probably wasn't the only one who was able to see that news feed. People from all over, even in different cities could see that piece of news with my family's faces plastered all over, including my brother's mug shot.

"I'm so sorry," she said again, crinkling the paper a bit in her shaky hands. "I truly am, sweetheart.   wish I could have…I should have done something sooner to put a stop to all of this madness."

I raised a brow at her, shuffling on my feet and feeling the uncomfortable atmosphere taking over me. "What do you mean?"

She looked around the hallway, watching the kids whizzing by with book bags slung over their shoulders and chattering away. Mary flickers her eyes back to mine uneasily and licked her lips. "Do you mind if we talk about this elsewhere? Maybe I can treat you to a coffee or something?"

I was so confused. What would Carter's mother want to do with me? I was Clay's little sister, but t's not like she owed me some type of explanation for anything. If ar yone owed explanations, it was me or my brother. I only thought about this encounter once before, figuring Mrs. Wayland would come up and slap me across the face or something for being related to the boy who killed her son.

Biting my lip I said, "I don't see why you would anything to do with me, Mrs. Wayland."

She waved me off momentarily. "It's Ms. I'd like to sit down and talk to you about some things I'm pretty sure you didn't know about. I owe you an explanation."

"Ms. Wayland…" I trailed off, looking around me for some type of escape. I wasn't sure I was ready for a conversation like this; one that I was sure would include tears and a handful of apologies.

"Please, Callie?" she pleaded, frowning. "It would mean a lot to me if I was able to explain myself."

I still didn't understand what she would have to explain. My heart ached for her, though. It was obvious that she wasn't married and from what I knew, Carter was an only child. She was now a lonely mother with no one else to talk to.

Against my better wishes, I agreed. "I have my car here. Where would you like to meet?"

Ten minutes and a panic attack later, I was seated in front of Mary Wayland with a cup of coffee she had just bought for me, again against my pleas. My hands were wrapped around the warmth of the cup, the steam rising from the lid and creating a mouth-watering aroma. I took tentative sips while Mary gathered her words, my stomach already in knots.

She ran a finger around the circumference of her coffee cup lid, glancing up at me every so often. Taking a deep breath, she finally looked up at me fully. "I'd like to apologize for my son's actions."

My eyes bugged out of my head and I almost spit out my tiny sip of liquid. "W-what...What do you mean?"

"I was aware that my son has bullied your brother in the past, Callie. I know my son. I wasn't ignorant to his actions."

Talk about a shock. I felt like everything anyone ever said to me in the past week was coming as a total slap to the face. I kept walking around acting like I knew the people in my circle, would know that they wouldn't hurt me or surprise me too much. I thought I knew all I had to know about this mess that was just about a month ago, now tired of running in giant circles to come back to the same conclusion.

After hoping I pulled my expression together enough to look normal, I cleared my throat. "How did you know?"

"One of the teachers at your school contacted me during their freshman year. He claimed that they both got into some type of argument and they were beating on each other. That was my first clue. But I also knew that your brother had a reputation for being a sweet boy. I figured that whatever it was about, was resolved in the best way young boys seem to know how. But then I got a call from his football coach at the beginning of this school year. He said that he caught Carter hitting your brother again at practice."

I winced as I thought back to that horrid day, filled with punches to the gut and blows to the face. I remembered how bloody Clay was and the expression on Carter's face when the coach finally walked away from us. He didn't seem to care in the least bit about what he'd just done.

"I tried talking to Carter about it when he came home from practice that day. But he was such an angry child. Ever since the divorce and his father caught him with that other boy that one day..." she trailed off, shaking her head again. "It was like you could never get through to him."

"Wait..." I interrupted, swallowing my sip of coffee. "You knew that your son was..."

She sighed heavily, like she was releasing a load of weight from her skinny shoulders. "He never confirmed our suspicions. His father only caught him the one time during his freshman year with a boy in his bed. While I was alright with it, his father was not. He was so hard on him before he left us. And Carter's been angry ever since."

This was all too much information to take in. So many hidden secrets were starting to come to light, some too little too late. I couldn't believe I was sitting in a coffee shop with Carter Wayland's mother, talking about his past like he was my friend or something. I never imagined myself in this position.

Leaning forward and moving my cup out the way, I said, "But I don't understand why you feel the need to apologize for what he did. It wasn't…"

She cut me off. "But it was my fault. I knew that my son was bullying Clay. He was such a sweet boy and I couldn't stop Carter from doing those things to him. I love my son, Callie. I always will because he's been my baby boy since the day he was born. But that doesn't mean that I agreed with what he chose to do with his anger and resentment towards his father and himself."

"Ms. Wayland," I tried to interrupt, but she held up her finger for me to pause and let her finish.

"If I would have tried harder to fix my son's issues, we all could have avoided this entire mess," she cried, the tears I hadn't noticed before now freely streaming down her bronzed cheeks. "Your brother would have never done those things that day if Carter stopped what he was doing."

She was fully sobbing now, hiding her face with a shaky hand. Mary had abandoned her coffee now, only focusing on her regrets and sorrows. Why was everyone feeling the need to blame themselves for what my brother did? Why was it that this one action held so many victims and so many bystanders who hadn't done a thing to stop it?

My heart broke for her. She didn't have a husband and was now left without her only son. She was putting all of this weight on her shoulders for something that was surely not her fault in the least bit. Although I felt terrible every single day for what Clay did to those kids that day, I knew Mary was taking this harder than anyone.

I reached forward and laid my hand on hers that was lying limp on the table. She looked up, startled, and tried to clear her glassy eyes. Her shoulders were shaking and it was all making me just want to jump up from my seat and wrap my arms around her to cure her from her worries. But I had the next best thing to say that I knew would make her feel somewhat better about this whole mess.

"Ms. Wayland," I started gently, keeping my hand on hers. "You were right. Your son and my brother didn't get along, by any means. For years, I wasn't sure why Carter always chose Clay to pick on. But for the past few weeks, I've been finding out a lot about your son and even my own brother who I thought I knew so well. From what I know now, Carter wasn't the first one to bully Clay. What happened back there wasn't in result of your son's actions. That was the outcome of many, many years of abuse Clay had gotten over the years. Clay's mind has been hazy from the start. He needed help before it all came down to this. If anyone is to blame for this mess, it's my brother. He didn't have to come to this conclusion. I know what your son went through everyday, for the same reasons my brother didn't get along with him. But please do not blame yourself for this. They both made decisions that neither one of them was ready for. You had nothing to do with that."

She watched me with wide eyes, surprised. Tears were brimming at her lids once more, but I was hoping it was for a reason other than guilt. "Thank you," she whispered. "Thank you so much dear. That was really mature of you to say. I know most of the children at school didn't see Carter for who he really was. But you do and you still have a leveled heart about this matter."

I smiled small. "I've been learning a lot of things since that day. One of those being that no one really knows someone like they think they do."

She nodded gently. She sipped at her coffee for the first time since she started to cry and said, "Thank you for being so understanding, Callie. I truly am sorry for what you've had to go through. And your parents as well. None of you deserve this mess."

"Thank you, Ms. Wayland," I smiled at her again.

"Oh!" she startled me for a moment, making me jump in my seat. "How is Grayson? I heard he suffered two gunshot wounds?"

I gulped, almost sick with guilt. She didn't know that it was because he jumped in front of the gun for me. No one really seemed to know aside from us and Clay. I decided to keep that fact to myself, hoping this topic of conversation would cease soon.

"He's doing...well," I settled with. "He's healing."

She smiled genuinely as she thought about him. "I'm happy to hear that. He's such a kind boy. He's been Carter's best friend since the day they started kindergarten together. He was by Carter's side every step of the way, with the divorce and the personal issues he was dealing with. I can't imagine why Clay would want to do such a thing to him," she murmured off for a moment, frowning at the image. "But that boy would do anything for the people he loves. That much I know."

I felt the tears coming forward, causing me to squeeze my eyes shut for a moment. "Yeah," I whispered. "Grayson really would."

20

CHAPTER 19

For the rest of the week, I couldn't stop thinking about what Mary had told me at over our coffee discussion. The shock from her sincere apology had worn off for the most part. It was refreshing to talk to someone who didn't label Carter as some type of God who couldn't do a single thing wrong. She knew who her son was and, despite his mistakes, loved him all the same.

I felt like it was a lesson that I had to learn. Bumping into Mary had to be part of fate's twisted path it was weaving for me, teaching me so many hard earned lessons. Every lesson I'd learned was part of some detailed and vigorous test, one that took me in tons of directions and made me really think of what I thought I knew. The truth was, I really didn't know anything about anyone.

You can spend your whole life believing that know someone and be completely surprised by them in the next second. People were made up of many different personalities, quirks and mischievous ways. They could change, grow and become a whole new version of themselves. Sometimes these versions weren't for the better, but they allowed you to make your own decisions on who you chose to surround yourself with.

Grayson had certainly changed. He was much more open to me and was talking to me for the first time in his life. I hadn't really thought about how this change in him was affecting the person that he was. He admitted that he was in love with me for the first time in years. For so long, he kept this huge secret to himself and put his heart on the line for me.

Frankly, it scared the hell out of me that he was always putting himself in danger, whether emotional or physical for me.

But it took me a little while to realize this, that Grayson would do anything for me; as I would for him. I felt like I owed him a chance to explain himself. A part of this new realization was coming from a bit of a selfish side for me, though I hated to admit it.

After school on Friday, I came home to my mother cooking up a storm. She was bent over the stove with sweat dripping down her forehead and her hair pulled into her signature messy bun. She was dressed in her work scrubs still, this time without any evidence of foul play against the blue fabric, which I was sort of grateful for. Whatever it was that she was cooking smelled great and I was finally up for eating something.

"Hey, what's the special occasion?" I asked, smiling gently at her when she looked up at me startled.

She weighed her words for a moment, an anxious look on her face. "I was hoping dinner would be done by the time you made it home," she stated, wiping her hands against a kitchen towel. "Your father and I had some things we'd like to discuss with you."

I raised a brow at her. "What things?"

My dad chose this time to interrupt, coming up behind me and placing his hands on my shoulders in greeting. "Hey sweetheart, how was school?"

"Fine…" I trailed off suspiciously. "Why is everyone acting so weird?"

He walked past me and into the kitchen, probably giving my mother a look only she would understand. They were communicating with one another silently, leaving me in the dark and a little annoyed.

"Maybe its best if we just wait for dinner. I'm making spaghetti and meatballs," she forced a smile.

"No, I want to know what you guys are hiding," I stated forcefully, almost feeling like a six year old who was about to stomp her foot to get what she wanted.

My mom looked to my father for a moment, giving him another silent look. He just shrugged at her, weaving around her and grabbing a plate from the cupboard above her head. She sighed and turned the burner off on the stove, making her way towards me and gesturing for me to sit at the kitchen table with her.

I sat down slowly, feeling the urge to bite my nails once again. I was just giving them the chance to grow but I knew the anxiety of this situation would change that quickly. She fiddled with her wedding ring without meeting my eyes.

"Your father and I went to vis t your brother today," she said.

And then all of the air left my lungs. All this time she kept feeding me lines on how my brother didn't deserve to get what he wanted, how he should be forced to rot in that cell for what he'd done to so many people. She swore to me once that she'd never go to see him because she couldn't bear to look at him in the eye without either crying or feeling the need to smack him.

She tried so hard to make me feel bad for even wanting to talk to him. When I asked her to visit him, she chastised me for giving into his wants. All the while, she was seeing him behind my back while I was at school. What had they talked about? Did the subject of him pointing the gun at me ever come up?

"We had a very long discussion about what he had done. He seems to be very…adamant on the fact that what he had done was bound to happen eventually. He doesn't feel any remorse about the shooting. He says whoever he hurt deserved it," she choked up a bit, still rolling her ring around her finger.

My dad appeared behind her, grabbing onto her hand as he sat down next to her with a plate of food. The tears were rolling down her cheeks in skinny streams, staining her pale blue scrub shirt. My dad kept squeezing her hand and murmuring positive words in her ear while I watched.

He took a deep breath before taking over the conversation. "He was about to tell us something else, something that was about you actually. But we were both so angry with him and the way he was talking to us, how he was behaving, that we just walked out. He was very persistent that we should talk to you about something that happened that day. We wanted to know…is there anything you've neglected to tell us, Callie? Anything that would give us a chance to understand this all better?"

I gulped, my breathing becoming panicky. I started playing with my fingers underneath the table and avoiding their eyes as I thought about the consequences of this. I was becoming desperate at this point, always pushing those feelings down that begged to come out. I should have told them from the start, made this an obvious point the moment I came home from school that day. Maybe they could have helped me sooner.

Behind my eyelids came the image of the barrel, staring me square in the face. The shiny, silver hole that encased one last life-ending bullet. I looked behind that barrel, to the face of my older brother with a vicious smirk on his face and a wicked glint in his eyes. Nothing was the same on that once precious face. I once found him adorable and dorky, too goofy to ever be serious most of the time.

But nothing on that face reminded me of that goofy brother I once knew. His eyes just read one ultimate goal, the death of his baby sister. There was no remorse on his face until he had realized he shot Grayson and not me. He didn't even try to ask for forgiveness, tell me that it was all just a big misunderstanding; he was never going to pull the trigger.

Then the sounds of him calling my name came back to life again, the strained and painful letters leaving his lips like his life depended on me. He was beneath those large linebackers, squirming on the floor and begging for me to come and help him. Silently, I was begging him to help me from the floor that day of the shooting, showing me that he still loved me and didn't plan on ending my life like that. The whole time my eyes were closed and my body was sweating at the thought of never seeing the light of day again, I was begging to wake up from this nightmare and return to the life where my brother wasn't this horrid monster.

I hadn't even realized I was crying until my dad had wrapped his arms around me, pushing my face close to his warm chest. He was holding me tight, just like he had done when I was a baby, before his rehab stint and the alcohol overrunning his life. I sobbed into his shirt, trying to use my hands as shields.

"Callie, what...what is it?" he asked, pain seeping through his tone as he clutched me to him.

Breaking away from his embrace, I wiped a hand underneath my nose and tried to straighten my shoulders. He didn't move, just opted to but his hand on shoulder in an encouraging manner to show me that he was still there. My heart was bouncing around in my chest, my stomach tied in utterly complicated knots.

"Clay..." I whispered, wincing when I said his name aloud, still thinking about that one moment. "He...he pointed the gun at me the day of the shooting."

The silence that erupted after that was so loud I'd never heard anything like it before. Every miniscule noise felt amplified, the sound of my parents' breathing, the bubbling of water in the pot of noodles, the dog across the street barking outside. My hands were shaking so hard I was sure they'd fall off soon. I tried to restrain them by placing them underneath my thighs, the tears streaming down my cheeks again far from controllable.

My mother finally looked at me, her hand that she was fiddling with now dropped to the table. Her mouth was slightly ajar and the crying ceased, but only for a moment as she took me in. My dad's hand squeezed my shoulder, causing me to look up at him. He brought his lips into his mouth, his eyes somewhat glassy and his jaw clenched.

"W-why..." my mom breathed. "Why didn't you tell us before?"

I shrugged helplessly. "It was too hard to say out loud to you guys, I guess," I murmured, my throat still thick with unshed tears.

"But this was important. If we would have known..." my dad piped up, his voice strained.

"I didn't...I didn't want to ruin your guys' image of him. You were already so tied up in this mess. If I told you guys, I thought it would only make things worse."

"Worse?" my dad bellowed. "Callie, you're our daughter. You will always come first, no matter the situation. As for our image of your brother," he shook his head. "That's been altered way before this news of yours."

We all sat in silence for what seemed like years, all of us thinking the same thing I was sure. Only, their tries to picture that incident more blurred than my own. I almost wished I could rip the image out of my head, paint it out for them and put it on display so they could somehow understand what I went through that day. A thousand words and a million gestures couldn't depict the way I was feeling at that moment.

Nothing seemed close enough to it.

"But why?" my mother cried, putting a hand over her mouth to try and suppress the sobs wracking her body. "He's your brother. Why would he do such a thing?!" she yelled.

I flinched at her tone, remembering asking the same question myself so many times before. If I would have known the answer to that question, it would have saved me a lot of time and a lot of heartbreak. I spent nights lying awake, thinking up reasons that never came close to good enough. The only person who knew the answer was Clay.

"I don't know," I whispered, keeping my eyes leveled on the kitchen table instead of at my mother's watery ones. I couldn't take seeing the pain on her face, how crushed and utterly appalled she looked. That was something I'd never wished to see.

"That settles it then," my dad said. "He's not seeing her like he wanted to." He walked towards the sink, rinsing his plate off in a signal that ended the discussion before it even began.

"Wait, he wants to see me again?" I asked, feeling my heart pitter-pattering once more, in an uneasy way.

"He asked us for permission to see you again. He said there was a lot unsaid between the two of you since the last time you visited. But now that we know this, you're never going there again." His hands gripped on the counter tightly, turning his knuckles white.

My eyes widened. For some reason I was feeling more determined than ever to go back there and talk to him one last time. No matter how much I hated to admit it, Clay was right. There was a lot left unsaid that only he could tell me. I'd never know the answers to my millions of questions unless I talked to him.

Maybe it was because I'd finally let it all out to my parents, freeing myself of the one secret I'd spent so long holding on tightly to. I felt almost empty, but full all at the same time. I was empty from doubt and fear, but full of determination to get this conversation I'd stalled for far too long, over with.

It would hurt, probably far more than the pain of reliving that day since the beginning, but it needed to be done. Or else, I'd spend the rest of my life wondering why he had placed the final bullets on me. I'd never get the closure I knew I needed.

"No," I said. "No. I want to see him."

"I don't care what you want to do, Callie," my dad said sternly. "You will not go see him again. He's a completely different person from the son I once thought I raised. He's not the same anymore. I won't allow you to go and see him anymore."

I shook my head. "I need to do this, Dad. I know he's changed, but that only gives me the upper hand in this. I know how he acts now and what makes him tick. I know how to handle myself now. I can do this. Just give me the chance, please. I won't be able to live with this over my head, the constant not knowing."

"Callie," he started to say, but my mom cut us both off by getting up from the chair and grabbing her purse from the kitchen counter.

"Let her go, Stuart," she whispered one last time before grabbing her keys from her scrub shirt pocket and walking out of the kitchen and right out the front door without a single word. We had no idea where she was going, what was going on with her, how she was handling this.

But I knew my mother. I knew something was eating away at her. What I didn't know was how long she could keep it all in.

From the moment my mother gave me permission to go see Clay; I knew what I had to do first.

The following morning, after our debate over my choices to see the one person who tried to kill me, I woke up early and took my time getting ready. Visiting hours at the prison were shorter today than during the weekdays, giving me little room to think of the way this script of mine in my head was going to go. I had so many questions listed, so many things I wanted to say just like the last time I saw him.

I just wasn't sure if I was able to say them aloud this time.

As I passed the wretched mirror in the hall that made me look like a haunted mess every time I looked into it, I noticed that things were a little different this time. While I still had some bags underneath my eyes and my skin was a little on the paler side from keeping myself locked up in my room for so long, I could see the color starting to come back once more. I looked like I was gaining life in me again for the first time in a while.

Although Clay's actions were still daunting and hanging over me like a dark cloud I couldn't get rid of, I felt a bit freer in a sense. Ridding myself of a secret I kept close to me for so long was relieving and made me feel somewhat fresh once again. I was more determined than ever to find out the answers and didn't want to end this final visit on a bad note.

But I needed one last thing before leaving for the prison.

I knocked on the familiar front door gently, feeling my determination from when I left the house lacking just a bit. The time I had to wait for someone to answer it felt like hours, causing me to shuffle on my feet and bite at my thumbnail nervously. I wasn't sure how this was going to play out, what would be said.

The door creaked open, revealing a tall brunette woman with curls framing her face. She was dressed in an apron splattered with flour and some of it was stained on her flawless cheeks. Her peach tinted lips curled into a smile as she greeted me.

"Callie," she beamed. "Well this is a pleasant surprise."

Every time I went to visit Grayson in the hospital, I never ran into his family. They always seemed to run on a different schedule than me, coming at times when I wasn't there. But Grayson always spoke about them with big smiles and positive words that I never felt like I needed to meet them.

He already made me feel like I knew them myself.

While I knew about his family, I wasn't quite sure how Mrs. Foster knew who I was. I hadn't visited the house when she was home recently and we had never met before this moment. I wouldn't doubt that Grayson probably mentioned me once or twice in conversation, but she greeted me like she had known me my whole life.

"Um, hi Mrs. Foster. How did you know it was me?" I asked unsurely, twisting my fingers as I squirmed.

"Grayson speaks about you all the time!" she boasted. "And his drawings of you are practically flawless."

My jaw dropped considerably. "He has...drawings of me?"

Grayson hadn't opened up on the side of his life just yet. He always kept his artwork hidden from me and whenever I asked about it, he said I wouldn't want to see it. He put himself down and complained that they weren't good enough to show off. But obviously they were meant for viewer's eyes if his mother could recognize me from a simple drawing.

She nodded eagerly. "They're quite beautiful actually. If you're here to see him, he's out at the store picking me something up for the cake I'm baking. He should be home any minute now. You're welcome to go up to his room and wait for him."

"Oh no!" I protested. "I can just come back later. I'm sure he's busy."

"Yes, but not too busy for you dear," she smiled at me like she knew something I didn't. What had he said about me to her?

After much retaliation on my end and persistence on hers, she finally convinced me to go up to his room and wait for him to come back from the store. It felt so weird walking past his doorway and entering into Grayson's world. But most of the things around me hadn't surprised me much. They was a poster of some professional ball player, a few sports trophies and some team photos on shelves that were stocked to the brim.

His bed was neatly made with crisp dark blue sheets, his two pillows pushed to the very edge. I tentatively picked up a frame of the baseball team's unprofessional photo, most of the boys sticking out their tongues and making rude gestures towards the camera. Some of the guys had their arms around one another's shoulders, two of whom being Grayson and Carter. They were smiling like maniacs, Carter gripping onto Grayson hard and trying to rub his head with his knuckles.

I felt a pang in my heart as I looked at the smile glowing on his face. Although the only times I'd ever seen him were based around scared moments, his face hard and his eyes on fire with fierce hatred, these were the moments other people remembered him for. He was known for his charismatic smile and his way with the ladies, despite his personal issues he was dealing with before he died. He was the biggest jock on campus and starred in all of the opening games. People adored him for the person he was that I hadn't gotten to know.

I almost felt bad that I didn't get a chance to know him in a different way than what I had. He had his reasons for acting out that way, reasons I couldn't really judge him for. Maybe he was trying to save Clay from himself, in his own sick and twisted way. Maybe he thought Clay really did play for the other team and he didn't want him to live like he had. He could have just been looking out for him, trying to change him before it was too late.

I could never imagine Clay hiding who he was because he was scared of what people would think. I would never be able to comprehend the physical and emotional toll it took on those who felt like if they showed who they really were, who they loved they'd be fearing some sort of consequences.

As I walked around Grayson's room, taking in the items around his room that seemed to speak volumes about his personality, I stilled when my eyes noticed the sketchbook on his desk. I tip-toed over to his desk and picked it up gently, afraid I'd hurt it if I was too rough with it. I ran my fingers over the edges of the leather bindings and made my way to his bed. Sitting down without making too much noise, I slowly flipped open the cover, my heart pounding nervously. I wasn't sure what I'd see sprawled out on all of these pages and I still felt a bit uneasy about going through his things without his permission.

I skimmed through the thin pages, passing by images of still life, some of people in his family that he once told me about. I found some designs of his that he must have thought up on his own and smiled to myself. I hadn't known he was this creative and talented. Each line looked so intricate, each stroke so passionately drawn out.

When I came to one of the pages towards the end of the book, I stopped cold. It was a picture of me, huddled in the corner with Clay pointing the gun in my face. It was odd, running my eyes over each line he made in graphite, noticing how much they differed depending on who they were outlining. When I looked at myself, stunned that it was so detailed and depicted me so well, I noticed that the lines were gentle and curved with ease. But when he got to Clay's body and his finger wrapped tightly around the trigger, his line were rough and almost jagged. I gasped as I noticed the familiar look in Clay's eyes, how easily Grayson portrayed this on paper.

It was what I'd always wanted to do, portray my feelings on paper and show the people I cared about most how I felt that day, the things I had seen. I wished I had the capability to do such a thing and somehow make it easier when I was explaining those harsh thoughts. And here Grayson was, putting pencil to paper and describing every moment with detailed vision. I never would have guess he was this talented with how little he spoke about it.

As I returned to flipping through the book, I realized I'd skipped over some pages I hadn't noticed before. I took in a deep breath, my heart thumping profusely when I saw that they were mostly of me. There was one of me in a desk in some classroom, laughing along with a blurred girl in the background. It looked so much like me, every detail on my face I hadn't quite noticed before on display. When I kept flipping, they were of all different moments I never remembered Grayson being present for, sometimes not remembering the moments themselves. They were so simple, times that hadn't really had much significance to me. But obviously there was some significance there for him if he was bringing them to life on paper.

I flew past the picture of the shooting, the one that made my stomach drop the longer I looked at it, and found the final drawing of me. It looked like I was seated in his hospital room, in that stupid plastic chair and looking out to something that wasn't clear in the picture. His lines were so refined, so delicate and simple. I felt a rumble of butterflies erupt in my stomach at the thought of him looking back on these moments and drawing me out.

For those years he spent hiding his feelings for me, I didn't have the slightest clue to how he felt. Tingles spread down my arms and throughout my body as I thought back to that kiss in my bedroom and how he pulled me roughly against him like he was afraid I'd reject him and he didn't want to let me go. When he first handed me that note in math class, I never knew it would be the start to something I couldn't predict the ending to. He talked to me like he knew me for years, but still stumbled over his adorable nervous words.

It only furthered my want to see him. I knew I needed to let him explain. These drawings, that kiss, his proclamation of his feelings didn't come wrapped up in a bow like I'd wished. Not everyone got fairytale endings and romantic confessions of love. While mine was far from romantic, covered in secrets and filled with feelings that didn't just include love, I knew he jumped in front of those bullets for me for a reason. He was the furthest thing from a bad guy and I realized that he wouldn't keep this from me as some dirty trick.

I just needed to know what I didn't let him tell me the first time.

As I ran my fingers over the thin lines of grey strokes, I almost fell off of the bed as a familiar voice broke through the peaceful silence.

"What are you doing here?" he whispered. I looked up at him quickly, snapping the sketchbook shut and almost throwing it across the bed. It landed with a thump against his pillows and he watched it fall before looking back to me.

"I shouldn't have done that," I squeaked, clearing my throat before starting up again. "I shouldn't have made you leave that night. I should have let you explain yourself. I want to know now."

He sighed, dropping his car keys onto his desk and shuffling through some papers to keep himself busy. "What's so different now? Why do you suddenly want to know what I have to say?"

I gulped, swallowing down my nerves that were threatening to jumble up my words. "Because I need you."

He dropped his papers and flicked his eyes to mine straight away. My heart was beating against my ribcage in a rumble of nerves. I had always been the strong one, protecting others around me like it was my job. I never needed anyone to loom over me and protect me from the world's demons like I thought Clay needed. For most of my life, I never needed help with anything because I thought I could handle it all on my own.

Now I was slowly realizing that I couldn't do this all on my own. I needed someone by my side to hold my hand through this and tell me that this was going to all be okay someday. I could remind myself that this was something I just needed to get through, but my own words just didn't seem good enough. I needed someone to hold me while I cried and protect me this time.

And I wanted that person to be Grayson.

21

Chapter 20

The silence that followed my first confession of the day was so nerve wracking. Grayson was just staring at me like I'd suddenly sprouted three heads and I was nervously playing with my fingers in my lap. My eyes darted to his now abandoned sketchbook, wondering if it was maybe too late to be the girl for him that he depicted in those photos.

"I know those pictures look creepy or whatever. It's not what you think," he said hurriedly, rushing across the room to pick it up and stick it on his bookshelf between two untouched sports books.

"And what am I thinking?" I quipped.

He gulped nervously and ficdled with more things around his room while he spoke. "It's not like I watched you all the time. I usually people-watch for inspiration. It helps clear my head sometimes. You just...have a beautiful smile and sometimes I get inspired. I don't know," he shook his head and kept averting his gaze from mine.

I blushed bright pink at that. I wanted to say so many things in that moment, all the things I'd spent so long pondering over all by myself. Grayson could answer a lot of questions for me. But I just kept watching him nervously meander around his room and do that nervous quirk of his.

"Grayson…" I whispered.

"It's not like you're the only one in that book. I mean…I draw everyone: my mom, sometimes my friends. I had a few of the baseball field but they're in my old sketchbook. I just like to draw people, they're more intricate and the detail is a challenge, which I like," he rambled on, gesturing crazily with his hands.

"Grays," I tried to interrupt again.

"There's only two or three pictures of you in there," he went on. I got up from the bed, making my way towards him across the room. "I honestly don't mean to draw you. It just…"

I put my hand on his back and he jumped in his spot in front of his desk. "Grayson, stop," I said.

He slowly turned around so he was facing me, dropping his fiddling and giving me his full attention.

"I love the pictures," I smiled gently. "They're beautiful. I'm actually surprised you would even draw me of all people."

"Really?" he murmured, running a hand down the back of his hair anxiously.

I nodded. His face configured for a moment, his cool coming back slightly as he dropped his nervous hand and took a deep breath. He put both of his hands on my hips, keeping me close to him just like last time. Now it was my turn to take in a breath.

He gulped, his voice coming back breathless. "You need me?"

I nodded again, not sure what to do with my hands. Part of me wanted to run them through his hair and bring him closer so I could have him all to myself. I knew there were still boundaries we needed to discuss and more things that needed to be said before all of that could take place.

"I have to visit Clay today," I started. "But I need you for more than that. I've been keeping up this front like I can do all of this by myself. I spent most of my life protecting Clay and the other people around me that I didn't take time out for myself. I'm not strong enough right now to deal with this myself. I need you. It took me a long time to realize that...but I really do need you."

He dropped his head a bit, his hair tickling my cheek. "Callie," he sighed. "This is probably just coming from the fact that I jumped in front of those bullets that day...."

I cut him off right there. "No," I protested rather loudly. I pulled back slightly so I could look at him in the eye. "I know that we weren't brought together under the best of circumstances but I'm positive that my feelings for you are real. Even though you risked your life for me, which I couldn't be more grateful for, it was you who I fell in love with, not just because you made that decision."

He didn't waste any time, quickly leaning his lips down to meet mine. He captured me in one of the most passionate kisses I'd ever experienced, slowly moving us so my back hit the wall behind me. My hands snaked their way up his chest as he started to move my lips apart, bringing themselves up and around his neck. One of his hands fell against my cheek, his thumb rubbing lightly against my skin. As my hands played with his hair, my heart was thumping on overdrive. Everywhere he touched lit a fire on my skin, every part of me erupting in goosebumps.

As the kiss started to fall to slower movements, he nipped at my lip slightly and I blushed the color of tomatoes after I realized I let out a whimper of sorts. With one final kiss, one that spoke volumes in that moment, he pulled away and locked me in his hot and heady gaze. His grey eyes pulled me into their waters, trapping me under the waves.

He raised his other hand so they were both holding my face in place as we both caught our breath. His chest was rising and falling underneath his navy blue t-shirt while my hand laid limp against it. I could practically feel his heart jumping in his chest.

"You sure you're ready to hear all of this? You won't change your…"

I cut him off with a shake of the head. "I know that whatever reason you had for keeping this to yourself is important. I trust you," I breathed, more certain than ever in my words.

He nodded a little unsurely, running his hand down my arm so he could grasp onto my hand. Following him to his bed, I felt my heart bounce nervously at the thought of what I was about to hear. Although I told him that I was ready for this, I wasn't sure how I'd handle it.

I wasn't even sure what I was in for.

Grayson sat down, bringing me with him, as I sat cross-legged on his sheets. His one leg was hanging off of the bed as I watched him calculate his words carefully. He was probably trying to figure out the best way to put this, find the gentler form of this story that wouldn't make me run like last time.

Letting out a deep breath, he clasped his hands over his knees and locked his eyes to mine. "During freshman year, Clay and I started talking because we got assigned as partners in Physics class. I had just started playing for the baseball team at that time and all of my friends were giving me shit for it. They were making fun of him, calling him a 'fag' and things like that. All of this was just because he was bragging about getting the lead during his first year of high school in the winter production."

I nodded along, my eyes falling shut as I recalled the memory too well. Clay was so excited. It was the first time he actually took the part in the play that he was rightfully given, the first time he didn't let the opinions of others around him sway his decision. He came home practically bouncing on the balls of his feet, fanning the fresh script in my face with a huge smile on his face.

It was the happiest I'd seen him in a while.

"I really looked up to him then. High school can be rough when it comes to doing whatever you want, whatever makes you happy. Being a freshman, I was scared to do anything that would label me as the 'uncool' kid. That was part of the reason I joined the baseball team, until I really started to love it as the years went on. But Clay was already teaching me that it was okay to be who you wanted to be, as along as it made you happy. To hell with the kids who didn't agree with you. It wasn't their life." He looked past me for a moment as a sign of recognition sparked in his eyes. His expression fell as he thought about his next sentence. "After that, Carter really started to get on his case. He'd just gotten a starting position on the team and he was walking around like he owned the place. I swear, it was genetically mastered in his blood for him to be a leader. When he saw Clay bragging about it in Chemistry the week after we were assigned that project, he wailed on him after school. He threw his face into the side of the dumpster and hit him so hard he was holding his side," he mimicked Clay's actions for a brief moment. "I wish I could have been there because then maybe I could have stopped it all. But I was in an after-school tutoring session that day.

The guys on the team were talking about it in the locker room after practice the next day."

"But Grayson, that's not..." I tried to cut in, but his shook his head and raised his finger for me to give him another minute.

"A few days later, Clay and I were in the library working on the Chem project. We were talking about his play and he was asking me about the next game we were practicing for. Next thing I know, he says, 'Do you want to know something?' I told him I did and he said that he was tired of being bullied all the time by everyone. He said he's been going through it since he was a kid. I tried to reassure him that it was all going to be okay soon. I told him I would talk to the guys on the team and try to get them to lay off. He said that for a long time..." he trailed off, his Adam's apple bobbing. He winced before he continued. "He'd been planning to shoot the people who hurt him. He said it was an eye for an eye. And if he could get rid of them then...he wouldn't have to worry about it anymore."

"Oh my God," I murmured, putting a hand to my mouth.

I thought his sudden change in his behavior happened over the course of his senior year. I never knew that he spent so many years plotting out ways to kill those who hurt him once. He put on this façade of sorts, pretending like he was happy whenever I saw him. There was never a time when he wasn't smiling like a mad man, pouring his heart out on stage or trying to make the people he knew happy. Was that all a lie? Was it all just a part of his plan to get rid of all of us?

Grayson's voice was strained as he said, "And then he told me that he was planning on doing it the next day in school. He said he knew where to get a gun and everything. He promised me not to tell anyone. I didn't go around telling everyone because after that, he was getting so much better. He was going out for roles, making friends in his drama class. He seemed like that was the last thing on his mind anymore. I thought...maybe he just needed someone to talk to and now he was okay. But I..." he shook his head.

"You what?" I prompted, begging him to just continue.

"I really think you should let Clay finish this story himself," he urged, moving his hand forward to play with my fingers that were lying limply on my lap. He didn't look at me, just kept his eyes on our hands that were intertwined.

My heart dropped. "You're really going to make me wait after all of that?" I asked, trying to keep my tone light to dim this heavy tension.

He peeked up at me through his millions of dark lashes. "Cal, you deserve answers. The rest is just something that Clay should be telling you, not me."

My mind went on a tailspin. I couldn't imagine what this final secret was, why it was so important for Clay to tell me and not Grayson, the one I was the most comfortable with. I was a little annoyed that I had to wait even longer for a story I was finally ready to hear, but I knew that Grayson was doing this for a reason.

Was it supposed to come out easier if it was from my brother and not him? Did Clay know more and could explain better than he could?

"Okay then," I stated. "Let's go give this one last shot."

The walk down the many halls, filled with a stench mixed of bleach and un-sanitized criminals, was still as hard as the last time I had walked through those huge black doors. My heart was still beating like crazy in my chest and my ears perked at the smallest of sounds. Grayson's hand was squeezing mine, his thumb rubbing small comforting circles on the top of my hand as we were led to the visiting room.

As I learned more and more about my brother, things I never imagined I could link to his character, I was realizing that it was now not so hard to group him into a label that all of these criminals had. He was borderline insane, thinking that what he did was the right thing. He was now a government-labeled murderer and would be locked away for the rest of his life. He deserved this. I didn't disagree with that fact at all.

Every action bore a consequence, whether small or large, simple or intricate. If Clay had spent so many years hiding away in his room, plotting the death of the people who picked him all his life, I was sure he thought about the punishment he would receive for doing so. It's not like he thought up this plan and didn't think he would be taken away afterwards.

Or did he?

A different guard was stationed outside of the thick door, tall and sturdy like he could carry the whole world on his broad shoulders. He was dressed in the same uniform as the last man who took his place the last time I was here. Only this time, he spoke to me, startling me.

"Alright Miss?" he asked simply, giving me a comforting look as I stared at him.

I wasn't used to the guards acknowledging my existence when I was here. Most of them were so used to pretending like they had seen these types of people everyday that they didn't bother to get personal with the visitors. They just led you to your destination and kept the criminals in check.

This guy must have been new.

I nodded with as much certainty as possible, feeling Grayson's grip on me tighten in an attempt to show me that he was still here if I felt like I was about to fall. He warned me before we walked in here that all I had to do was squeeze his hand if I wanted to leave. He said it would be a better way for me to say that I couldn't do it, without saying so out loud and feeling like I'd failed myself.

He was about to walk through the door with me, but I stalled us both. The guard was watching us with curiosity.

"I want to do this alone," I said firmly, giving him a look that read I still cared that he coming here for me. I knew he hated sitting in the waiting room for an answer to what happened. But I knew if I went in there with Grayson, Clay would sense my fear straight away and I wouldn't be able to get what I came here for.

But Grayson didn't protest. He just nodded his head and leaned down to give me a chaste kiss. When he pulled back, I gave him the biggest smile that I could, which wasn't much on my part. He grinned back at me, squeezing my hand reassuringly one last time before I went in.

As I watched his back retreat towards the waiting room chair, a similar plastic one like the one I used in his hospital room, the guard cleared his throat to get my attention.

"Ready to go in, Miss?" he asked hoarsely, his voice strong and masculine.

I nodded my head again, this time with more bravery than I'd showcased before. I squared my shoulders off and smiled kindly at the guard who held the door open for me. It buzzed as he scanned his ID card, signaling to the other guards that the criminal was having visitors.

The room was just the way that I had left it last time. A table was bolted to the floor, two metal chairs on either side of it. The large window that was a two-way street stared me in the face threateningly, almost like the people on the other side were begging for me to give them something to work with to keep Clay locked up for the rest of his life like they wanted.

I slowly sank down into the chair, keeping my back firm against it to show no fear. Not too long after I settled in, the opposite door opened and two guards were hauling my brother in with two hands wrapped around each of his arms. He smirked snidely at me as they sat him down in front of me.

"Well, well, well, look who decided to change her mind," he remarked.

Stiffening my posture, I said, "I only came here for answers, Clay."

One of the guards handcuffed his hands around the pole underneath the table and left us in the room alone, but not unwatched. He lazily sank down against the back of the chair and eyed me with such strength it was almost scary.

"You know, I'm surprised that they even passed on the message to you. They left all haughtily like that..." he trailed off; shrugging like it all hadn't meant a thing to him. He could honestly care less.

"Because you act like that," I pointed at him, not letting his brave nature get to me this time. I knew his tricks now and I knew how to respond. I wasn't letting him overrun me anymore.

He sat up a bit straighter. "I believe I'm entitled to act this way. I've earned the right."

I rolled my eyes. "You didn't earn anything! Taking someone's life gives you the right to act like a cocky asshole?"

"Whoa," he smirked at me again. "Callie, where is all of this newfound attitude of yours coming from? You never used to talk to me like that."

"Yeah, well things change," I said firmly, keeping my face sturdy.

He nodded, pursing his lips for a moment. "Why the hell are you here? Came to rip on me again?"

I shook my head. "I came to find answers. And then I'm gone."

"The answers to what exactly?" he asked, sitting back in his seat again and getting comfortable.

He seemed to getting more in tune with this criminal act than I ever imagined before. He wasn't itching in his orange jumpsuit, didn't care that he probably didn't have a proper shower in weeks. He pretended like the metal chair he was locked in was the comfiest couch in the richest of living rooms.

What had happened to him?

"Grayson told me that he was the first one that you told about your plans," I started, planting my hands on the table. "He said I should come to you for the rest of the story."

He shrugged. "What else is there to know? I told him what...during freshman year? I needed someone to talk to about it. I felt like I was going crazy, keeping it to myself."

"You spent all those years plotting people's deaths?" I asked, appalled.

Clay only nodded at me like none of it mattered. Nothing held any amount of care for him. He didn't have a sympathetic bone in his body any longer. "I was waiting for the right moment, I guess."

"The right moment?" I scoffed. "You should have never done it in the first place!"

"Okay, spare me the self-righteous bullshit, Callie. I'm giving you answers here. I don't need a life lesson," he held up his hand for me to shut up.

I scrapped my teeth together, trying so hard to ball up the anger boiling in my blood. A part of me just wanted to jump over the table and shake the life out of him, asking him what the hell happened to my brother. But I was only here to get my closure.

Nothing more.

Clenching my hands into fists against my lap and with my jaw hard, I said, "Then I don't understand what's left to the story. He said he didn't tell anyone because it seemed like you were getting better. He thought you just needed someone to talk to. But he said he did do something, or said something. He just won't tell me what."

"Oh, he told Mom."

22

Chapter 21

I couldn't even find the words to respond to that. I just sat there, jaw probably sitting in my lap and my fingernails curling into the skin of my palms. Everything seemed to freeze and I felt nothing but...stupidity. Clay was perched in his chair, a smug grin on his lips as he watched it all unfold on my face.

"It's a shock to you, huh?" he asked, using the tips of his white sneakers to lift him up and push the chair back slightly.

I shook my head but didn't know why I did it. I wasn't disagreeing with his statement because I was exactly that, shocked. Not to mention confused, disgusted, and a little hurt. Maybe it was just my subconscious way of mixing up the jumble of thoughts in my head to make some sense of this.

"I don't..." I trailed off as soon as I began. "She knew?"

He just nodded his head, shrugging like it didn't matter to him. It probably didn't, the fact that my mother knew about his mental instability and how she chose to ignore it all this time. She could have saved Carter's life; saved Clay's...saved mine. She sat around the house blaming Clay for what he'd done, when it reality, she was the one who allowed him to do it.

How do you let your own son go on with those types of thoughts?

I could feel my skin ripping beneath the ends of my nails, the more emotional I was getting. As this moment, I wanted to run from this room and get home to question her. I wanted answers, just like I'd been searching for since this all started. I wanted to confront her and make her state what she had done wrong. Did my dad know too?

"Does Dad…" I went to ask, but Clay immediately shook his head.

Clay and my father had a rocky relationship from the start. During Dad's rehab stint when he was emotionless and didn't want to interact with others, Clay was hurt without his dad there to stick by his side, especially during one of his worst times when he was dealing with Carter. But growing up, my dad was Clay's go-to, his confidant. Clay wanted to grow up to be my dad before all of this mess happened.

Even if he hated my mother right now, he'd never be able to hate my dad. He could talk to my mom and I anyway he wanted, but he'd never be able to talk to my dad that way.

"How could she keep a secret like this? She never came to you to solve this?"

"She never said a word. She just kept coddling me like I was a baby, like she'd done for years. It's one of the reasons I resented her so much. She was never there to listen, just to dust me off and throw me back to the wolves. She treated me like I was a child and I was overreacting about all of these things at school."

As Clay rambled on, I found myself even more awestruck than I already was. All this time, I figured that those nights where Clay and my mom were sheltered away in his bedroom, him with his face down in the pillow and her stroking his back was just my mother sending him soothing words and comfort. Meanwhile, she was babying him and telling him that his problems weren't as big as he made them seem.

What, were the black eyes and bruises not enough for her to believe that he had hit rock bottom?

He took a breath, the smug smirk gone from his face. "She hid the fact that she knew very well, I'll give her that. I didn't have a clue. I was under the assumption that Grayson hadn't told anyone. I figured I was in the clear."

I closed my eyes as I tried taking all of this in. "I don't understand. I was under the impression that Mom was always comforting you when you guys were alone in your room those nights when you came home from fights. You're telling me that she just told you to stop overreacting?"

He nodded simply. "Why is that so surprising to you, Callie?"

I shook my head. None of this added up. My dad had always been the one to tell Clay to shape up and didn't send him the comforting words. But it was only because he wanted Clay to learn how to fight for himself. Mothers were supposed to be the ones who held you and promised that everything would be alright soon. They scared the monsters away, listened to you ramble on for hours and gave you the motherly advice you sought out for.

My mom was never cold to us.

"She's our mom, Clay. I've never seen her act cold like that towards either one of us. That doesn't make sense that she would tell you your stories were overdramatic. She always seemed like she was trying to help you and not tear you down. Now you're saying our mother's ignorant?"

Clay sighed heavily, bringing his cuffed hands onto the table in a forced manner. "Look, I'm not persuading you to believe me," he stated, still no trace of a smirk on his face. "You don't have to believe a single word I say. Quite frankly, I wouldn't blame you if you didn't believe me right now. But I wasn't the one who told you come find the rest of the story. Grayson was the one who told her, not me. I always thought he was bluffing when he said he told her. All I have to say is, if there's one thing I know for sure about Grayson...it's that he doesn't lie, Callie."

As much as I hated to admit it, Clay was right. Grayson wasn't known to lie about things like this. He was the truest form of himself and didn't lead others on. He could have kept his story to himself our entire relationship, but he chose to open up to me even under the risk that I wouldn't like the end result.

But Clay was also right about another thing.

"You're right," I hissed. "I don't have to believe a word you say because everything up until this point has been a lie between us," I finished, glaring at him underneath the flickering lights.

Clay squared off his shoulders but didn't try to make me squirm underneath his gaze. "I know," was all he said.

"If Mom had tried to stop you, maybe get you help with what you were...struggling with," I began, my voice shaking slightly and losing its edge. "Would you have reconsidered your decision?"

The silence that fell around us then was soul-shuddering. The room suddenly felt icy cool, the mood between us drifting back and forth between positive and negative. He just watched me intensely, thinking of the honest answer I believe we both knew was about to come. The guard stationed by the door that Clay came out of was staring ahead at the wall behind me, but I knew he paid attention to every word. Even the people behind the two-way window were taking notes, thinking of diabolical ways to take my brother down.

"No."

That's all Clay said. The word, two letters and the shortest response you could ever give, just hung around us hauntingly. He knew that this would go against him on the record, was fully aware that other people were listening into this conversation. But he didn't lie. It was the first time I saw my brother come to light before me, not the monster that overtook his body and claimed him. It was just my petty brother, the one with the once heart of gold and kind smile.

I just wanted to get out of here, no matter the conversation turning points and the fact that my brother was finally coming through that rough exterior he built. My body was pulling me from the chair before I even realized what I was doing, my mind already heading for another agenda of the day. I had to see my mom and get the answers to the rest of this story.

This ever long, horrid story.

I felt Clay's eyes on me as I started to make a path towards the door. They were burning two, large holes in my back, making the urge to turn around even more potent. Right before I'd reached the door and the guard was taking out his ID to scan in order to let me out, I froze.

I'd forgotten the most important question.

"Clay?" I said gently, my emotions rising to the surface.

"Callie?" he asked, sitting up straighter and looking like he was preparing himself for a slap of some sorts.

I walked back to the table and placed my hands on the cool, metal surface. He looked down at my hands and then back up at me beneath his dark lashes. His face was a lot gentler, which seemed odd to me now that I'd gotten so used to the monster that was his alter ego.

"I have one last question," I started, wanting to dig my nails into the hard top table. I was now sweating in the small room, my heartbeat taking over every sound I heard. I wasn't sure I was prepared for the answer to the question I was about to purpose, but I knew that I needed to hear this. "But before I ask, you need to know that this will be the last time I ever come to see you. I'm done with this back and forth game of yours and you're not the brother I grew up with. It hurts too much to come back here and know that when I'm in this room with you."

He brought his lips into his mouth and bit on the inside of his lip. "As much as I hate to admit this to you of all people, you're right. That's the one thing you've been right about all along. I'm not the same brother you used to know. I haven't been that boy for a long, long time, Callie. You just never took the time out to see it. But who I am now...it's what has been created over the years. It's my way of defending myself now. You have to understand that."

I shook my head in disagreement. "That's where you're wrong. On both accounts. You were in there somewhere in these past few months. I could see it. Although I was the one protecting you, you were still there to protect me...when I fell out of that wagon out front when we were kids, when Carter was in my face in the halls that last month before you came here." I took in a deep breath as I thought back to all of the times that my older brother was the vision of perfection in my eyes, the moments where I admired him the most. "But I will never have to understand the monster that you've become."

His eyes lit up in a roaring fire in that moment, signaling that he was ready to pounce for a fight. But I saw the way they softened when I spoke about how he used to be, before all of this mess occurred. Even if he would never be able to admit it, he knew he was wrong and he knew what he was now missing out on.

Clay knew that this wasn't the answer he was searching for from the beginning.

"Callie," he said through gritted teeth.

I held up my hand. "No, I didn't say that to fight. I'm done fighting with you, Clay. Before I go, I have one last question I'd like you to answer."

"What makes you think that I have to-"

"Why me?"

My words came out slowly and surely, but quiet as a church mouse. Those two small words, so silently whispered, seemed to echo against the brick walls in the room. They bounced to and fro, like they were hitting us both in the face over and over again. I could feel my heart wanting to burst out of my chest in fright, could feel my hands shaking and my knees wobbling. I almost wished I had Grayson in here to catch me when I was almost certain I would fall.

But I knew I had to stick around for the end. I had to understand this before I left him for good.

Clay watched me for a long while, making me feel like I'd been here for days instead of just an hour. He shifted uncomfortably in his seat for a moment, licking his lips and replaying my words over and over in his head. His face was hard with emotion I couldn't quite place and his eyes were still blazing.

"I'd managed to convince myself that you were biggest bully of them all. Those guys on the team, Carter and them, yeah they beat me up a lot and they tossed me around like I was a fucking dodge ball, but you were always there deflecting the punches," he stated in a firm, leveled tone. "I never got a chance to fight back all those times like Dad told me to. I couldn't make Dad proud because of you. I couldn't shut Mom up because of you. I swore to myself sometimes that...that you were the reason I got chosen so many times, because they got a laugh out of the fact that my little sister would come save me time and time again."

"I mean, fuck Callie," he continued. "You couldn't just let it go. You couldn't let me fight for myself. You always had to be there when it happened, every single time."

I was breathless, my chest bouncing as I panted for a breath I couldn't find. "I did it because I loved you, Clay, not because..."

"You said that all the time! I heard it too many times to count, Callie. It was almost like...the over-protection drove me over the edge," he mumbled, looking down at his cuffed hands and making my heart drop further into my stomach.

"So you're saying that...I was the one who caused you to-" I went to say, but my voice was so shallow and breathless and he cut me off before I could finish. The tears were threatening to spill over any moment and I was hoping I could get out of here before he caught me.

"No," he shook his head, his voice low as well. "You weren't the one who drove me to do that. But it...all added up. Brick after brick, mess on top of mess," he moved his hands in a gesture like he was building a wall in front of him.

The tears spilled over before I had the chance to stall them any longer, making me curse myself. I quickly wiped them away with the back of my hands and tried to gather some courage to get me through this without breaking down fully in a prison visitor's room with my alleged almost-killer staring me in the face.

"That was enough to kill me?" I gasped, my voice wretched with sobs that were begging to come to the surface.

He paused for the longest moment imaginable. Clay picked at his fingers without looking at me. I watched him bite his lip in contemplation, making me want to run over there and grab him by the jumpsuit, shaking the life out of him for an answer. The longer I had to wait, the more I felt my heart crack into smaller and smaller bits. My own brother planned to kill me because of something I'd done to protect him. He thought this was enough to take my life and sever our life-long relationship.

"I was never going to tell you this..." he started, gulping. "I've been trying so hard to keep up this exterior I'd built up, but you...you need to know that..." he trailed off, stumbling again and again over his words. He had my heart in his hands then, squeezing further the longer he waited. "I wasn't...going to go through with it. When I'd aimed the gun at you, I had a...moment. This moment made me realize that I couldn't do that to you."

"B-but Grayson..." I stuttered, finding it difficult to form words.

"He scared me, okay?" he got a bit louder this time, banging his hands down onto the table. "I had my finger on the trigger and he jumped...it just all happened so fast and I'd already killed Carter...I just got scared and it...it happened."

Clay's face had lost its tough mask, mirroring the image of the older brother I used to once know. His eyes were soft and his face was falling in a stream of guilt and confession. I couldn't believe him, didn't know how to believe him. These past few months that I'd drilled over the situation time and time again, prying my brain for a reason as to why he would do such a thing to me...and this was the answer all along. He wasn't going to do it. He planned it, but at the last minute he was going to back down.

This revelation, although life-altering and heart-wrenching as it was, wasn't enough to make me forgive him. I may have believed him because he was my brother and my heart still held a piece of him in it, but all of this wasn't enough. He could tell me repeatedly how he wasn't about to go through with this, didn't mean to shoot the last two bullets in his gun towards his sister, but I'd never be able to forgive him for what happened before his last minute decision.

I used my fingers to wipe the remaining tears from underneath my lids and took a deep breath to let this information soak in. "I've spent so long wondering why you ever chose to point that gun at me that day. I wracked my brain for what I could have possibly done wrong to make you hate me so much that you actually wanted to end my life like you had planned. I appreciate you telling me this. It changes things. It changes a lot. But what it doesn't change is the fact that I'll still never be able to forgive you for pointing the gun at me in the first place. That...I'll never forget," I murmured off, turning towards the door and planning on leaving with that.

"Callie, please..." he begged, his voice reeking with desperation. It was the first time I heard him use my name like he'd actually cared for me some time before this. I froze in my walk and waited for him to continue. "You have to..."

And there it was, his signature response. You have to understand.

That was the thing he didn't understand. Not everyone in his life would have to understand anything. There would still be things years from now that we wouldn't be able to wrap our brains around. People did things without reasons and people would never understand them. People didn't things with reason and still others wouldn't be able to understand. I didn't have to understand a thing.

No matter how many times he would explain his feelings to me, why he'd done the things he had or how he managed to conjure up such an action, I would never be able to understand this. I'd never be able to forgive him. I'd never be able to forget this.

So that's why I turned around to face him fully, giving him my attention one last time to utter my last ever sentence to my brother because I never planned on seeing him again. This was it, the moment of truth. This was the last and final time I'd be able to say anything to him and I wanted him to remember it for the remaining years of his life that he'd be thrown into his hell-hole.

"I don't have to understand a single word you tell me anymore, Clay. I've gotten my answers and now I have to live with them. I have to live with the fact that my older brother is the town's murderer. I have to walk down those halls at school with people pointing me out as the 'sister of the boy who brought a gun to school.' Every time I touch the boy I love, I have to remember that my own brother was the one who put those holes in him. I have to realize that Carter will never come back because of you. I have to deal with Mom and deal with myself. I have to get on with my life knowing that you created this mess that I will never be able to forgive you for. But the most important thing is: I don't have to do anything for you. I don't owe you a single thing and I never will. You may have been my brother and picked me up when I was down as a kid, but I'll never begin to understand what you've become. Mom and Dad won't be back. I won't be back. No one will be back to see you ever again. And all I can hope is that one day you realize how wrong you were for what you've done to me, those kids at school, Mom and Dad…this whole town."

"Understand this, Clay. What's happened to you was horrible. You didn't deserve a single punch that was given to you while you grew up. I'll stand true to that for the rest of my life, no matter what people say. I wish I could go back and change what's happened to you, but I can't and neither can you. If this was your way of rectifying that, it didn't succeed. Millions of kids get bullied everyday, some for years. They commit suicide, hurt themselves, and hurt others. But none of it helps what's happened. They're just ways to dodge what's right in front of them, which is exactly what you've done. You backed down. You tried to be the underdog, but it failed. You didn't become the bigger person in that scenario. If that's what you wanted, then you should've tried to stick up for yourself, talked to me or someone who could help. Be the bigger person and create a better life for yourself. But you chose this…" I gestured around me. "A dirty prison cell with people who are now just like you. And that's gotten you to be no one but a boy with a label as a killer. I hope you think about that for the rest of the time you have left in here, because that's all you have left. Goodbye, Clay."

I walked out of the room without another word, letting the door buzz shut behind me. After that, everything was just a blur of tears and heavy hearts as I immediately found Grayson pacing the waiting area, where he stopped as soon as he saw me, letting me fall into his arms without me having to say anything.

This seemed to be just enough right now to help carry the pieces of my broken heart and the severed tie between my former brother and me.

23

Chapter 22

On the drive back to my house, the car was silent. Grayson was driving my car back because he didn't trust me behind the wheel in my condition. I tried keeping my eyes trained out the passenger side window, but I could see Grayson casting glances at me every so often out of the corner of my eye.

"I'm not going to blow up again, if that's why you keep staring at me," I commented, making him jump in his seat for a moment. "I'm just saving that for my mother," I mumbled underneath my breath where I was sure he didn't hear me.

He shook his head. "That's not why. I'm just worried about you."

I sighed heavily, already annoyed with this conversation. I was tired of everyone around me waiting for me to drop, like I couldn't control myself. My brother was the one who created this catastrophe. He was the mentally unstable one. So why was I being looked at like I was about to be admitted into a mental institution?

"You have nothing to worry about."

Grayson clenched the steering wheel a bit harder before he spoke. "You've just been putting up this front for so long, pretending like you've been okay when it's obvious that you aren't. No one's going to judge you for breaking down, Callie. What you have been forced to go through is hard, really hard."

I sat up further in the seat and turned to face him with a slightly reddened face. "Why is it that everyone's acting like I'm going to end up like him or something? Everyone's got their eye on me like I'm the one hiding a gun in my purse now. When I say I'm fine, I mean it. I'm fine."

He smirked, his lips turning up at the corner of his mouth. That small dimple in his right cheek appeared as he rubbed a hand underneath his jaw.

"What the hell are you smiling about?" I grumbled.

I didn't like the fact that I was so grumpy and irritable, taking all of this frustration out on Grayson of all people. He's already been through enough with me so I knew he didn't deserve it. My mind flashed back to Clay's words:

But it...all added up. Brick after brick, mess on top of mess.

In that second, stuck in the engrossing silence of the car with the one boy who could do me no harm, I knew exactly how Clay felt for the first time since this incident happened. Every time I fell deeper into this story, more people kept piling on my list of who to be mad at. I always thought this story began and ended with Clay's selfish and unstable thoughts. I never once imagined all of these people playing parts in such a situation.

"I'm trying to remind myself that you're not angry with me, but with someone else," he said, casting a glance in the rearview mirror as he changed lanes.

"I'm sorry," I grumbled again, sliding down into my seat and crossing my arms over my chest. "I'm just tired of chasing this story. It's like everyone in my life was living a lie or something. I feel like

I was the only one who didn't know about his idea to bring a gun to school that day. And here I thought I was the closest person to him."

A frown replaced the sweet smile on his lips. "I don't think I've been living a lie per say..." he trailed off, shrugging while keeping his eyes on the road ahead of him.

"I didn't mean you!" I protested, feeling my heart drop into my stomach for the tenth time that day. Grayson was the only one who was holding me up in this and I was always beating him down in return.

He pursed his lips. "It's alright. I understand why you said it."

We reached a red light and for a moment there I figured he would avoid eye contact at all costs. I watched him swallow before he turned to face me slightly. His one hand was clenched around the gear shift still, turning his knuckles a ghostly shade of white.

"Grayson, I really didn't mean you. I'm just frustrated that so many people knew about this and didn't say a word about it. I mean, my brother could still be home and going off to college soon if this hadn't happened. We'd still be able to be close," I murmured.

Grayson looked like he was about to say something, but someone beeped from behind us, making him flicker his eyes up to the now bright green light. He stepped on the gas without saying any further. I wanted to reach forward and turn on the radio, do something to make this silence feel less awkward.

He and I never had awkward silences.

I started biting at my thumbnail while I stared at the trees passing by, my vision almost blurred by the fast paced street-lines. I didn't know what else to say to him that would make him feel better. He always wanted me to be honest, keep things out in the open between us. This was my honesty brimming over the edge. I couldn't change that unless he was comfortable with me lying to him about how my heart felt.

And I knew I wasn't comfortable with that.

"Sometimes I feel like I shouldn't have told you," he interrupted the silence with a grimace.

My eyes snapped to his. "But I thought you said that..."

"I know what I said. But after watching you having to go through all of this...I wish I didn't tell you that I knew. Now you're going crazy over what your brother said and you're about to call out your mom. It seemed so much easier to just leave you out of the loop. I mean, what good has this done? It just left you with a shattered look of the people around you, me included. I feel like I tore apart your family, Cal."

The new tears were starting to cloud my vision as I watched his face crumble, his heart on his sleeve which always seemed to match his character. He was never one to take things lightly, always being completely honest with those he truly cared about. Why were so many people blaming themselves for something my brother had done? Shouldn't he be the one crying in his prison cell, wishing he could have a do-over and regretting his decision?

Clay wasn't even this upset about what had occurred these past few months.

"Grayson..." I whispered, but he cut me off as he pulled into my driveway, shutting off the car and looking over at me.

"We're here. Are you ready?"

I gulped, already feeling my hands shaking in my lap at the thought of what I was about to do. This was my mother, the one who was supposed to keep the monsters away and shelter me from the cruel world. Not only did she play a part in this fiasco, but she could have been a hand to stop this before it spiraled out of control.

Taking a deep breath I said, "As ready as I'll ever be."

Grayson walked me through the front door and into the living room, where he stopped cold as soon as he saw my mother's half-smiling face while she was sitting on the couch. She was flipping through the newspaper with the television playing some soap opera of the afternoon. She had her hair down for the first time in a while, her scrubs nowhere to be seen and a pair of yoga pants on paired with a purple t-shirt. She was the vision of content.

And I was about to ruin it.

"I'm going to head home," he whispered near me ear behind me.

He was starting to walk back into the foyer, intent on leaving without as much as a goodbye. I followed suit quickly, pulling him by the sleeve of his sweatshirt before he made it to the door.

"Grays," I called to him, making me freeze in his steps but he didn't turn around until I gave his sleeve another tug. "Come on, look at me."

He winced briefly before capturing me with those bright grey eyes of his, already sending me underneath his waters. I felt almost breathless as he watched me for a moment before conjuring up the courage to speak.

"This is something you need to deal with alone and with your family," he started. "I'd only be getting it the way. You really need some time to deal with all of this without me tagging along."

I shook my head, squeezing my eyes shut like I was in a dream. I was begging for someone to pinch me so I'd wake up and just be in his arms once again. "I don't want you to go," I whispered, looking behind me to catch a peek at my still comfortable looking mother on the couch.

"Callie," he breathed, making shivers run up my arms at the sound of his voice. He always said my name like it was the one thing holding him down to this earth. I never felt so special until he started doing that. "I really think that you and your family need some time to cope with this before we," he gestured between us. "Really shouldn't start something you're not ready to get into. I know what you're going through is tough and it's frustrating. I just don't think I can take knowing that I was part of the cause of all of this."

"Grayson, we already talked about this. This isn't your fault," I said firmly, just now realizing that I was still holding onto his sleeve, a pathetic attempt to make him stay.

He grimaced. "But it partially is. I feel like the least I owe you is to give you time to deal with this on your own, with your family and the people who were so horribly affected by this. So I'm going to go for a little while, give you what you need."

"But Grays, I..." I wanted so terribly to finish that sentence. I wanted to pour my heart out to me, tell him that over these past few months I've fallen in love with him. I've become immersed in his golden boy charm. Everything about him; the heart of his sleeve, his incredible artistic abilities, the way he smirks and that dimple appears and how always seems to know what I'm thinking without me having to say a word, has become pretty much all that I think about. Aside from overanalyzing the hell out of this current situation with my brother, the thought of Grayson always seems to pull me out of the gutter when I've fallen too far in. How could he leave now?

He came towards me, putting his hand on the back of my head and bringing me forward. Placing his lips on my forehead and stroking the back of my hair with a gentle hand, he finally pulled me all the way under with no lessons on how to swim. I hated that he had the ability to do that, make me mush beneath his appearance. But when he pulled back, all I could do was stay drowning in those grey, choppy waters.

"It's what you need to do. You need to be able to be with your family right now, especially after what you're about to do. And I need some time to sort through the crap that he left behind for me. No matter what you say, it is partially my fault. There's no way I'm leaving you behind after this. I've waited far too long for this," he pulled my face close once more so our foreheads were touching. "To let it all go now. We just both need time, that's all. And I'll be waiting when you're ready," he whispered finally.

But I'm ready now, is all I wanted to say.

But maybe he was right about all of this. From the beginning of the aftermath of the shooting, we had both dove right into one another without a second thought. We became so close so quickly and trusted one another to be the fall back for the other. People became strong by learning how to cope on their own, learning how to stand on their own two feet. I couldn't very well have him holding me up for the rest of my life.

Maybe we did need to learn how to move on...alone, for just a little while.

"Okay," I whispered, my lips almost a ghost-whisper away from his. "Time sounds like a good idea."

He smiled that beautiful smile of his, his lips pulling back to coax out that right dimple of his. "See you soon?"

I nodded, our skin creating friction against one another's. "See you soon," I stated firmly, matching his grin.

He kissed me one last time at the top of my hair, pulling me tight before he let go. I watched him walk out the door with a heavy heart, but a heart that knew this was the right thing to do. You couldn't go on in life always keeping someone at your feet, waiting to pick you up when you fell. Life was about learning to go on by yourself, in case that person decided not to be around anymore. You needed to learn to fight for yourself and understand on your own.

Casting one last glance to the door, I took another much needed deep breath before turning on my heels and walking into the living room to face my mother. I hated seeing her so at peace with herself, so comfortable and unaware of what was about to be asked of her. It made it that much harder for me to just sit down on the chair beside her and start this conversation.

I mustered up as much strength as I could before sitting down across from her, leaning forward with my elbows on my knees and looking over at her. As I was putting together the words to say to her that wouldn't be too mean or too striking, she flipped down a corner of his newspaper and peered at me over the edge.

"Is everything okay, sweetheart?" she asked. I didn't have to say anything more for her to notice my change in emotion since the last time we had seen each other.

I shook my head, my lips in a straight line. "No Mom, everything's not okay. Is Dad around? I'd like to talk to him, too."

She nodded silently, calling for him to come into the room to join us. He padded into the room, his eyes tired and his face lighting up as he saw me. It faded quickly as he noticed the tension in the room that suddenly seemed to stretch between my mother and me. My dad sat beside my mother, his hand on knee while they both looked to me to continue.

"So I visited Clay today," I started, playing with my fingers while I tried to keep my eyes on theirs. My dad nodded curtly and I saw my mother squirm the longer she watched me. "I found out something today that I didn't know before."

"Callie," my dad sighed, rubbing his hand over his face in exasperation. "Whatever detailed story your brother decided to make up is probably a lie. I wouldn't trust anything that comes out of his mouth anymore."

I felt a small pang in my heart for Clay, but only momentarily, as my dad's words sank in. The last thing my parents saw when they visited was the monstrous side of Clay that he had been using as a mask for his overwhelming feelings. The last thing I saw of him was the brother I always remembered.

Our views of him would forever be brought to different definitions.

"I'm not so sure that this one's a lie, Dad. I found out that someone knew what he was planning on doing before it happened. This person could have saved us all this pain and this embarrassment if they had just spoken up and gotten him help before everything went south."

I couldn't even look over at my mom as I spoke. I just kept glancing at my dad as I continued, my eyes practically begging to just peek over at her. But then she would know I was talking about her, she'd probably get up and leave the room before I could finish everything I had to say. If this past month's actions hadn't spoken volumes about her character and speaking up to tell the truth, I don't know what could.

My father's jaw dropped. "He told someone before that day?"

I nodded, now wavering in my decision to just point at my mom. Although my blood was boiling just at the thought of her hiding such a thing and harming people because of her secrets, I felt somewhat guilty for putting her on the spot like this. But I knew that my dad had a right to know what had been going on behind his back, just like I deserved the right.

"Was it that Grayson boy?" he asked, his voice still full of shock and disdain. "He always seemed like he was too good to be true."

"No!" I immediately shouted, putting a hand up to stop him. "I mean, Grayson knew but he told someone who could help. He tried to get Clay help."

He raised a graying brow at me. "Well out with it, Callie. I don't know who he could have possibly…"

"Mom…" I coaxed gently, making her jump in her seat. My dad's eyes fell down to her, squeezing at her knee to give her a boost of comfort. She had already put down the paper so she now had nothing to hide behind. She sat up a bit straighter, putting her hand on top of my dad's.

"Yes?" she asked, feigning any knowledge about what I was about to say. I figured I would give her a minute to join in, speak up for herself before I finally laid out the truth to everyone involved. But now she was pretending like she didn't have a clue.

"Dad…" I caught his attention again. "Mom knew," I whispered so quietly I could have sworn he didn't hear me. But I immediately trashed that idea as his face fell dramatically. He looked over at her with such sadness and betrayal, like he didn't know her at all.

He dropped his hand from her knee, even after she tried to hold onto it. "Gail," he gasped. "You… You knew?"

She shook her head rapidly, trying to put her hands on his shoulders, but he pulled away before she could. "I...Stuart I didn't..."

Dad got up from the couch and started pacing the floor. My mother watched him with wavering eyes, calculating his every movement. "You knew that our son was struggling like that and you didn't say a word?!" he shouted this time, throwing his hands in the air.

She put a hand to her mouth, her eyes wide. That look of content was completely erased from her features. "I didn't know he'd go through with it, Stuart! I didn't know! How was I supposed to know that he would actually go out and buy a gun?" she countered back, his voice rising and shaking.

"It doesn't matter if you questioned his intentions and his capability, Gail! You should have come to me and we could have planned something to help him get better. We could have made a plan to avoid this!"

"You saw how he was, Stuart! Who in a million years could think that he would do such a thing?!" she protested, getting up from her seat to stand her ground now.

He stopped short, eyeing her down. "No, Gail. Tell me how our son was," he seethed.

She started pacing the floor like he had just done, a hand over her lips and trembling limbs. "He was getting picked on all the time for being...well you know!" she shouted once more. "How could anyone have known he had the courage to do such a thing? It's not like the strongest of the bunch..."

I couldn't believe her. This was her son she was putting down, pointing all blame to the fact that her son was labeled gay so he couldn't possibly have the strength to do this. What did one have to do with the other? Why did his label matter?

"Do you hear yourself?" he boomed. "This is your son you're talking about! Who cares what those kids at school labeled him! Being gay has nothing to do with picking up a gun and pointing it at another person. You don't have to be strong or brave to do things like that. Children even get their hands on guns and shoot them! For Christ's sake, Gail! Even if our son was gay, it didn't mean his strength was diminished."

"I know, but..." she tried to begin, but my dad cut her off.

"No! You don't know anything! You're standing there labeling our son and saying that just because he was thought to be gay that he didn't have the capability to do this! You were wrong!"

"Stuart!" she protested once more, moving over to him to grab onto his arm just like I'd done earlier to Grayson to keep him here with me. But she must have known now wasn't the time and even the forceful grabbing couldn't make my dad stick around after that. "I loved our son! I just didn't know that..."

He ripped his arm from her grip and gave her the deadliest of glances. "I can't even look at you right now," he spat, turning from her and going downstairs to his office with a final slam of the door behind him.

My mom just stood there, frozen from where the ties of her husband and herself had been cut down the middle. I heard her crying but didn't even make a move to console her. That woman standing before me was nothing like I remembered her to be. She was a whole new person to me now, just by this situation alone. She was labeling her once bullied son, doubting him and hurting all of those who were supposed to be the closest to her. If she hadn't been so simple-minded, so judgmental and mentally abusive to Clay, then we could have all avoided this.

The bullying hadn't started when Clay decided to be himself. It hadn't started when Carter set his eyes on him and started to torment him for those three and half years of high school. Without me knowing it until now, the bullying started from a totally different place I had never expected.

It started at home, where those you love were supposed to wrap you in their arms and tell you that you were perfect just the way that you were. Home was supposed to be a safe haven where you could speak your mind and feel the most comfortable.

Now I was almost at a point of understanding. Clay hadn't done this because of some kid at school. He didn't do this to get back at just those who picked on him while he tried to express himself in plays and in class. He did this for an escape.

And that type of escape didn't come from home like he always wanted.

24

CHAPTER 23

The next few weeks in the Tollson household were intentionally quiet and almost disturbing. I was so used to my parents cuddling on the sofa on Friday nights, watching movies on Netflix and talking about their hectic weeks. My mom would be cooking up something different every night while my dad stayed tied up in his office, planning out new schematics for his mechanic's shop. Everything was at peace, with nothing but love and admiration in the house.

Since the shooting, the peaceful nights and nightly dinners came to a short halt. My mom was a bit quieter than normal and my parents didn't seem too touchy-feely the days following the arrest of their son. I didn't blame them for not wanting to just act normal around one another. This whole situation in itself was so life-altering that it still didn't make sense, even four months later.

But after the night of the confession from my mom, my dad wasn't around much at all. He was staying late after work to 'finish up on some labor' and bring in more money. My mom was keeping time at the hospital, where the girls at work were still giving her the stink eye and making her out to be like she was the odd one out, even though she had been apart of that hospital team for almost twelve years. It was mostly just me roaming around the house by myself, with just my incessant thoughts and no one else to talk to.

My dad's reaction was nothing short of what I expected. The fact that the woman we both trusted with our lives was so judgmental and out of character that day was a major shock to the both of us. Neither one of us understood why she thought that being gay was such a problem. His label that was brought onto him by the kids at school wasn't something she should have been worried about. She should have been worried about his mental state and the fact that he actually warned somebody that he was planning on killing someone someday soon.

Whenever she came home from work and was catching me slipping into the kitchen for a midnight snack or a drink of water, she just looked at me like she was scared to come near me. She stopped in her tracks and gently placed her stuff down on the dining table, giving me an uneasy look and then just deciding to shake her head and flee from the room.

It felt like none of us had spoken a word to each other for months, even if it had only been weeks.

Now I was finding myself missing Grayson more than I'd like to admit. It wasn't just because I felt like I couldn't hold all of this on my own, because I was becoming more sure of myself in the past few weeks than ever before. Although all of this was hard to wrap my brain around, being without Grayson for a while gave me a chance to breathe and realize that I needed to handle this on my own. Just like he said, I needed to deal with all of this with my family and on my own terms. But I still wished I had him to run to so I could throw all of this out of my head and hand it off to someone else just for a little bit.

The scary part was, he was waiting for me to make the first move. I was used to him being there when I fell, picking up the pieces and putting me back together to move onto the next agenda on the list. Normally, it was him knowing exactly what I wanted to say and how I was feeling. It scared me more than I was willing to admit that I actually had to put my feelings out there and make it known that I needed him more than ever.

I'd already done it once, confessed how much I truly needed him to help me out. But this was the first time that I realized I was in love with someone and wanted them to be a major part of my life. While Grayson still had doubts that the only reason I was falling for him was because he saved my life that day, I knew it was much more than that now. He knew me better than anyone else, could sense how I was feeling and always seemed to know what to say at the worst of times.

And he was the only thing, aside from the battle with my parents, that I could think about since he walked out my front door that day and declared that we both needed time. While I felt like time was up and I was ready to have him walk back into my life again, I still wasn't sure where he was or how he was doing.

As I reached above the stove for a pot to cook my dinner in, my mother startled me by sneaking up behind me and clearing her throat. A clashing sound erupted around us as I dropped the pan onto the counter and threw a hand over my chest.

When I turned to look at her, I wasn't sure if I should say anything just yet. We hadn't spoken to one another at all since the fight and I was still angry at her for keeping such a thing like that a secret from everyone.

"You scared me," I whispered, finally deciding that was the only thing I could come up with after weeks of silence.

She dropped her tired eyes from mine, only to look back up at me again when she spoke. "I'm sorry. I just felt like...I feel that we need to talk, Callie."

"I think we've talked enough, don't you think, Mom?" I dead-panned, turning from her and putting the pot over the flickering flame.

She sighed heavily, placing a hand on my shoulder to make me face her again. "I don't think I ever had the opportunity to finish what it was that I had to say."

I ran my hands through my hair and turned down the flame, taking a deep breath and pointing towards the dining table so we could sit. She followed me quietly, keeping her hands together in front of her and watching me with weary eyes. When she pulled the chair out and sat down, she wouldn't look away from me.

"Callie, honey...I'm so sorry," she started, her voice thick with oncoming tears. She swallowed them down quickly, shaking her head. "It wasn't my intention to keep this from you all."

"Then why did you?" I snapped, flinching just as I had done it and watched as she pulled back a bit. "Sorry," I muttered. "But why would you keep something like that from me and dad? Why didn't you get him help?"

She let out a shaky breath, twisting her hands. "I was already having trouble dealing with that fact that the woman at work were labeling him as a 'gay'," she finger quoted. "I didn't want to believe that he was capable of this, too."

"What does he being gay have to do with anything? Just like Dad said, his label doesn't handicap him. He still had the ability to..."

My mom cut me off. "I know that now! And I couldn't have more guilt and regret than I do at this very moment. No one wants to believe that their child...the baby that they raised from birth, can do terrible things or get themselves into trouble. We all want to believe that our children will just swing through life with no worries and become some incredible human being that can't do a single thing wrong."

The more she continued, little by little, it was clicking as to why she decided not to do something. Although it was a terrible judge of character and wrong on her part to not get him help, I could see why she never expected him to actually pull the trigger that day. Every parent just wants to see their child grow up to be something great, not the monster that my brother made himself out to be.

"Then why..." I started, my brain still fuzzy on her first reaction when the truth came to light. I shook my head as I tried to flee the thoughts that came about when I was transported back to the day. "Why did you judge him so much for being labeled gay?"

Her dull eyes watered as she put a hand to her mouth. "I've always had trouble with people like that. I grew up in an all-catholic family that believed in different sex partners. You know how stubborn Grandmom is about her beliefs." I nodded my head, but was still far from understanding. "The fact that my own son could be one of those...people," she cried. "I couldn't imagine it. He never hinted that he was, nor did he tell anyone about it. But I couldn't escape those evil women from work that kept making comments about my own son, saying that he'd rather be with a man, against their religious beliefs. I was just having trouble with it. I still have trouble with it."

I was almost disgusted with how ignorant she was to the changing world around us. Not everything was black and white and people weren't like everyone else. We all had different viewpoints and beliefs, ones that sometimes put us against one another in battles. But this was her son. Religion or not, she should still have had an open mind about his feelings. It was almost like our roles were reversed and she was stuck as the high-schooler with rumors swirling around about someone she loved.

"That's not right, Mom. You should have still loved him all the same. Just because people decided to pick on him and give him a label that he didn't pick for himself-"

She got up from the chair quickly, making the table almost fall over. "I know! I still loved your brother! The label that was thrust upon just rubbed me the wrong way. Even if I hated the thought of him being that...way," she shuttered a bit. "I still loved him because he was my son. Nothing could ever change that."

"Then why did you just brush off his pain like that when he was around?" I shouted this time, getting up from the chair as well. She stalled in her pacing and stared at me with a slacked jaw. "He came home most nights, close to crying because he was getting beaten up so much. He just wanted a safe place to fall, somewhere that he could relax. You just ignored his pleas and pretended like they didn't mean anything!"

"I said I was sorry, Callie!" she threw her hands up in frustration. "I can't take back the way that I treated him! I wish so much that I could take it all back and have a do-over. I could have helped him and wrapped my brain around him...being the way that he was. I made mistakes. I just thought he was being over-dramatic, because he known for that sometimes. He could spin a story farther than anyone, sweetheart. That's why he was so good at what he used to do. But I'm so sorry for all of this. I know I was wrong..." she started to sob. She had a hand over her mouth and tears streaming down her slightly tanned cheeks.

As frustrated as I was with her choices and how she treated Clay, a small piece of my heart broke for her. She, like so many others included in this story, felt so guilty for what they hadn't done. Everyone played parts, small and large, in the end result of Clay's downfall that none of us could take back, no matter how badly we wanted to.

"But you have to stop finding people to blame, Callie," she spoke back up, her throat thick with tears once more. "As guilty as I feel about this whole thing..." she gulped. "I wasn't the one who pulled the trigger that day."

I winced as the words left her mouth, a sudden rush of that day coming to light once again. His eyes were there, staring me down like he was a whole different person. I watched the way his hand was sturdy and how his finger curled viciously around the grey trigger.

And it all reminded me that she was right. There were so many people involved in this incident that I hadn't taken the time out to sit down and really find the culprit. I wanted so many other people to blame because it was so much easier than pointing the finger at my own brother, the one who used to protect me instead of hurt me. I kept thinking of old memories and not actually placing the face with the shadow in my nightmares that pulled the trigger that day.

I nodded, the tears brimming over my lids. "I know. As much as I want to find someone else to blame so that I can't stay mad at him, I know that he was the one who made the decision that day. I wish I could go back and change his mind, get him help before he finally decided that he had to do that. I wish I could have gotten everyone to stop picking on him and make him realize how much potential he had. But I can't..." my voice broke. "And I hate that."

She immediately came for me, wrapping me in her arms as we tried to make the tears subside. My mom rubbed my back in comfort, squeezing me tight as I just sobbed into her shoulder. I hated how twisted this whole situation was, how much it ruined our lives and how much hatred was portrayed in just a couple of months. It all didn't seem fair. Not to me, my family, Grayson, Marnie, Carter...and especially not Clay.

When she pulled apart from me, she placed her hands on my shoulders and smiled small to try to calm me down. "I have something for you."

I watched as she went over to her bag that was hanging from the dining chair and pulled out a white envelope. She held it out for me and I lost my breath as I saw the handwriting.

It was Clay's.

"I know I promised you that I wouldn't visit him anymore, but I felt like I owed him an explanation...and apology of sorts for everything I'd done wrong to him. We had a very long talk about how I treated him and the reasons behind his decision. Although I will never agree with that decision as long as I live, I needed to see my son one last time. We both decided that he needs help, which the prison will supply for him. They have a psychiatric ward where mental prisoners go. With the help of his lawyer, we're able to get him help. We're not sure what that means for his sentence but..." she took a deep breath, running a finger underneath her eyes. "He wanted me to give you this. He promised that these are his last words to you before we officially cut ties for the time being."

I took the envelope from her hands and held it shakily, the paper crinkling as my nerves went on haywire. I didn't have the willpower to open it right that second, so fearful as to what it was he had to say to me that we didn't already cover in our last visit. Was this from the Clay I grew up with or the monster that had been created in the process?

"I um…" I stuttered, grabbing my things before turning back to my mom who was giving me a questioning look. "I have to do something. Well…things actually. There are a few missing puzzle pieces that I haven't recovered yet. But…thanks Mom," I whispered. "For making me see the light in all of this mess."

She smiled small at me again before waving at me as I fled from the house and right out the door to visit some people who could help me fill in the final missing blanks.

"Wow…" Marnie breathed. "We really had some catching up to do."

I nodded silently, still fully aware of the unopened letter stuffed in my bag. I came to Marnie first because there were still things about her and Carter that I hadn't connected the dots to just yet. Plus, I really needed my best friend after a day like this.

It had been so long since her and I had sat down in an elongated conversation like this, far deeper than our normal heart to hearts. She sat across from me on her bed without saying a single word until I was finished, only nodding her head and making agreeing noises as I continued.

"I know it seems like I was always on Grayson's side or Carter's…but I always had your brother's best interests at heart, Cal," she whispered, that guilty look that had become so familiar to me washing over her features.

"We all did to a point, I think."

"I just wish we could all go back, you know?" she continued as I nodded along this time. "We could have helped him out if we had just known."

"Trust me…" I sighed. "No one wants to take this all back more than I do. But, Marn?" She looked up at me, her doe eyes wide with concern. "There's still something I don't understand. If Carter was gay…why was he so invested in your guys' relationship? I mean, he almost hit me because he thought I was jeopardizing it."

She smiled small at the memory she had of him, the nicer ones that I hadn't gotten to be a part of. Reaching into a drawer that was beside her bed, she took out a letter was folded into threes. When she opened it up, she glanced at it before looking back up at me.

"He gave me this a few days before he died," she said, her voice small. "He wasn't trying to win me back anymore but he said he still had more he wanted to say to me. In it…" she breathed. "He told me how he was struggling with the fact that he liked other guys. He didn't feel like he would be accepted if he came out to his friends on the team and to those who idolized him so much. But he said that I made him feel like he was loved…no matter who he chose to be. While I didn't know at the time that he was struggling with that, he still kept me around because he said I was the only person he felt like he could be himself around. He didn't want to let me go because he was afraid he wouldn't find anyone else like me, even if we weren't officially in a relationship."

Her eyes watered as she locked back up from the paper, gripping onto it like her heart was laid on that sheet. I smiled at her, giving her the smallest form of comfort that I could, knowing that whatever

I said in that moment wouldn't measure up to the power that was in the letter he wrote for her.

"He was a good guy, you know," she sniffed, folding it back up and placing it on her lap. "He just made some bad choices."

I rolled my eyes playfully. "That seems to be the definition for a lot of people these days."

She laughed lightly, wiping the remaining tears from her eyes. "Are you going to read your letter?" she deadpanned.

I shook my head, looking down in my lap as I spoke. "There's one more thing I need to do before I get to that. Something that seems to be a long time coming..."

Marnie got up from her bed, the springs squeaking beneath her as she walked towards her bedroom door. She opened it up and pointed out into the hall. "Go get him, Cal," she smiled.

25

EPILOGUE

When I got to Grayson's door, I still wasn't sure what I was going to say. I wasn't planning on declaring my love for him in some overly dramatic speech or flailing my arms around like an idiot. I knew that the both of us still had a lot that needed to be discussed, especially the fact that we were supposed to be giving each other time and I certainly wasn't abiding by that rule.

Taking a deep breath and preparing myself for what could potentially be a wrong turn in this winding road of mishaps I'd gotten myself into, I knocked on the door a few times. I half expected to see Mrs. Foster answer the door in her apron and floured cheeks once more, but was shocked to see someone I didn't expect.

"Oh! Callie, dear, I'm sorry," Mrs. Wayland sputtered, laying a hand on her heart as she almost walked right into me. I guess no one heard me knock on the door.

"It's alright, Mrs. Wayland," I smiled. "Came to visit with Grayson?"

She nodded, a grin spreading across her face. "Grayson and I visit once in a while when I find some things he might like from Carter's room. They were best friends so I figure it's only right to allow him a piece of Carter that was left."

"That's really nice of you."

She just shrugged, brushing her bangs out of her eyes and side-stepping to get around me from the doorway. "Grayson's such a sweet boy and he helped Carter so much. It's the least I can do. Have a wonderful day, Callie."

I waved to her as she smiled at me one last time before walking to her car. She had an empty cardboard box, probably once full of little things of Carter and she placed it in the passenger seat before driving off, gesturing a wave.

Before I could sink into the awkwardness of this situation, noting that I couldn't just walk inside Grayson's house without being welcomed in, Grayson's mom met me at the door with an overbearing grin. She didn't have an apron on this time and she wasn't covered in baking goods. She was just dressed in normal soccer mom attire, a pair of stretch pants and a v-neck t-shirt that hugged her waist.

"Callie! It's nice to see you again," she beamed. "Grayson's up in his room."

I nodded, biting my lip as I realized what I was about to do. I hated that I was so stubborn and couldn't manage a few simple words to tell Grayson how much I needed him. Not just for that one moment back at the prison, but for all the days after that. I wished I could just go up there and put it all out there without hesitation.

But bravery left the building as soon as I knocked on his bedroom door, the letter scrunching up in my hand as I waited for him to let me in. He cleared his throat from the other side of the door and called out for me to come in nonchalantly, probably expecting his mom or something.

When I opened the door and he looked up from his sketchbook, he dropped the pencil from his hand and his mouth fell open slightly. "Cal?" he breathed.

I waved awkwardly, still chewing on my lower lip. I wanted to be able to sit down on a chair somewhere and act as casual as possible about all of this. But I was frozen by the doorway with his eyes set on me. "Hey..." I mumbled.

"Uh..." he started, putting his sketchbook and pencil off to the side of his bed and giving me his full attention. "What are you doing here? I mean...not that I'm mad that you're here or anything," he rambled on. "I'm just surprised.'

Shifting on my feet I said, "I just sort of felt like our time was up," I deadpanned. "It's been a while."

He nodded, getting up from the bed and moving around the room to hide away his pad. As he tucked it into his bookcase he said, "It has. I missed you, you know," he grinned.

And just like that the awkward tension that was lingering in the air disappeared in a puff of smoke. We were back to our old selves once more, able to talk to one another without feeling like certain things couldn't be said. I made my way into the room and sat down on his bed. He decided to take the desk chair and pulled it across the room so we were sitting not too far away from one another.

I almost forgot about the letter until he pointed at it while it was sitting in my lap. "What's that?" he asked.

My eyes fell down to the unopened envelope, my breathing now becoming rapid. I kept thinking of all of these different things Clay could say to me. It scared me to think that this could be from the monster he had created himself and not the big brother I used to admire. I couldn't even think about looking at the words without feeling like every letter would sting as my eyes glided across them.

"A letter from Clay..." I breathed, looking back up into his melting grey eyes. They widened as I spoke, but fell back to normal like he didn't want to make me feel more nervous than I already was.

"What did he say?"

"That's part of the reason why I'm here, actually." I cleared my throat, holding it out to him. "I was hoping you would be able to read it to me. I can't muster the strength to read it myself."

He pursed his lips, waiting a moment before he reached out and took the envelope out of my hands. It crinkled as he ripped open the flap, taking out a couple sheets of paper. Unfolding it so it was finally on display and ready to be heard, he cleared his throat before reciting it out loud:

Callie,

I know this letter may come as a shock to you. I know I wasn't expecting to write you something like this, probably ever. But Mom came by to apologize for everything she's said to me over the years. Dad even came by and told me about everything that happened at home. He apologized for Mom and apologized for himself for not realizing how far deep I was into this thing. He said he hopes one day we'll be able to reconcile and I'll get help. He also hopes that he and Mom can overcome the fact that she kept such a secret like that. This all made me realize that I probably had a lot of apologizing to do myself.

I'm not going to say that I regret my decision to do what I did that day, because I don't. Everyone can try to convince me that what I did was wrong but I don't think I'll ever be able to believe that. I always believed that revenge and karma were tied into one another. They treated me like shit, Callie. Was I really that wrong to give them a taste of their own medicine? I wanted to escape all of the things they put me through, especially Carter. I couldn't think of a better way to do it. In a way, I was hoping to save all of those other people in his life that he would potentially hurt.

Mom says that once I get into therapy that the shrink will begin to convince me that I actually was wrong. He or she will try to make me believe that there were better ways to escape the pain, ways that involved no one else getting hurt. I don't know if I necessarily believe that, but it's worth a shot I guess.

But if there's one thing I regret, it's pointing the gun at you that day. I planned on it, but not for those months that I was planning on getting revenge on Carter. It started after football tryouts, when you and him both embarrassed me in front of Coach. I wanted so badly to find a way to fit in with these people that I felt like you guys ruined that chance for me.

Being locked up in this place for so long really gives you time to think. And for the longest time I kept thinking about your face and how fucking scared you were when I did that. I couldn't shake it. I still can't to this day. I don't know why I chose to take out my pain and anger on someone who I now see was just trying to save me. Although you were a bit over-protective most times, I knew you only did it with the best of intentions.

I only wish to take back putting you through that. I told you the last time you came to visit that I backed out on the last second, especially after seeing that look in your eyes. You're my baby sister and I'm supposed to protect you. I'm not going to blame it on Grayson for scaring me and making me jump that second. I'm only going to blame it on myself. I shouldn't have even thought about pointing a gun at you. I failed at my job to keep you safe, Callie. And for that, I couldn't feel guiltier. You didn't deserve that.

I'm not looking forward to doing this stupid therapy thing. After all, I already know where all of this pain and anger comes from. I already realize why I resent everyone. Maybe I was too giddy or too 'out there' for those kids at school. But I don't for a second regret acting the only way I knew how. Like myself.

So I want to leave you with two pieces of advice. Not that you have to take it, because you have every right not to listen to someone like me. But I felt like you needed to hear this.

The first is: Never let anyone talk you down from being who you really want to be. Don't let others trample on you and tell you that who you are is wrong. I know that you've always been the stronger one in the family, the one who takes the brunt of everything and isn't afraid to speak her mind. But please keep that in mind.

And the second one is: Don't let your stubborn air stop you from asking for help. Grayson had always been a good friend of mine. He accepted me when no one else did. I saw the way he looked at you and noticed how you always came up in conversation. He admired you a whole hell of a lot. And I also saw the determination in his eyes when he jumped in front of the bullet for you that day. He loves you and I know that you'll find it in your heart one day to let him in and share the same feelings for him.

This last part is really ironic but it fits. After Grandpa died, Grandma always used to tell me: "Love's like a bullet. It's fast. It's furious. Sometimes you can't see it coming. You can run from it. But you can't dodge it. Unless someone stands in your way..."

I guess I'm the one standing in your way, as he stood in the way for the bullet that day. Don't let the shit I put your through and what others are probably putting you through get in the way of you and Grayson. He'll take care of you while I'm not there. I know he will.

I'm so sorry for doing this to you. I'm messed up. I know that. After so many years of going through all of this, it makes you crazy to the point of no return. I never imagined hurting you like this. But I hope one day that I can return back to the person that I was, a little less cynical and far more compassionate. And I hope that you can somehow find it in your heart to forgive me one day.

- Clay

Grayson folded the paper back up, placing it on his leg as he released a heavy breath. By now, I was a mess. I was crying so hard that my shoulders were shaking and I couldn't stop them no matter how hard I tried.

That letter wasn't from the monster that he morphed into. But it wasn't from my big brother either. It was almost like an in-between, a place that he was stuck in for that moment. He was still cynical but that heart that I admired so much was poured out onto those pages for me.

The anger I had for him that always boiled in my blood was still there, making me far from the forgiving person he wanted me to be. But I was still filled with a small patch of hope that he would actually get the help that he needed. I wanted him to be able to see the error in his ways and actually regret killing Carter. As disgusting as it sounds, I liked that he was feeling remorse and wishing he could be forgiven, even if it was from just me. It meant that the old Clay was coming back, little by little.

I knew that it would take more than just a heartfelt letter to mend the broken strand between us, but it was a small start. It showed me that the old Clay was capable of coming back to life once again. After therapy and a lot of realizations, he would someday be able to see that just because someone hurt him; it didn't give him the right to hurt them, too.

Bullying wedged holes into so many people's hearts, leaving them with a large feeling of emptiness that sometimes were too hard to overcome. It made people weak and made them feel helpless. If people just found the courage to get help, it would create so many differences.

That was the only thing I regretted, not being able to get him the help he needed before making a decision like that. I was filled with so many 'what if' thoughts that I was left with just the same simple outcome: he wouldn't have made that decision.

Grayson took me into his arms, sitting next to me on the bed and letting me cry on his shoulder while he rubbed soothing circles on my back. I noticed that he seemed a bit embarrassed at what Clay said about him in the final pages of the letter, but he ignored his blushed cheeks and just kept silent while I let it all out. We didn't say anything for a long while, just let his words hang heavy around us.

After a while when I finally managed to wipe the snot from my face and muster up a couple of easy breaths, I gave him a lack-luster smile that seemed too forced. He brought his hand up to my cheek and rubbed it with his calloused thumb. His hand was covered in grey shading from his pencil, but I didn't even care. Grayson pushed back my hair so it was nestled behind my ear and took another deep breath.

"Well that was a lot to take in," he said. "What are you thinking?"

Sniffling, I said, "I'm thinking that...I'm not able to forgive him right now. I'm not sure I ever will. But I'm thinking that therapy will give him a wake up call that he really needs. I'm thinking that with tim e...my dad will hopefully be able to forgive my mom for overlooking Clay's decision. With time, I'll hopefully be able to forgive myself for not being able to help him in time. Most importantly, I'm thinking that...I'm still not cut out to deal with this all on my own."

He raised a furrowed brow. "Yeah?"

I nodded carefully, assessing him. "I know we agreed that we both needed time to sort things out, but I already know how I feel. I was able to go through these past couple of weeks without you, but it wasn't easy. I realized that I could deal with these things on my own. But I still need you."

"Cal," he shook his head, getting up from the bed. "As much as I love the thought of you needing me as much as I need you, I still can't over the fact that this all boils down to one thing. You didn't even start talking to me until after the shooting, after I did that for you. How do I know...?"

I already knew what he was about to ask, so I beat him to the punch. "How do you know that I'm not just in this because you were some knight in shining armor? Well for starters, I can open up to you more than I can to anyone else. I wasn't even able to talk to my parents about all of this until months after the fact. You were the first person I able to talk to right after the shooting. You always know what to say when I'm upset. You always seem to know when I need someone to lean on, even when I don't know it myself. You're so sweet, sometimes too sweet for your own good. You're an incredible artist and I love that about you. You're so talented and you don't even know it sometimes. Not only did you save me from the bullets that day, Grayson..." I breathed, getting up from his bed and walking over to where he was paused in the middle of the room. When I was in front of him, I said, "But you saved me from myself."

He put his hand to my cheek again, looking like he was trying to contain a grin he so badly wanted to let come about. "As much as I wish I was able to stop him that day, get him more help than just telling your Mom, I don't regret jumping in front of those bullets that day. I would do it all over again if I had to. I just wish that I was able to get to know you in a different way than..."

I cut him off by shaking my head, a smile taking over my features this time. "None of that matters. All that matters is that you helped give me the strength I needed over these past few months. I wouldn't have been able to get through this without you. I love you, Grays. And as much as we both wish this happened under different circ umstances...it brought me to you. I can't thank you enough for all that you've done."

He leaned his forehead down to mine and finally let his signature dimpled grin come to light. "I love you, too."

Then, without hesitation, he pressed his lips to mine. He put both of his hands on either side of my face and kept me near him for as long as he could. As his lips moved against mine, one of my hands wrapped around his neck and fell into his hair while the other landed on the part of his shoulder that housed the home of the bullet wound he'd gotten for me.

The weight that I had been carrying around for so long was far from being fully lifted. There was forgiveness that needed to be built upon and relationships that needed mending. I needed to work up the courage to talk to my brother again, in time, and when I was absolutely ready to do so. I needed to forgive myself for not getting to Clay in time to fix his sorrows. My parents needed to fix the tear in their trust and learn to forgive one another as well, while they somehow searched for a way to forgive their son in the process.

Clay would never be able to come up with the ultimate apology for what he had done to not just Carter, but his family and everyone who knew him as well. He altered so many lives with just that one bullet, creating a havoc he could never put back together.

But even though he decided to pull the trigger that day, the people who chose to put him down piled pain onto him until he couldn't take it any longer. While none of us would be able to forget what happened in the halls of Riverton on that horrid day, we all needed to realize where all of the anger was stemming from. He didn't just wake up one day and decide to become a monster.

That all took time and pain that he couldn't seem to escape.

I hoped that one day he would be able to realize what he had done wrong. I hoped that he was going to see that using a gun to solve his problems only made him equal to or worse to those who picked on him while he grew up.

Some people may never be able to forgive him for what he had done. What he chose to do that day wasn't conjured up from the freshest mind and the heart that I'd always known him to have. But lessons were meant to be learned from this, no matter how hard it all was.

While sometimes it just took one person to send someone over the edge, there was also a process of building blocks that just crushed the person on the receiving end. There always came a time when the weight of those blocks, as they started to pile higher and higher, that the person beneath them wouldn't be able to breath any longer. They'd become incoherent and crazy from just a few jumble of words from multitudes of people.

You never truly knew how deep someone was sinking until it was too late.

As Grayson pulled away, lifting just a small amount of weight from my shoulders that I had been harboring for so long, he smiled. "I have something I've wanted to show you."

I raised an eyebrow at him, a matching grin on my face as I watched him walk over the bookshelf by his bed. He fished around for what he was looking for, making a small thrilled noise when he picked it out from the mess of books. He sat down on his bed and gestured for me to come and sit next to him.

When I did, I realized that it was a sketchbook that I hadn't seen before. It was somewhat old and the pages were slightly wrinkled from years of being lugged around by a probably much younger Grayson. He flipped through the pages slowly, letting my eyes linger momentarily on each work of art.

"When your brother and I used to be friends, he'd let me draw him for my art class sometimes. I always remembered him being so excited about the next project he was working on and constantly flipping through scripts so he could get his part just right. This one, I think, really paints his picture."

In delicately scratched lines and shades of grey, was my brother's lit up face. He was in the midst of waving his hands around in mock gesture, reading from a script in his hands. His face was channeling a character I couldn't even place from that time and the smile on his face and in his eyes painted, just like Grayson said, my brother's picture.

It was the boy who I admired once again; the one I hoped would come back one day. He probably wouldn't be near the same exact boy he was in that picture, but I wished he would come close to it.

And as we laughed on while Grayson told more stories of the brother that I used to know, I made a point to remember that there was always more beneath a story line than what was just at the surface. There would always be more secrets that hadn't come out of hiding and people who wouldn't be able to confess that they had done the wrong thing.

But I remembered that Clay had changed, for the worst. The boy who I thought I owed everything to wasn't the one on my receiving end any longer. The one I really owed it all to was sitting across from me, a boyish grin lighting up on his face and a passion glimmering in his eyes as he told me more stories of the boy we both used to know.

Grayson was the boy who taught me that not only was love like a bullet, fast and furious and coming without warning most times; but people were also like bullets as well in a way, crashing furiously into your life without warning but making you realize things in ways you never imagined before.